# DESERVING CORA

The Refuge, Book 4

## SUSAN STOKER

# CHAPTER ONE

Pipe stared straight ahead as he stood in a line with a dozen other men, listening as the MC worked the audience into a frenzy when he introduced the next guy to be auctioned off.

He wondered for the hundredth time how the bloody hell he'd let himself be talked into this. Being in the spotlight was literally his nightmare come true. Pipe had spent so much of his life living in the shadows that it made his blood crawl to be onstage in front of so many people.

But his friends Brick, Tonka, and Spike had women and families to care for now. And out of the remaining owners of The Refuge, Pipe had literally pulled the short straw...so here he was.

Soon, the announcer would be introducing him. Would be taking bids from people in the audience willing to pay to have dinner with *him*. It was ridiculous.

"It's for a good cause," he reminded himself under his breath.

And that was the only reason he was in Washington, DC. To raise money for veterans.

He watched as the guy before him preened and strutted about the stage, playing to the audience, who loved every second of his posing, his muscle flexing. Pipe had the fleeting notion that maybe the man thought he was in a strip club or something, before the MC excitedly announced that the bidding was over.

The woman who won him let out a small scream and turned to her friends, who hugged her as they all jumped up and down in their excitement. Pipe refrained from rolling his eyes...barely. The woman had won a dinner date, not a boyfriend or a husband or whatever it was she thought she was bidding for.

He was cynical, for sure. All the more reason that it should've been Owl up here, not him.

Well...no. Not Owl. His friend and co-owner of The Refuge was too introverted. Still wary around most people after being held captive when his chopper had been shot down years before.

All of the men Pipe worked with were damaged in their own ways. It was one of the reasons he was here right now, in fact. He wanted to raise money for other veterans like him and his friends, who'd given their all for their countries and found themselves mentally broken in return. It wasn't that he didn't think the powers that be in the US—or in his case, in Britain—weren't thankful for the service of their military members. For the most part. But it was a herculean task to run a country, take care of those currently serving, and keep up with the hundreds of thousands of men and women who'd gone back to civilian life.

Which was where events like this charity auction came in. They were raising money to assist veterans attempting to reacclimate after their service. Pipe and his friends had each other, and The Refuge, but many people didn't have any support at all.

Ultimately, that was why Pipe was there. Feeling uncomfortable and out of place, and definitely not thrilled about parading himself in front of a roomful of over-dressed men and women who judged him based on superficial parameters. He knew what they saw. A man with hair that was too long, a beard that was too bushy, tattoos on his hands and fingers that many people assumed meant he'd been in prison. It was stereotyping at its worst, and he'd experienced it too many times to count.

Yes, he was wearing a tuxedo, but it was obvious to everyone that he didn't belong here. Not even close. These people wouldn't give him the time of day if they saw him on the street or in a grocery store. In fact, they'd probably cross the road or leave the aisle to avoid being anywhere near him. It was definitely ironic.

But he said he'd do this—would represent The Refuge, hopefully bringing more attention to their business out in New Mexico—and he didn't go back on his word.

All too soon, the man in front of him was sauntering off the stage to meet the woman who'd paid a ton of money for his time. And now it was Pipe's turn.

Since it was way too late to get out of this farce, he stepped forward into the circle taped onto the floor of the stage, where they'd all been instructed to stand when it was their turn. Unlike the man before him, Pipe didn't smile and preen as he was introduced. He stared into the audience, sweat beading at his temples as he imagined someone in the audience, an enemy he couldn't see because of the bright lights in his face, pointing a rifle at his forehead.

"Next up is Bryson 'Pipe' Clark. He's forty-two, and

one of seven owners of the world-renowned The Refuge resort in New Mexico. I know you've all heard of the amazing facility that caters to those who suffer from PTSD. He and his fellow co-owners have been huge supporters of our military men and women. Mr. Clark was a member of the infamous Special Air Service in the United Kingdom, and he's offering to escort whoever's lucky enough to win the bid to The Inn at Little Washington. As I'm sure you all know, The Inn is the first and only restaurant in our area to have three Michelin stars, and an additional green star. The food is unparalleled and the atmosphere cozy and intimate, with space for only twelve guests at a time. Now, who wants to start the bidding?"

For a moment, the room was silent, and Pipe had the hope that maybe, just maybe, no one would bid on him at all and he could get out of this ridiculous situation unscathed. Unlike many in his situation, that would be the ideal. He wouldn't feel humiliated or rejected if he got no bids...he'd be relieved.

But then a woman in the front row called out, "One thousand dollars."

The bid wasn't exactly impressive, considering the six men before him had gone for anywhere from two to seven thousand, but the chance of him leaving without having to take a stranger to dinner died along with her bid.

Trying to squint through the bright light shining in his eyes, Pipe couldn't see the woman all that well...until she stepped closer to the stage. She wasn't very tall, from what he could tell, and had long brown hair. She wore a simple dress that came to mid-thigh, and unlike the other women packed into the room, she wasn't expertly coiffed or wearing a ton of flashy jewelry. She was just another woman in a little black dress. If not for the bid, he'd have thought she was trying not to stand out. He probably would've looked right past her if she hadn't spoken up.

"A good start for this brave Brit. Who's up for two thousand?" the announcer cajoled.

There were a couple other bids, but the first woman kept upping her offer by a hundred dollars every time anyone outbid her.

The more Pipe watched the woman in the black dress, the more intrigued he became. He wasn't sure what it was about her that piqued his interest—maybe her understated appearance in a roomful of glitz; or her quiet, determined bids—but suddenly he was rooting for her. Wanted her to actually win so he could get to know one of the few women in the room who looked...normal.

And that kind of reaction wasn't normal for *him*. He'd mostly given up on the opposite sex. Of having what a few of his friends had recently found. But he couldn't deny that the woman in the black dress held his interest...and something deep inside him, something he'd long thought dead, sat up and took notice.

Pipe would've missed what happened next if he wasn't staring at the woman in the black dress so intently. Another woman—a tall, gorgeous redhead, wearing four-inch heels and a forest-green dress molded to every inch of her curvy body—stepped up next to the brunette and jostled her so hard, she almost fell over.

"Ten thousand," the redhead called out, sounding bored.

The announcer got very excited, since that was the highest bid of the night. Pipe kept his eye on the brunette and saw devastation flash across her face before she bit her lip and dropped her gaze. Her shoulders slumped just slightly...indicating that the bid was too high for her to top.

The redhead smirked at her, not even looking at the stage.

Pipe frowned in confusion. Why had she bid on him if she didn't seem the least bit interested in what she was spending a hell of a lot of money on? He watched as the redhead leaned down and said something to the other woman, who frowned and abruptly turned, pushing her way through the crowd and walking away from the stage.

Then and only then did the redhead look up with a very satisfied grin on her face.

Disgust swam through Pipe's veins. It seemed obvious she'd only bid on him so the other woman *wouldn't* win. That meant the two women probably knew each other, had some sort of bad history.

He realized he was way too interested in the dynamic between the women than he should be. But he couldn't help remembering the hopeful look in Brunette's eyes when she'd briefly held the winning bid...and the devastation when she realized the amount had gone over her price range.

"Looks like the winner is Ms. Eleanor Vanlandingham. Congratulations! Have a wonderful time at dinner!"

The MC gestured for Pipe to walk off the stage to the left. He did so, but couldn't get the woman in the black dress out of his mind, the way she didn't fit in at this event. How he knew that, Pipe wasn't sure. Mostly, he was judging her exterior—exactly what people did to *him*. But still, he was rarely wrong in his assessments of others. It was an important skill to have as a special forces soldier, and he'd always been the one his team relied on when they needed to determine if they could trust an informant or not.

He didn't think he was wrong in his assessment of that woman either—yet, she had thousands of dollars to blow at an auction.

The fact that she was such a dichotomy intrigued Pipe. That she stood out to him, for the very reasons she *didn't* stand out to others. And that spark of...something...flared again. It was a foreign feeling, but he wasn't willing to ignore it.

He needed to know more about the woman in the black dress. She may not have won the date, but Pipe was going to track her down the second he got off this stage... and try to figure out why he was so drawn to her.

# CHAPTER TWO

It was taking every ounce of pride and strength for Cora Rooney not to burst into tears. She'd planned tonight so carefully. When she'd heard that one of the owners of The Refuge was going to be in Washington, DC, at a charity auction, she'd been elated. Like most people, she knew about the resort catering to those who suffered from PTSD. There had been a lot of articles written about the place—and the men who owned it—when it had first opened, and even now, more than five years later, they were still getting interviews and press coverage because of how generous they were with their time and money.

She'd been distressed enough to spend some of her own hard-earned money on a ticket to the gala tonight. She'd have preferred not to, wanted to hoard every dime to use for her main objective, but the gala was a means to an end...namely, the chance to have a conversation with one of the former special forces soldiers who owned The Refuge.

It was a desperate decision. She'd contacted private investigators, all of whom wanted too much money to take her case. Private security firms were out, for the same reason. Cora had even dug around on the Internet, trying to find a former police officer or FBI agent to consult, but the few she'd found made the hair on the back of her neck stand up, and not in a good way. They were quick to offer help, but like everyone else, demanded thousands of dollars—up front. Which made her think they were scammers.

If there was any other way to get help that didn't require money she didn't have, Cora would've taken it. But she was out of options. Even if the representative from The Refuge had refused to help her, at least she could say she'd tried everything.

Thinking about why she was at this auction in the first place made her heart hurt.

Lara.

She'd known her best friend since they were teenagers, so over twenty years now. Lara had been the only girl at school who'd tried to befriend Cora when she'd arrived as a newcomer in the tenth grade. Cora hadn't fit into the upper-class school at all. A foster kid with no designer clothes, a bad attitude she wore like a shield, and an expectation that everyone would hate her on sight. She wasn't exactly wrong on that last count...except for Lara.

Lara Osler had literally saved her life. Had overlooked her lack of money, lack of parents, and lack of trust for anyone and everyone, and simply taken her under her wing, not caring that their peers made fun of her for it behind her back.

They were opposites in so many ways. Lara was tall at five-ten, compared to Cora's five foot five. Cora had boring brown hair, while Lara's was shiny blonde. Cora was brash and didn't hesitate to speak her mind. Lara was far more diplomatic and almost shy. Despite that, Lara fell for men hard and fast, convinced each one could be her happy-ever-after, while Cora was too distrustful to offer most guys more than a single night.

They were like oil and water, but somehow they'd immediately clicked. Despite their differences, or maybe because of them, Cora and Lara had become best friends. She owed Lara everything.

That was why she'd bought a dress and two-inch heels, attempted to put on some makeup, and attended this fancy shindig.

And she'd failed.

She hadn't been sure she'd have enough money to win the man from The Refuge to begin with. The six thousand dollars she'd scrounged up was the most money she'd ever had in her bank account at one time. And she'd spend every dime to help Lara, even if no one other than Cora believed she actually *needed* help. And when most of the winning bids for the men in front of him had been in her range, she began to think she might have a chance.

The bidding had slowed at five thousand dollars, and for a second, Cora had thought she'd done it. That she'd won. That she was one step closer to helping her friend.

Then Eleanor Vanlandingham appeared, practically knocking Cora to the floor. From the second she realized who was standing next to her, Cora had known her nemesis from high school was going to ruin everything... and she'd been right. She didn't know why the other woman hated her so much. She'd been a bitch back in high school, and she was still a bitch twenty-two years later. They didn't run into each other often, but when they did, nothing good came out of it.

Like tonight.

Eleanor had crushed Cora's plan with two little words. Ten thousand dollars was way above what she could afford to spend...more than she had in her account. She'd failed. She wouldn't be able to talk to Mr. Clark, wouldn't be able to try to convince him to help her.

Cora wanted to cry...and she wasn't a crier. It never helped, only made her feel stuffed up and weak, and made her look like crap.

It wasn't as if Eleanor even wanted a date with the man. He wasn't her type. Not even close. Too rough around the edges, too many tattoos. Not pretty enough. Not a millionaire. The list went on and on.

But it didn't matter. Eleanor simply wasn't going to let Cora win something that she'd so desperately wanted.

She huffed out a breath as she blindly pushed through the crowd. She needed to get the hell out of there. No way was she going to give Eleanor the satisfaction of seeing her cry.

Detouring to the coat check area at the back of the grand ballroom, then down a short hall to the bathrooms, Cora locked herself inside one of the stalls and leaned against the wall as she desperately tried to keep despair from overwhelming her.

She'd been so sure she'd be able to convince Bryson Clark to help. All she needed was an hour or so to talk to him. To plead her case. The police hadn't believed her. Lara's own parents dismissed her concerns without thinking twice, and she'd exhausted all of her other options. But Cora knew down to her bones that her friend was in danger. An ex-special forces soldier could easily get to Lara. Talk to her. Find out if she was safe or not.

Taking a deep breath, Cora straightened. Fine, Eleanor might've ruined her plans tonight, but she still had six thousand bucks. She could fly out to New Mexico, go to The Refuge in person, and see if she could talk to one of the men who owned the place. It would be better if she could get a reservation for one of the cabins so she could seem like a visitor, but that was impossible. They were booked up for months.

Cora wasn't even sure why she was so fixated on the men who ran The Refuge. They were no longer in the military. They all suffered from various degrees of PTSD. Hell, they were resort owners now, not mercenaries for hire or something. But from the moment she'd visited their website...seen their pictures and read their bios...something about the men had struck a chord deep within her. They'd all suffered, and yet they'd gone out of their way to help others. And from the news accounts she'd read about recent situations with some of the women who now lived and worked at The Refuge, the owners seemed to have a soft spot for women in peril.

So maybe, just maybe, they'd be willing to look into Lara's situation. It was worth a shot. Cora would do whatever it took to help her friend.

She dismissed going straight to Phoenix to try to see Lara herself, because she had a feeling that would be an epic failure. She didn't have the strength or skills needed to succeed. No, she needed someone like Mr. Clark or one of the other men who worked at The Refuge.

Deciding that going to The Refuge would've been a better plan than trying to win the auction anyway, Cora reached into the bag she'd checked earlier and began to change clothes. She'd never been one to dwell on the bad shit in her life; if she was, she wouldn't be able to function. Her life had never been easy, and why she'd expected tonight to be any different was a complete mystery.

Cora quickly changed into the jeans, T-shirt, old, comfy sweatshirt, and sneakers that she'd brought with her, and stuffed the black dress and heels into the bag. She wasn't stupid enough to ride back to her crappy part of town wearing something so nice. She'd be picked off by one of the many drug dealers or creeps who prowled the Metro looking for victims before she could blink.

She used the bathroom for good measure while she was there, then exited the stall. After washing her hands, Cora pushed open the restroom door and headed down the hall that led back into the ballroom. Her plan had been to slide out of there unnoticed by the crowd, whose attention was still on the stage for the ongoing auction. But of course, like all her carefully crafted plans that night, that was also destined to fail.

Eleanor Vanlandingham and two of her Barbie followers were waiting for her as soon as she stepped into the dim lights of the ballroom.

Of course, Eleanor looked beautiful in the dark green dress she'd poured herself into. The bitch duo flanking her, Valentina and Scarlett, also looked as perfect as ever in their almost-matching strapless black dresses and four-inch heels. Their makeup was perfectly painted onto their Botox-injected faces. Valentina rocked her curves, filling out her LBD like a Marilyn Monroe lookalike, while Scarlett was her opposite, rail thin like a runway model.

The trio might be beautiful on the outside, but they were rotten to the core. They took every opportunity to step on anyone they considered beneath them...which was just about everyone.

Eleanor didn't give Cora the chance to speak, simply jumped in with the insults she was known to use every time she opened her mouth. If words were colors, Eleanor's would've been pitch black.

"Yeah, that's right, bitch, go back to the hole you crawled out of. I don't know how you got a ticket for tonight's event, but you aren't good enough to be here."

"Funny, my money's just as green as yours, El," Cora said, straightening her shoulders. Now that she was wearing clothes she was more comfortable in, she felt more sure of herself. As if she'd redonned her armor.

"What money?" Eleanor sneered. "Your dress was from Walmart, and those shoes you had on? You get those at Payless?"

Valentina and Scarlett giggled as if Eleanor had said the most hilarious thing ever.

Cora refused to be ashamed that Eleanor's guesses on where she'd gotten her clothes and shoes were spot on. She'd been saving her money for more important things.

"Why are you such a horrible person?" Cora asked. "I mean, seriously, I would've thought you'd grown out of being a mean, bitchy, stuck-up snob after you graduated from high school. Instead, more than two decades later, you've just gotten worse. The world doesn't revolve around you, El."

"Stop calling me that," Eleanor growled, taking a step closer.

Cora stood her ground. No way would she ever back down from this bitch. If she wanted to throw down right here, right now, Cora was ready. In fact, she wished she would. Eleanor would get her ass kicked in front of every-one, just like she deserved. She could take this stuck-up bitch in her heels and tight dress in a heartbeat. Hell, could take on Frick and Frack standing next to her, as well. All she needed was Eleanor to make the first move.

She'd learned the hard way that being the aggressor never turned out well after a fight...but if she was protecting herself, that was a different story.

But of course, Eleanor wouldn't use physical force. Her words were her weapons.

"You're trash, and you always will be, Cora Rooney," Eleanor hissed. "You're an embarrassment. Everyone was laughing at you tonight, wondering why the hell you were here, who made the mistake and sold you a ticket. Even if the only way you could *ever* get a man to look twice at you is by buying one, you were never going to win an auction. The second we saw you, we decided if you bid on anyone, you'd be the loser you already are."

The old feeling of rejection hit Cora hard. None of her foster families had ever wanted to keep her, so she'd shuffled from home to home, school to school. Consequently, it was impossible to make friends. People she'd thought had her back turned on her the second someone more interesting came along.

Except for Lara. It had been hard for Cora to trust her for a long time, but whenever she did or said something to drive her away, Lara never even flinched. She'd stood by her time and time again. Had helped her get a job when she'd needed one desperately, had let her live with her when she was one day away from living on the streets.

Pushing down the pain of Eleanor's words, Cora glared. "Fuck you," she said between clenched teeth.

"Oh, yeah, that's elegant," Eleanor sniped with a roll of her eyes. "So classy. Why don't you just die already?" she added. "No one liked you in high school, and no one likes you now. You're weird, ugly, and pathetic!"

*Those* words didn't hurt. None of them were a new insult from Eleanor. She'd been spouting the same crap for years. Besides, Cora *was* weird, plain enough to probably be considered ugly by a lot of people, and she'd been pathetic more often than she wanted to admit over the years.

"Why are you here, Eleanor?" she asked. "It's not like you give a shit about anyone other than yourself. Homeless veterans, our military heroes addicted to drugs and alcohol, needing psychiatric help? That's not your jam. I can't imagine you wanting to give *money* to those people."

Eleanor tittered. "You're right...for once. I don't give a shit about them. They're all a bunch of fucking losers, using their so-called PTSD as a crutch to get free money and services from the government. If they'd just get jobs like the rest of us, they wouldn't need a handout."

"As if you have a job," Cora couldn't help but mutter.

"Bitch, I'm an influencer. I have more followers than you could even imagine. Do you know how much money I make every day? With every video I post, I could buy whatever hellhole you live in," Eleanor said with a sneer.

Thing1 and Thing2 next to her nodded in unison.

"That's not a job," Cora informed her.

"The hell it's not!" Eleanor protested. "I work damn hard to be beautiful. Witty. Fun. Three things you *aren't* and will never be."

"You're right. I'd rather be a good person. Charitable. A loyal friend. Someone people can rely on. You aren't any of *those* things."

"As if I care," Eleanor said with a flick of her head.

Cora was tired. And done trading barbs with Eleanor. The woman wouldn't change. Ever. And Cora needed to figure out what her next steps would be. See if she could get an inexpensive plane ticket to New Mexico, find a cheap hotel near The Refuge, and figure out how to get on the property and come up with some way to get ten minutes to talk to one of the owners.

"Right," Cora said with a shrug. "Whatever. At least your ten thousand bucks will be helpful, even if your heart is as black as your soul."

"So naïve," Scarlett said with a giggle.

"Stupid," Valentina agreed.

Cora frowned. "About what?"

"I'm not giving anyone money."

"But you have to. You won the bid," Cora said adamantly.

"So? No one can force me to pay. I just wanted to outbid *you*. No harm, no foul. Besides, if you think I'd be seen anywhere near that freak with the tattoos, you're crazy. No way would I sully my reputation by being seen out and about with someone who looks like a gang member. Nope. I'll just push out a few tears and act confused when I can't find my checkbook. Then I'll ignore their efforts to collect the money. It's not as if they'll even use it for anything they said they would. It'll go right into some CEO's pocket."

Cora saw red. What a fucking *bitch*. She wanted to march over to the table where the money was being collected and give them her six thousand to try to cover for what Eleanor refused to pay...but she needed every cent of her money to get to New Mexico.

"You're going straight to hell," Cora blurted. "And that man on the stage is worth a *hundred* times more than you. He risked his life for his country. Put himself in harm's way. Suffered to try to help others. What have *you* ever done for anyone other than yourself? Not a damn thing. You judge everyone by their looks, when you're the ugliest person who's ever lived. His tattoos, beard, and long hair don't make him a gang member or a violent person, just as your *lack* of tattoos doesn't make you an upstanding citizen. Personally? I think his tattoos are sexy as hell. They tell me he's a man who doesn't give a shit about what other people think. People like *you*, who look down on him because of a little ink on his skin. You'd sully *his* reputation if he was ever seen with you."

Eleanor rolled her eyes. "You're such a dumb bitch, Cora. You have no idea how things work in my world. Go back to the gutter where you belong."

Cora's fists clenched. It had been a long time since she'd gotten into a physical altercation with anyone, and she was itching to punch this bitch in the face. But it wouldn't change anything. In many ways, Eleanor was right. She didn't belong here. In her cheap dress and shoes, with an actual soul.

There was so much she wanted to say but nothing would make a difference. Eleanor and her silly friends were who they were. Mean, entitled bitches who truly thought the world revolved around them. They wouldn't change, especially not because of anything she had to say.

With Lara's words about rising above those who seek to bring her down to their level ringing in her ears, Cora turned to leave.

Only to stop in her tracks when she saw two men standing about ten feet away.

She recognized them immediately. It was Bryson, the man she'd unsuccessfully bid on, and Callen Kaufman, who, according The Refuge website, went by the nickname Owl.

She stared at them in confusion. What were they doing? And how long had they been standing there?

Then she blushed, remembering that she was in her ratty jeans and sweatshirt.

Eleanor turned to see what she was staring at, and Cora actually felt the shift in the woman. Her mask was back on and she smiled at the men, jutting a hip seductively.

"Oh! Hi, gentlemen. I'm so excited about our date," she simpered.

Cora was disgusted. At Eleanor, the auction, and humanity in general. She'd had enough. Eleanor had won, like she always did. Bryson could go out with the witch and marry her, for all she cared. There were other men at The Refuge who would work just as well for her needs.

Of course, she didn't feel the attraction toward them that she did for Bryson, but whatever.

She hadn't wanted to admit to herself that she was drawn to the man she'd bid on. She'd studied his short bio on The Refuge's website until she'd memorized it, then dug further, finding as much information as she could about him on the Internet. In one particular picture, the tattoos on his arms had been on full display. He looked nothing like his friends, which intrigued Cora. He had an edge, which had always appealed to her. She didn't want a pretty boy. She wanted someone who made people walk the other way when they saw him. Someone who wouldn't put up with anyone talking shit.

Someone who looked as if they could, and *would*, protect their woman.

Internally rolling her eyes, Cora headed for the ballroom's exit. Romance wasn't for her. She wasn't the kind of woman men found attractive, which had been hammered home more than once in her lifetime. She didn't need a man to rely on, anyway. They'd only ever disappointed her.

She had several foster dads and siblings who'd proven that true.

There was only one person in her entire life who'd never let her down. Lara. And Cora would do whatever it took to help her now.

# CHAPTER THREE

Pipe ground his teeth together so hard, it felt as if he would crack a tooth. He couldn't believe the things the redheaded bitch was saying.

He hadn't even recognized the woman in the jeans and sweatshirt until the redhead had said enough for him to realize she was the woman in the black dress. The one who'd been outbid.

His blood ran cold at hearing the awful things the redhead—Eleanor, apparently—had said about veterans. What she truly thought about them. Pipe knew there were people in the world who thought the way she did, but he honestly hadn't expected any of them to be here tonight, or to actually bid.

And to hear that she had no intention of actually paying the money she'd promised was the last straw. Every muscle in his body was tense, and he was two seconds away from going off on the bitch.

"Easy, Pipe," Owl said, grabbing his arm.

"Take care of this for me?" he said to his friend.

"Of course. I'll make sure the organizers know she has

no intention of honoring her bid, thus voiding your responsibility to take her to dinner. I'll donate the money in The Refuge's name. Go on. Go after the other one."

Pipe should've been surprised that Owl knew exactly where his head was at, but he wasn't. They might not have served together, but they'd worked side-by-side for years. "Thanks, man."

"Shut up," he said, tightening his fingers around Pipe's arm for a moment. "For the record...I like her." He nodded toward the woman—Cora, the bitch had called her—who'd just reached the doors to the ballroom.

Something within Pipe loosened at hearing his friend's approval. It made no sense, except that he valued Owl's opinion. Nodding, he took a moment to send a glare Eleanor's way, before turning and jogging toward the exit, where Cora had disappeared.

He was supposed to go back up onstage after the last man had been auctioned off, for the final announcement of how much money had been earned and for the closing remarks, but Pipe felt no guilt about bugging out early. He couldn't lose sight of the woman who'd not only stood up for him, and seemed to honestly care about the veterans she was here to support, but who he'd found himself strangely attracted to since he'd first seen her standing near the stage, looking so out of place.

He had to talk to her. Find out why she'd seemed so desperate to win a date. He needed to know her story.

He wasn't sure why, but he had the bizarre thought that if she slipped away, he'd somehow lose something precious.

Looking both ways in the hall outside the ballroom, Pipe didn't see any sign of Cora. She'd been moving quickly, and he instinctively knew he had only seconds to make a decision on which way to go to find her. Left or right?

Right. Toward the lobby. He had a feeling Cora wasn't staying in this fancy hotel.

To his relief, his instincts were proven correct when he rounded the corner. He saw Cora across the lobby, talking to a man standing at the entrance to the hotel. He was smiling at her, and as Pipe headed in their direction, Cora reached into her back pocket and hand the man some money.

Seeing her tip the doorman made Pipe's respect for her rise even higher.

He'd heard the women's entire conversation, and the only thing that bitch Eleanor was correct about was the quality of the clothes Cora had been wearing. He wasn't an expert, but even he knew her dress from earlier wasn't designer. The jeans and sweatshirt she now had on looked comfortable and well-worn. Yes, she'd bid quite a bit of money for him, but he had a feeling that every cent had been hard-won.

Pipe picked up the pace, jogging toward her. He made enough noise as he neared that both Cora and the doorman turned to look at him. Pipe approved when the man stepped in front of Cora as if to protect her. He wasn't going to hurt her, far from it, but neither of them knew that.

He slowed as he approached and subtly held his hands out, making sure they both saw he was unarmed. Which wasn't exactly true, but he also wasn't packing anything that could harm them.

"Cora, right?" he asked.

She looked surprised. Then wary. "Yeah?"

"I'm Pipe, as you probably know. Can I walk you home?"

Instead of looking relieved or impressed, the suspicion in her eyes grew. "Why?"

"Because it's late. And dark. And you shouldn't be out alone."

"I can take care of myself," she said with a small lift of her chin.

To his surprise, Pipe found her stubbornness refreshing. Maybe because he'd been around so many women tonight who tittered and giggled at anything he said. He hated women who simpered, and he had a feeling this woman would rather die than play coy for a man.

"Right. Then maybe you can give me a reason to get out of here, instead of going back into that ballroom and saying or doing something I'll regret in response to that bitch who has no problem stiffing veterans who've risked their lives for their country."

She stared at him for a long moment before asking, "You heard that?"

"I heard everything," Pipe told her.

He saw the dismay and embarrassment in her eyes before she straightened her shoulders. "No offense, but you in that tux would make me more of a target than if I was by myself," she said with a glint of humor in her eyes.

Without hesitation, Pipe shrugged out of the tux jacket. He ripped the stupid bow tie off his neck and held both out to the doorman, who was probably used to the quirks of the wealthy people who attended events at the swanky hotel. The man took them without a word. Pipe then undid the buttons at the top of the white shirt, then took off his cufflinks, stuffing them into his pocket. He rolled up the sleeves of the fancy shirt, exposing the tattoos on both arms. Finally, he ran a hand through his hair, mussing the strands. "Can't do anything about the shiny shoes, but maybe this is better?"

His skin tingled as her gaze ran over him. He didn't see any judgement in her eyes, instead it felt as if she approved of him more like this than in his expensive duds. "I don't live near here. I have to take the Metro," she warned him.

Pipe shrugged. "Not near here is fine. It'll give me more time to calm down."

For a moment, he thought she was going to refuse. Tell him that she was perfectly able to get home by herself, which he had no doubt she was. He had a feeling this woman could do any-damn-thing she wanted without anyone's help. But for some reason, he wanted to ensure her safety. Wanted to be someone she could lean on, even if just for tonight. For the time it took to get her home.

"Okay," she said after a long pause.

Relief flooded Pipe's veins. It was a surprising feeling. He'd been numb more often than not since getting out of the military. He'd gotten most of his tattoos as a way to feel *something*, even momentarily. Even if it was the pain of a needle. He'd begun to think he'd be stuck in this weird nothingness forever.

But somehow, this woman had managed to do in seconds what years of therapists and tattoos hadn't...she'd broken through the ice encasing his entire being without even trying.

It was confusing and exciting at the same time.

Pipe turned to the doorman. "I have a buddy, his name is Owl...sorry, Callen Kaufman. Red hair...beard. He kind of looks like Ed Sheeran. If you can get my jacket and tie to him, he'll take them off your hands."

"Are you staying here, sir? I could give them to the front desk staff and they can put them in your room."

"I'm not. Is that a problem?" Pipe asked.

"Not at all. I'll find your friend."

"Thanks."

"It's my job," the doorman said.

Pipe could've let that go, but he didn't. "No, it isn't. Not really. And I didn't miss the way you stood in front of Cora to protect her when I approached. Working in the service industry isn't easy. I know, since I'm in it myself. I appreciate your assistance and working with me to make sure this woman gets home safely." He pulled out his wallet and selected a fifty-dollar bill, holding it out to the man.

The doorman looked surprised, but reached for the tip. He nodded at Pipe. "Thank you."

Pipe returned the nod, then turned to Cora.

She was staring at him with a confused expression. Was his being a decent human being that surprising? He had a feeling it was. At least to her...which pissed him off. "Ready?" he asked, gesturing to the street outside the doors.

She jerked as if surprised by the word, then nodded and turned to the door. The doorman immediately opened it and held it for them.

"Be safe," he said as they exited into the night.

Cora turned left and started walking at a fast clip. Pipe immediately lengthened his strides until he reached her right side, closest to the busy street. They walked silently for a minute or two before she looked up at him.

Pipe stood at least half a foot taller than Cora, but for some reason she seemed larger than life. She walked with confidence, her eyes constantly scanned her immediate area, and he couldn't help but grin when she refused to step aside as they neared a pair of men who were walking toward them. They both almost walked right into her before veering to the right to go around her. Obviously, they were used to women giving them the right of way on the sidewalk, which was extremely sexist and misogynistic, but so engrained in society, everyone simply accepted it.

Everyone except for Cora, apparently.

Pipe looked down and caught her eye, before she turned her attention to the sidewalk in front of her again. He had a feeling she was working herself up to say something to him, and he wasn't wrong. She began to speak moments later. Fast and staccato, like if she didn't get out what she wanted to say right that second, she'd chicken out and not say anything at all.

"I came tonight to bid on you and *only* you. I looked you up online. You and your friends. I know you co-own The Refuge out in New Mexico. That you guys were special forces. I know you were in the SAS, and I even saw the news articles about Alaska Stein, Jasna McClure, and Reese Woodall, about what each of them went through. I saved up every penny I could to win that bid."

"Then bitch-face won," Pipe said in a flat tone, a little leery that she seemed to know so much about him and his friends.

A snort escaped Cora. "Yeah. She's hated me since high school. Would do anything to make my life miserable."

"Why?"

"Why does she hate me? Um...because she's a bitch?" Cora said with a shrug.

"No, don't give a fuck about her. Why *me*?"

Cora stopped walking, and Pipe turned to look at her. She took a deep breath and said, "I need your help."

"With what?" Pipe asked.

Instead of answering, Cora sighed and looked past him. "Shoot. This isn't going how I thought it would."

His lips twitched. "How'd you think it would go?"

"You're full of questions," she accused.

Pipe shrugged and realized he was actually enjoying himself. He hadn't thought anything about this trip would be fun, but meeting this woman was more enjoyable than anything else had been in a long time. She was so unusual, and with every word, he was more and more intrigued. "Yup. I am. But I'm not the one who was willing to spend five thousand bucks to go to dinner with me just to ask for help."

"Six," she muttered.

"Pardon?"

"I had six thousand dollars," she admitted, looking him in the eye. "And if I could've come up with more, I would've spent that too."

"What's so important that you were willing to spend so much?" Pipe asked.

"Not what. Who," Cora corrected.

Surprisingly, disappointment hit Pipe. The only person he could imagine Cora spending that much money on was someone she loved. "Right," he said. "I'm thinking we need to have this conversation somewhere else, not in the middle of the sidewalk in the dark."

As if she could read his mind, tell that he'd mentally taken a step back from her, Cora reached out and put her hand on his arm. "It's not like that," she insisted.

"I don't know what you're talking about."

"Her name is Lara Osler. She's my best friend. The only person in the world I trust with my whole heart. She's in trouble and no one will listen to me. No one believes me.

Not her parents, not the cops. They all think I'm crazy, that I'm just upset because she's left town and I don't have her around to mooch off anymore. Not that I would do that. Mooch off her, I mean. She's helped me in the past, I won't deny that, but she's literally the only person in the world who gives a damn about me, and I refuse to believe she up and left without a word."

The desperation and honesty in her tone made Pipe tense. She was genuinely worried about her friend and believed she was in danger. Anxious enough to go out of her comfort zone to attend a fancy bachelor auction, just to talk to him. The least he could do was give her a moment of his time. But not here. He didn't like the dark, especially in a city he didn't know.

"Come on," he said, putting his hand at the small of her back and urging her to start walking again.

She did so without complaint, even though her brow was furrowed.

They walked for a few blocks until Pipe saw what he was looking for. When she tried to head toward the entrance to the Metro, he steered her to the left instead.

"Pipe?"

He couldn't help but smile. He liked that she called him that. Brick and the others might prefer their women to use their given names, but he'd never felt like a "Bryson." He'd been Pipe for as long as he could remember; it felt right for her to call him by his nickname.

"It's not The Inn at Little Washington, but with the way we're dressed, it's probably a bit more appropriate," he said, while nodding at the twenty-four-hour diner on the corner.

Cora stopped again, and Pipe was forced to stop with her. She looked up at him in disbelief.

"What? You want to eat somewhere else?" he asked.

"No, it's fine. I just...you're taking me to eat?"

"Yup."

"Why?"

"You wanted to talk to me. I'm here and willing to listen."

"Why?" she asked again, this time in a whisper.

Pipe decided to level with her. "Because something about you screams honesty. I'm a little wary that you know so much about me and my buddies, but what you said about your friend? That's how I feel about the men I work with at The Refuge. If something happened to them, I'd do just about anything to make sure they were safe. I'm not promising you anything other than a free meal, but I'm intrigued enough to want to hear more."

Cora swallowed hard and closed her eyes for a moment. Then they snapped open and she stared at him with narrowed eyes. "I'm not sleeping with you."

Pipe frowned in confusion. "I don't recall asking you to."

"Many men don't."

Pipe didn't understand for a beat...then he got pissed. "Taking you out to dinner doesn't entitle me to sex. Doesn't entitle *any* guy to a shag."

"Sorry," she said, not looking or sounding sorry at all. "I just had to make sure we were on the same page."

Pipe was furious that Cora had such a low opinion of men.

No. It wasn't that. He was mad that she obviously had a *reason* to think such things right off the bat.

If anyone needed someone she could trust, it was this woman. And he wanted to be that person for her. He knew without a doubt that once she let someone in, like her friend Lara, she'd defend him or her to the death if necessary.

She was the kind of woman he'd always wanted by his side. Someone who wasn't scared to be with him, who would stick up for him, love him for who he was. It was almost a shame he wasn't from DC. Not that Cora was interested.

But then...he remembered how she'd defended him to the bitch Eleanor, when she didn't even know him.

*His tattoos, beard, and long hair don't make him a gang member or a violent person, just as your lack of tattoos doesn't make you an upstanding citizen. Personally? I think his tattoos are sexy as hell. They tell me he's a man who doesn't give a shit about what other people think. People like you, who look down on him because of a little ink on his skin. You'd sully his reputation if he was ever seen with you.*

"We're on the same page," Pipe said gruffly.

The relief in her entire body narked him off further, but also made him want to reassure her. Tell her that she could trust him, that he'd help her. But he kept his mouth shut because he didn't know if he *could* help her. He needed more information. Once he knew what the situation was, he'd decide on his next steps.

They walked to the door of the diner and Pipe held it open for her. The waitress who came to greet them took one look at him and stiffened slightly. He wasn't sure what she objected to—the full sleeves of tattoos, his longish hair and bushy beard, or maybe all those things combined, juxtaposed with the tuxedo pants, shiny shoes, and button-down shirt.

"Two, please," Cora said firmly, subtly leaning into him. Without thought, he wrapped his arm around her waist as he kept his face as blank and unthreatening as possible.

He could see the waitress relax a fraction as she said, "Follow me."

She led them to a booth in the back of the room, nowhere near the windows, which was fine with Pipe. He wanted Cora's complete attention, and here in the back of the room, where the light was a bit dimmer, he'd have that.

"Stupid woman doesn't realize that if the shit hits the fan while we're here, you'd be the person most likely to run to her rescue." She shook her head with a sigh.

Again, her defense of him made Pipe smile. She was like a mouse protecting an elephant, but somehow he knew down to his bones that her loyalty would be the greatest reward he could ever earn.

They made small talk as they looked over the menus then gave the waitress their order. When she walked away, Pipe put his forearms on the table and leaned in. "You wanted to win dinner with me to tell me your story, to ask for help for your friend. We're here. Talk to me. Tell me all of it."

Interestingly enough, she'd seemed nervous up until now. Had fiddled with her napkin, sipped the water the waitress had brought as if she needed something to do. But now that she was asked to talk about her friend, she lost some of her edginess. She copied his posture and leaned on the table as she began to speak.

# CHAPTER FOUR

"To explain, I have to go back," Cora told the man across the table.

She couldn't believe she was here, having dinner with the very person she'd been semi-stalking since finding out he'd be in DC. She'd been prepared to pay big bucks for this moment, but somehow, thanks to Eleanor's bitchiness —she'd be pissed if she knew her big mouth had given Cora exactly what she wanted, rather than having it stolen out from under her nose—she was sitting at a greasy diner, for free, getting a chance to potentially help Lara.

"I met Lara when I was fifteen. I'd changed schools, again, and things weren't going well for me in the new place. I didn't fit in...which wasn't really a surprise, as I rarely fit in anywhere, but I *really* didn't mesh with the kids at Harrison High."

"Why not?" Pipe asked.

"They mostly all came from rich families. Ones with political ties. I was a nobody. A foster kid who was shuttled from one house to another. I had a huge chip on my shoulder, didn't give a crap what anyone thought about me, and honestly, I'm not all that smart."

"Now *that* I don't believe," Pipe said with a small smile.

Cora studied the man, still a little stunned that she'd ended up sitting in a restaurant with him. His hair was longer in front, with a curl flopping onto his forehead. His beard and mustache were full and a little unkempt. His nose was long and narrow, his cheekbones high, and his dark eyes were focused on her with an intensity that was a little disconcerting. She instinctively knew this man didn't miss much, which both intrigued and scared the crap out of her.

Both arms were covered with tattoos, and she could see them peeking out behind the few open buttons of his white dress shirt as well. Some people would be turned off by all his ink, but not Cora. They fit him.

"Cora?" he prompted.

Realizing she'd been staring at Pipe without talking, Cora felt her cheeks heat and she forced herself to stop examining the man sitting across from her and kept talking.

"I'm not being derogatory toward myself, just telling the truth. I was a solid C student in high school. I'm sure it didn't help that I had to change schools every time I had to switch foster homes, but still. Anyway, I'd been there a week and the popular kids, like Eleanor, had already homed in on me as a target. I didn't care. I was used to being bullied. I'd learned to mostly ignore the juvenile insults and attempts to make me feel like shit.

"But at lunch that particular day, apparently Lara had heard enough. She stood up for me. Told Robbie McCallister to stick his head in a bucket of cow dung. She said it just like that too," Cora said with a fond chuckle. "Too

34

sweet to swear properly. And she looks like an angel. Tall, blonde hair, blue eyes, slender...all the boys were in love with her, and Robbie immediately backed off.

"Then she sat down next to me, and when the attention turned away from us, she started shaking a bit. I thought she was having a seizure or something. But she assured me it was simply delayed reaction. She *hates* being the center of attention. It literally makes her have a panic attack. Ironic, since her gorgeous looks are like a beacon to everyone around her. Anyway, to try to help, I talked to her about stupid shit, just babbling really, until she felt a little more in control.

"Eventually, she held out a hand to me and said, 'Hi, I'm Lara Osler. Your new best friend.' She was kidding, but little did we know how true that would become. We spent the next two and a half years of high school fending off the cruel bitches who ran that place and have been thick as thieves ever since."

The words seemed so lame, considering how close Cora and Lara had truly become over the years. Nothing happened in either of their lives that the other didn't know about...until recently. And Cora couldn't, *wouldn't*, believe that Lara had simply moved on. They'd been best friends for over two decades. A friendship like that didn't simply disappear because of a man.

"Neither of us dated in high school. I didn't have any interest in the assholes who came after me because they thought I'd be easy, and Lara was too shy, too focused on getting good grades. We spent every extra moment we had together, which was a godsend. After graduating, Lara headed off to college, and I moved with her. I found a job to help support us. We got a small, crappy apartment together, and things were pretty good. When she graduated with her early childhood degree, she got a job at a preschool near our place. I worked a bunch of different jobs as she continued to get raises and more and more responsibility."

"After a few years, we decided the time had come for us to find our own places. I was all right with it, although I knew it would be tough to swing the rent by myself. But I could tell Lara really wanted to spread her wings. She was finally dating a little bit, as was I, and it felt like what we were supposed to do...you know, grow up, get a job, get your own apartment.

"It was okay for a while. Until my douchebag landlord decided to come into my place at two in the morning to," she made quotation marks in the air as she spoke, "check my fire alarm batteries, and found himself staring down the barrel of my pistol. He wasn't too happy. The next morning, after the cops left and I'd gotten some sleep, I found an eviction notice on my door."

"That's illegal," Pipe growled.

Cora shrugged. "Of course it was, but who was going to defend me? It wasn't as if I could afford to hire a lawyer or anything. And no one in the complex was going to stick up for me because they needed a place to live just as much as I did. Anyway, Lara didn't hesitate to take me in. I slept on her couch for almost six months, and she never, not once, made me feel as if I was a nuisance." Cora paused, a slight smile on her face. "For someone who'd been a foster kid, you have no idea what a big deal that is.

"Eventually I found a new place to live and moved out again. Of course...a couple of months later, I lost my job. My boss decided she liked me, and when I wouldn't go out with her, she came up with a reason to fire me."

Pipe growled across the table. Cora looked up and was

surprised to see how angry he looked. Reaching out her hand without thought, she gripped his arm. "It's okay."

"It's *not* okay," he said between clenched teeth.

"It's the way of the world," she said with a small shrug.

Pipe put his hand over hers on his arm. He leaned forward a little more and shook his head. "*I've* never been fired from a job for not returning someone's interest. *I've* never had a landlord come into my flat in the middle of the night."

"You're a guy," she said immediately. "And you have friends. I'm thinking Ned—and yes, that really was my landlord's name—knew that I didn't have a lot of visitors other than Lara. Family, other friends, boyfriend, that kind of thing. I was an easy target and he knew it. Same with my boss. People can sense when someone doesn't have a support network. Especially in this town. Of *course* no one messes with you, Pipe. Even without your badass tattoos, you ooze confidence and fuck-off vibes."

He continued to frown.

And for some reason, Cora really wanted to soothe him.

"I was a foster kid. I wasn't wanted. I had fourteen foster homes, and not one family ever gave the slightest indication that they wanted to keep me for good. I wasn't a bad kid, I didn't cause trouble, but they still always sent me packing after a while."

Her chin came up at the look of sorrow on Pipe's face.

"It's fine. *I'm* fine," she insisted curtly. "I survived, and I had Lara. I'm not telling you all this for your pity. I'm telling you so you truly understand that Lara was my family. *Is* my family. I'd do literally anything for her. She's been my rock since I was fifteen. Even *she* probably doesn't know just how much she means to me. She's the sister I never had, and I wouldn't be here today if it wasn't for her."

With a sigh, she continued. "Moving this boring-ass story along, when I was fired, she got me a job at the preschool where she worked. By then, she was the executive director. She hired me as a teacher's aide. It's like the lowest member of their staff, but I refused to let her down. And a funny thing happened..." Her voice trailed off.

"What?" Pipe asked.

Cora realized then that he was still basically holding her hand. His large palm was resting over hers, where it was still lying on his arm.

"I realized that I loved it. Loved working with the kids. I'd been a waitress, a stripper, a valet, and what feels like a hundred other things...but I'd found my niche. Kids that young don't care about your skin color, your sexual orientation, your weight or height, if you have a family or not...all they care about is whether you're nice to them. If they feel safe in your presence.

"So not only did Lara stick up for me in high school. She gave me a place to stay when I needed it, she fed me, and then she gave me a job that I love more than I ever thought possible. And now she needs my help—and no one will listen to me." Her voice cracked on the last few words.

"*I'm* listening," Pipe said gently.

Looking up at him, Cora stared for a long moment.

"Talk to me," he ordered. "Why do you think she's in danger? Where is she?"

Cora opened her mouth, but the waitress returned at that moment. "Here we go," she said perkily. Cora was forced to let go of Pipe, and she sat back as the plates were put down on the table. "Can I get you two anything else?"

"No, thank you," Cora said.

"We're good," Pipe agreed.

"All right. Enjoy, and if you need anything, don't hesitate to let me know."

Cora studied the food in front of her, but she'd completely lost her appetite.

"Eat," Pipe said in a low, growly voice.

She looked up at him.

He nodded to her plate. "It'll make you feel better."

"Actually, it might make me puke," she grumbled.

Pipe's lips twitched. "When was the last time you ate something?"

She tried to remember if she'd had lunch that day, and realized she'd been so nervous and worked up about the auction, she hadn't. "Breakfast?" she said, the word coming out more as a question than a true answer.

"You need some calories," Pipe said in a gentler voice.

"It feels wrong to eat when I can't help but wonder if Lara's okay. If *she's* getting food."

Pipe tensed. "Look at me," he said in a tone Cora hadn't heard before. It was harder, more commanding. She couldn't help but lift her gaze to his.

"Would Lara want you to starve yourself just because she wasn't getting enough to eat? Would she really want you to suffer along with her?"

"No," Cora whispered.

"Right. Eat, Cora. We'll talk after. And if I can help your friend, I will."

Her eyes widened. "You will?" she couldn't help but ask.

"Yes."

"But you don't know the situation. I mean, I might be wrong. She could be perfectly fine."

Pipe stared at her for so long, Cora squirmed in her seat. "You aren't wrong," he finally said.

Her eyes closed as she struggled to process what was happening. *No one* had believed her. Not the cops, not Lara's family, not their co-workers. They all told her she was jealous, or overreacting, or just plain wrong. But she knew better.

The extremely short email Lara had sent to Human Resources with her request for a leave of absence was shady as hell, but no one other than her seemed to even think twice about it. Lara wouldn't just up and leave without talking to her first. Cora knew that without a doubt.

And this man, this stranger, believed her without even really hearing what had happened.

"Eat," Pipe said again, a little gentler.

Cora's eyes opened and she looked down at the turkey club sandwich she'd ordered. Suddenly, she was ravenous. She reached for the ketchup bottle on the table and smothered her sandwich in the stuff. She also poured it all over her French fries.

Looking up, she caught Pipe smiling at her. The change it made in his countenance was astounding. It was like a completely different man was sitting across from her.

"I take it you like ketchup," he drawled.

"I don't like it, I love it," she told him. "It makes everything taste better. When I was little and forced to eat food I didn't like, putting ketchup on it made it palatable. When I was on my own, and short on cash, I could put this stuff on just about anything and it somehow made me feel fuller."

He frowned at that, but Cora simply smiled. "It's okay, Pipe. Really. I survived. A lot of people have been way worse off than me. And ketchup is honestly the world's perfect condiment."

He didn't look so sure, but picked up the hamburger he'd ordered, one without any sauce or condiment on it whatsoever—heathen—and took a large bite.

They ate in companionable silence. When she was nearly finished with her meal, Cora felt herself smiling. "What do you think they would've served at that fancy restaurant? I mean, if I'd won and we were there now?"

In response, Pipe put down his hamburger and reached for his phone. Cora frowned in confusion. He typed for a moment before his lips quirked upward. "According to their website, 'carpaccio of herb-crusted elysian fields baby lamb loin with Caesar salad ice cream, or pecan-crusted, mushroom-stuffed loin roulade with mustard and drunken prunes.'"

Cora couldn't stop her nose from wrinkling. "Do you know what any of that is?"

"Nope," Pipe said breezily.

"What the hell is Caesar salad ice cream? And drunk or not, prunes are not my idea of a good meal."

This time, he chuckled. "Agreed." He put his phone back in his pocket. "I'm much happier with my burger, and I don't think putting ketchup on the prunes would help them sober up any."

Cora giggled. As soon as the sound left her mouth, she felt guilty. Here she was having a wonderful time, eating a great sandwich, when she had no idea what Lara was going through.

"Don't," Pipe said, his brows drawing down.

"I can't help it. I'm so worried about her."

Pipe pushed his plate to the side and reached for her

hand. Cora let him take it. His thumb brushed over the skin on the back as he spoke.

"I don't know your friend, but to have inspired such loyalty in you, I know she has to be an amazing person. And she's tougher than you're giving her credit for."

"You don't know her. She's...not like me," Cora finished somewhat lamely. "I'm not afraid to say what I'm thinking. She's nice. Sweet. I told you before that she didn't date in high school, but even after that, she didn't go out much, despite wanting desperately to find her Prince Charming. She always sees the best in people, and they frequently take advantage of her. She doesn't like to rock the boat, in a relationship or in her professional life. I think that's how Ridge hooked her. He pretended to be a gentleman. But he's not. I mean, from what I've seen, that is."

Pipe stared at her for a long moment before reaching for his pocket. He pulled out his wallet and threw a couple of twenty-dollar bills on the table. Then, without a word, he stood and reached for Cora's elbow.

She was too surprised to resist when he pulled her to her feet. He grabbed her bag and put it over his shoulder. With his hand still under her elbow, he walked to the door. When they were on the sidewalk, he turned right, back the way they came.

"Pipe?" Cora asked. "Where are we going? The Metro is the other way."

"My hotel," he said shortly.

Cora stopped in her tracks, surprising Pipe enough that his hand slipped from her arm. "I already told you that I'm not sleeping with you," she growled. Disappointment swam in her belly. Had she really been so wrong about this man?

Pipe ran a hand through his hair, mussing it further. "I'm not good at this stuff, Cora."

"What stuff?" she asked, confused.

"Planning. Figuring shite out. I'm the muscle. I'm sent in to do the dirty work. My mates are better at the pre-mission details. I don't know what you're going to tell me about your friend, but my instincts tell me that it would be better if Owl was there...the guy who came to DC with me."

Cora nodded. "Callen Kaufman. Former Night Stalker Army helicopter pilot. He was shot down in the Middle East with his copilot, Jack 'Stone' Wickett—who also co-owns The Refuge with you and your other friends. They were held for a couple of weeks while the terrorists tortured them and filmed it all."

Pipe blinked. Then smirked. "Stalker," he joked.

Cora couldn't help returning his smile, but it quickly faded. "I needed to know if you guys could really help me find and rescue Lara."

The humor fell from Pipe's face. "If you truly believe she *needs* to be rescued from wherever she is, and our skills are needed, trust me, you want Owl to hear your story. He doesn't have as much experience as the rest of us with boots on the ground, but he's smart. It'll help to have his input."

Every instinct was screaming that Cora could trust the man in front of her. He'd been nothing but gentlemanly and courteous. He didn't have to walk her home. Didn't have to buy her dinner. But here he was. Though...she didn't believe for an instant that Pipe couldn't plan a rescue mission by himself.

"Okay," she said after a long pause. This had been her goal from the moment she'd realized one of the owners from The Refuge would be at the auction. She'd wanted a chance to talk to one of them, to plead her case. To explain what was happening to *two* of The Refuge owners was more than she ever dreamed she'd get.

They continued to walk, stopping at a hotel just down the street from where the auction had been held. It wasn't fancy. A chain hotel Cora herself sometimes stayed at when she traveled, which wasn't often.

Pipe opened the door and he led her up an escalator to the deserted restaurant on the second floor, toward a table in the back. He sat, gesturing for her to do the same.

"Um, are we supposed to be here?" Cora asked nervously, looking around at the empty tables and the semi-dark room.

"It's fine," Pipe assured her. "Not going to take you to my room, that would be disrespectful," he said as he typed out a text on his phone.

Cora stared in surprise as his concentration remained on the screen in front of him. Many men wouldn't have thought twice about taking her to their room, even if they *weren't* planning on making a move on her. In her experience, guys were largely clueless to the things women went through to stay safe. It wasn't that they were unsympathetic; they just had no reason to worry about walking across an isolated parking lot, getting in an elevator with a man, walking up an empty stairwell, being anywhere alone in the middle of the night, getting gas, and a million other everyday scenarios.

But she probably shouldn't have underestimated Pipe. He wasn't like most men, which was precisely why she'd wanted his help.

"Owl's on his way," he told her.

"I'm still not sure why you think he needs to be here."

"I told you, I'm not a good planner."

"I don't believe that for a second," Cora said firmly. "You wouldn't have been in the SAS if you sucked at that kind of thing."

Pipe shrugged. "You'd be surprised. The military the world over is the same. They need foot soldiers. Men and women willing to give their lives if necessary, without question. Just like any organization, there are those who excel at thinking and those who are best at doing."

Cora frowned. "And you're saying you were an unthinking robot who simply did what he was told?"

His lips twitched. "Not exactly."

"I know you realize by now that I did my research on you and your friends," she said, wanting him to understand why she was here with him.

"Yeah, you made that clear."

"I don't think I did. Pipe, I live in Washington, DC. You know how many military guys there are around here? Generals? Special Forces? Even private security, people who've spent years guarding the freaking President of the United States. Not that I know them personally, but I could've used my six thousand dollars to hire one or more of them. I didn't. You know why?"

She had Pipe's full attention now.

"One, because the people I *did* contact only wanted my money. Didn't seem to care about Lara as a person. But mostly because I wanted the best. I wanted someone who would take this as personally as I do. Who would believe me when I told them my best friend was in trouble. Not someone who'd just take my money, do a shit job researching her situation, maybe a little recon, and then tell me they couldn't help."

"How do you know I won't do just that?"

"Because of Alaska," Cora said softly. "And Jasna. And Reese. You and your friends...you're protectors. Not only of all the men and women who come to stay at The Refuge, but especially for the people you love. I've read all about how you guys used your skills to help the women who now live at the resort with you. And while you don't know me, or Lara, I instinctively knew without a doubt that you'd do whatever it took to help me bring her home."

Pipe stared at her for so long, Cora struggled not to squirm in her seat. But she tilted her chin a touch higher and refused to give in to the unease swimming in her veins. She'd spent her life being judged, and she didn't care about this man's opinion of her, as long as he agreed to help Lara.

Refusing to admit she was lying to herself about caring what Pipe thought about her, Cora waited for him to say something.

"I can't promise you anything," he finally said.

"I know."

"And we aren't in the military anymore. We're civilians. We can't exactly use guns, grenades, and the might of the government to break laws."

"I know that too. I'm not asking you to do that. All I'm asking is for you to use the tactics you've learned to help me get in to see my friend, and possibly get her out of a bad situation."

"And you're sure she's *in* a bad situation?" Pipe asked.

Thankful he didn't sound skeptical, just curious, Cora nodded firmly. "One hundred percent."

When he didn't respond, Cora said a little desperately, "And I still have my six thousand dollars. It's all yours to use for flights or supplies or whatever you need."

"If we decide to help you, we aren't taking your money," Pipe said firmly.

Cora wasn't certain how to respond to that. He had no idea what she'd done to come up with that amount of money. The fact that he'd let her keep it meant the world to her. She could use it to get Lara counseling, to move them to another city...whatever it took to make sure her friend was okay after whatever she'd been through.

And that was the most terrifying thing—Cora had no idea *what* was happening to Lara. She might be fine. Might be perfectly safe and being treated kindly.

She mentally snorted. She didn't believe that for a moment. Whatever her friend was experiencing, it wasn't good. Cora had no doubts about that.

The sound of footsteps startled her, and she turned toward the entrance to the restaurant. She half expected an employee to be standing there frowning, but instead, the man she'd seen earlier that night, Owl, was walking toward them.

"He really does look a little like Ed Sheeran," she mused.

"If you want to get on his good side, whatever you do, don't bring that up," Pipe said before standing and greeting his friend.

Owl pulled a chair out from one of the empty sides of the square table and nodded at her. "So you're Cora."

"And you're Owl," she returned.

He grinned. "That's me." He turned to Pipe. "You didn't miss much. The MC was a little peeved that you weren't there, but since they raised over a hundred thousand for veterans, he'll get over it."

"And the bitch?"

"Ran off with her equally bitchy friends," Owl said with a shrug.

"You made it clear that I wasn't taking her to dinner?" he asked.

Owl smirked. "I don't think that was ever a part of her plan."

"Right. What was it she said?" Pipe asked, looking at Cora. "'No way would I sully my reputation by being seen out and about with someone who looks like a gang member.' Right?"

"I don't remember every word, but that sounds right," Cora said. It was a lie. She remembered exactly what Eleanor had said as she'd insulted Pipe. His memory was spot on.

She once more doubted his claim that he wasn't a good planner. Anyone with that good of a memory had to be an asset when planning some top-secret op.

"Anyway, she left, I paid her bid, all's good," Owl said. "Now...what's up?"

Pipe looked at Cora. Having both sets of eyes on her was a little disconcerting, but she did what she always did. Straightened her shoulders and refused to show that she was intimidated.

"My friend Lara was kidnapped by her so-called boyfriend, and I need help breaking her out and bringing her home."

# CHAPTER FIVE

Pipe wasn't completely surprised at Cora's pronouncement. He'd had a feeling it was something like this from the little she'd said earlier. "Go on," he encouraged.

He was impressed with the woman sitting across from him. The accusation she was making was serious, and he supposed if there was proof of what she was saying, the police would've acted by now. But despite the lack of such proof, instead of giving up, going home and getting on with her life, she was digging in her heels. It was more than obvious she truly believed what she was saying.

"About three months ago, Lara met this guy. To me, it seemed a little too coincidental. They bumped into each other at the coffee shop she goes to every morning. I've told her more than once that she needs to change up her routine every now and then. You know, not go to the same place at the same time every day, not take the same route home, stop going to the grocery store every single Sunday at ten in the morning, that kind of thing. But Lara's always been a little naïve.

"Anyway, she came to work all excited about the tall, dark, and handsome guy she'd met. Within just days, she was spending all her free time with him. He said all the right things and apparently was very generous. He showered her with gifts, which she loved. Her family is rich, and she grew up having everything she wanted. Not that she's spoiled, far from it, but she's never really known hardship. I think having this guy give her little presents because he supposedly cared about her was very flattering for her."

Cora stopped, and Pipe could tell she was thinking back on her own hardships. His hands clenched in his lap. He hated that this woman had obviously suffered. That she'd had to be tough and look after herself since childhood. Being in the foster care system wasn't easy, and he recalled the pain in her voice when she'd talked about being rejected by family after family.

"I wanted to meet him, but every time we planned to hang out, his plans suddenly changed. And not just a few times, but over and over for weeks. But Lara continued to sing his praises. And to be honest...he simply sounded *too* perfect. Good looking, rich, completely devoted to Lara after just days...not that I think she couldn't attract a guy like that, and she certainly deserves one. But when I looked him up on social media, there wasn't much there. And the little I did find consisted of pictures of him with beautiful women, or posing alone in front of expensive cars and boats. Look, I get it, social media isn't real life, but there was nothing there that made me think he was anything but a playboy, let alone a good match for Lara.

"I also thought it was a bit weird that she fell for someone who wasn't sticking around. Apparently he travels a lot, and he was here on a project for his dad. That didn't seem like the best set-up for a long-term relationship, especially when Lara's job was here.

"I was already suspicious of his feelings for her, but by the fifth time he'd had something come up unexpectedly when we were supposed to go out for drinks, I knew something wasn't right. Most men who want more than a casual fling would want to meet their women's friends, wouldn't they? But he was going out of his way to *avoid* meeting me. It didn't sit well, but Lara kept making excuses for him and reassuring me that he *did* want to meet, but the timing never worked. She was head over heels in love with this guy by this point, and she had serious stars in her eyes.

"He finally agreed to go out for dinner with us shortly before Lara disappeared from town. Believe me, I honestly wanted to give the guy the benefit of the doubt, because Lara had nothing but great things to say, and she was crazy about him. But meeting him face-to-face didn't make any of my concerns dissipate. If fact, it only made me more sure that he was a total dirtbag."

"How so?" Pipe asked.

"He wouldn't meet my eyes, not even when he shook my hand. His phone kept going off with notifications and texts, and he wouldn't put the damn thing down to talk to me or Lara. He made a few off-color, inappropriate jokes, and he subtly put Lara down. She didn't even notice, but I did. I'd lived with my share of foster parents who did the same thing, so I recognized what he was doing right away —a power play. Everything he did and said was about control.

"And to top it all off, when our waitress came to the table, he couldn't take his gaze from her tits. The guy made my skin crawl, and I honestly hated everything about him. I couldn't believe Lara didn't see any of it.

"Of course, right before our meals came, he got another text and told Lara that he was sorry, but he had to leave. He didn't say why, just simply got up and left."

"Please tell me he paid for your meal on his way out," Owl muttered.

"Of course he didn't," Cora snorted. "I could tell Lara was upset that he'd left, but she pretended everything was fine. Told me he was a very busy man with a lot of important deals he was working on.

"When we got back to her place...we had a fight," Cora said softly. "I told her that he was no good, that he was going to hurt her. Lara very rarely raised her voice, especially to me. But she yelled at me that night. Told me I was just jealous, that she wasn't going to let my bitterness ruin the best thing that had ever happened to her. It hurt. I don't think we'd ever fought like that before. And I *wasn't* jealous. If she found someone who honestly loved her like she deserved to be loved, I would be pushing them together. Would do everything in my power to help that relationship along. But this guy...no. He was self-centered and immature and a womanizer, and I didn't want my best friend anywhere near him."

"What's his name?" Owl asked.

"Ridge. Ridge Michaels. I tried to do more research on him, but most of the stuff I found online was about his rich parents. I discovered where he went to high school, and saw a ton of pictures of him in tuxedos at one fancy event after another, but nothing really substantive."

"Can you describe him?" Pipe asked.

"Of course. He's younger than us, maybe around thirty? He's tall; about the same height as Lara, so five-ten or so. Short dark brown hair, brown eyes. His nose has been broken at some point because it's a little crooked. He's built, muscular, not fat at all. The night we went out for our unsuccessful dinner, he'd dressed casually in a pair of brown slacks that had perfect creases and a polo shirt. He looked like a successful businessman, but..." Her voice trailed off.

"But what?" Pipe asked.

Cora shook her head. "You'll think it's stupid."

"No, we won't," the men said at the same time.

Cora's lips twitched before she sighed. "I'm not sure that he actually works at all. I mean, according to Lara, he allegedly owns some kind of technology company...she wasn't sure of the details...but he didn't seem to know how to use some of the features on his own phone. Hell, Lara had to show him how to adjust the font size when he complained he couldn't read his texts.

"Anyway, our fight was on a Friday night. I didn't talk to her all weekend, I was still too upset that she wasn't taking my concerns seriously. That she wouldn't even listen to me. By Monday morning, I was anxious to see her. To apologize, even though I didn't think I had anything to be sorry about. I wanted to have a rational conversation about Ridge. Spell out my concerns and make her understand that they were coming from a place of love and concern, but she didn't show up for work."

Cora looked at Owl, then Pipe. "You have to understand, Lara very rarely misses work, and then only if she's sick, because she doesn't want to pass any kind of illness to the children. She lives and breathes her job, and she has something like three months of vacation time built up. I immediately knew something was wrong. The office told me there was nothing to worry about, that there was an email sent Saturday morning to HR about her taking a leave of absence. I immediately knew that was bullshit. Lara wouldn't just leave without talking to me."

"But you fought," Owl reminded her.

Cora shook her head vehemently. "No! I mean, *yes*, we did, but there's no way Lara would have just left work without arranging it well in advance. She's too responsible. I immediately texted her, and she responded, but the wording was wrong on her reply."

"How?" Pipe asked.

Cora looked away briefly. "She didn't use punctuation," she said quietly. When Owl gave her a skeptical look, she straightened. "And before you tell me that's not proof, you don't know Lara like I do. She got a hundred and four percent in her advanced English class in high school. And in college, she continued to get A's in all the classes where she had to write papers. Look, I'll show you," she said almost desperately.

She pulled out her cell phone and clicked on a few buttons before practically thrusting it at Pipe. He took it and scrolled through the messages on the screen.

"If you go back, you'll see that before she took this so-called leave of absence, she used periods, commas, exclamation points every now and then. Her punctuation is always perfect. It's a point of pride that I've teased her about for years. But in her more recent texts, there's nothing. It's just *not* like her."

Pipe had to admit she had a point. He handed the phone to Owl.

"I went to the cops. They said she was an adult woman and could decide to take a spontaneous vacation with her boyfriend if she wanted. The fact that she was still texting me was enough for them to conclude she was fine. They dismissed me as if I was just being paranoid. I'm *not*. This

Ridge guy kidnapped her. He's not letting her talk to me. And I'm scared to death that he's going to do something awful to her, if he hasn't already."

"When did all this happen? How long has she been gone?" Owl asked.

"A month and a half," Cora whispered. "He's had her for almost two months."

Pipe didn't want to ask his next question, but he had to. "Do you have any proof that she's still alive? Have you talked to her at all?"

"She's alive. At least, she was two weeks ago. I kind of lied and texted that the Phoenix police would be knocking on their door if she didn't call me, if I couldn't see or hear for myself that she was all right. I went through her apartment—and no, I'm not sorry—and found an address for Ridge in Arizona. The phone rang two hours later. It was Ridge. He wasn't happy. Told me that he'd press charges for harassment if I didn't stop. I told *him* that until I spoke to Lara, I wasn't *ever* going to stop. He turned FaceTime on, and Lara was there. They were sitting on a bed together. She wasn't herself," Cora said in a shaky tone.

"In what way?" Owl asked.

"She seemed really...*off*. I apologized profusely for our fight, even though I still felt more than ever that I was right. Her voice was wooden. Monotone. Her gaze kept drifting away from the screen. But she accepted my apology, and told me she was happy and that she wasn't returning to DC. I panicked. I mean, she's spent her entire life here. She loved her job. Her parents are here. But more than that, she just seemed so unemotional about it all. As if she wasn't really there. It was Lara, but it wasn't... if that makes sense."

Pipe nodded.

"Then Ridge pointed the camera back on himself, told me now that I'd seen Lara and knew she was fine, I needed to leave them alone to live their lives. He told me to butt out and hung up."

"So what do you think *we* can do?" Owl asked.

Cora turned to him. "Go in and get her," she said without hesitation.

Owl frowned. "We can't just kidnap her."

"I know! I mean, I *technically* know. But a part of me still wants to do just that. He's hurting her. I know it. The person I saw on that video phone call wasn't my friend. It looked like she was drugged or something. And she's protecting me. I have no doubt about that. I think Ridge threatened her to say what she did."

"You can't actually know that—" Pipe started.

"I *do*!" Cora interrupted fiercely, then paused, taking a few deep breaths to calm herself. "Look...Lara and I watched a movie together once. A woman was kidnapped and held hostage by her mafia boyfriend. When her mom finally got to see her, she sent her a secret message, letting her know that she wasn't there of her own free will. The movie was horrible. Really cheesy and stupid. But we watched until the end anyway...then we talked about what *we'd* do if we were ever in a situation like that."

She stood, as if she needed to burn off nervous energy. She paced briefly behind her chair, wringing her hands. "Of course, we both insisted we'd never be so stupid, but we were having fun, discussing something we assumed would never happen. We even came up with a signal. Something only the two of us would know—and when we were talking, *she gave me that signal*.

"I'm not crazy, Pipe. I'm not jealous of my friend. She's in trouble, and I'm the only one who cares. Her parents are actually *thrilled* that she's finally found a man. The police think she's there of her own free will. But she's not!" Cora was practically yelling by the time she finished.

Pipe hated seeing her so upset, even as he admired her fierce defense of her friend.

He didn't care what people looked like. Didn't give a rat's ass how much money they had in the bank. What he *did* care about was loyalty. The lack of it was why he'd finally left the SAS. He'd seen too many of his superiors— who were supposed to ensure the safety of the men under their command—make decisions to further their own careers instead of protecting men and women in the field. And he'd worked with plenty of people who were more concerned about saving their own skins than about the soldiers fighting alongside them.

He knew he had PTSD after everything he'd seen and done. Not nearly as badly as some of his friends at The Refuge, but he was thrilled nonetheless that he was no longer regularly put into a position that involved a hail of bullets. Or knowing someone may or may not have an RPG pointed at his chopper. He'd been loyal to the military, but seeing others not care about the lives of soldiers under their command had affected him deeply.

The six other men who owned The Refuge were as loyal friends as he'd ever known, and he finally felt like he'd found his place in the world. Now, seeing Cora fight tooth and nail for her friend, her extreme loyalty toward her, even when most signs pointed to the fact that Lara was with this Ridge guy because she wanted to be, made his heart turn over in his chest.

"What was the signal?" Owl asked.

Glancing at his friend, Pipe noticed he was leaning toward Cora as if he could pull the information out of her simply by staring. He was also visibly tense. More so than Pipe had ever seen him before.

Then it clicked. Owl been a hostage himself. He knew exactly how Lara was feeling...if she really was being held against her will.

Pipe wasn't sure what he believed at the moment. Oh, he was completely sure *Cora* believed her friend was in danger, but whether she was or not remained to be seen.

Cora took a deep breath and did her best to regain her composure. She clutched the chair in front of her with both hands as she met Owl's gaze. "She scratched her ear with her pinky," she said calmly, as if she wasn't just yelling at them a moment ago.

Pipe frowned.

"Like this," Cora said, demonstrating what she meant. She raised her hand and, using her pinky finger, kind of stuck it inside her ear and twirled it in a small circle. "It was quick, but I know what I saw. And trust me, that's not something Lara normally does."

It wasn't much...but Pipe started to believe her. What were the odds Lara would use the exact signal they'd devised if she *wasn't* in danger?

"All I'm asking for is help getting her out of that house in Phoenix. I know without a doubt that if I show up and knock on the door, Ridge will deny me entry. I'd try to sneak in, but I looked up the address on the Internet and checked out the satellite view. It's a sprawling estate. He probably has cameras and dogs and trip wires or something. I'd never get close, and then I'd end up just like Lara and we'd *both* be screwed. You guys have training. You can get in and out of places without anyone knowing. From that point, I'll take care of her. Hell, you don't even have to get us out of the city. I swear I won't bother you further if you can just get her out of that house."

She gave Pipe a pleading look. "I'm *not* crazy. And every day that goes by and she's there..." Her voice trailed off once again, and she slumped, head dropping between her shoulders as she continued to clutch the chair.

"Lara's the only family I've ever had," she said after a moment, her voice low. "And I won't abandon her." Her head came back up, and she looked at both Owl and Pipe. "If you won't help me, I'll figure something else out. But I feel like you're my best hope." She flicked her gaze to Owl. "I can pay you. I've got the six grand I was planning on using at the auction, to win a chance to talk to Pipe. I know it's not nearly enough, but if you tell me your price, I'll pay you back. Even if it takes me the rest of my life, I'll get you whatever you ask."

Pipe didn't like the desperation he heard in her voice. It was worrisome and simply...wrong. And he had a bone-deep instinct to fix it.

"Can you give Pipe and I a moment to talk?" Owl asked her.

She nodded and turned immediately, walking to the other side of the deserted restaurant to stare out the windows. Her back was ramrod straight, and it looked as if all it would take was one more stressor on her shoulders and she'd break into a million pieces.

"What do you think?" Owl asked softly.

He turned his attention to his friend. "She's telling the truth."

"I agree. But I'm not sure what we can do. It's not like we can actually go to Phoenix and storm the house," he said.

"Why not?" The words out of his own mouth surprised him, but he didn't take them back.

Owl lifted a brow.

"I don't mean kidnap her. If we put enough pressure on this Ridge guy, like going to his house every day, he'd have to let us see her eventually."

"Or he could call the cops and claim we're trespassing and harassing him and his girlfriend, just like he threatened to do to Cora," Owl reasoned.

"We need more intel," he said after a moment.

Owl nodded in agreement.

"We don't even know if Ridge is this guy's real name."

He nodded again. "And if her friend really *is* being held against her will...we can't turn our backs on her."

Pipe wasn't surprised at Owl's thinking. He, more than most, wouldn't be able to turn a blind eye to someone who was being held hostage. He knew how it felt. He and Stone had been through hell, and nothing would keep him from helping anyone else who might be enduring a similar situation.

"I agree," he told his friend.

"You think there's any way *she'll* agree to stay here in DC, while we look into things in Arizona?"

Pipe snorted. "Not a chance in hell."

"Yeah, that's what I was thinking. I'll call Stone. Give him a head's up on what's happening, and that we'll probably have a guest coming back with us. Maybe I'll give Tex a call to see if he can start looking into this Ridge guy too."

Pipe nodded, turning to look at Cora. She hadn't moved. She had her arms wrapped around her belly as if she was holding herself together. It looked like the weight of the world was on her shoulders, and he almost desperately wanted to carry that burden for her. "I'll meet you in the lobby tomorrow morning," he told Owl. "I'll see if I can get her to stay in DC and let us do some recon, but if she balks at that and insists on coming with us, she'll need to go back to her place and pack."

"Sounds good. Shoot me a text if she's coming with us, and I'll take care of getting her a ticket to New Mexico." Then Owl cleared his throat, and Pipe turned to look at his friend.

"We're all in on this, right?"

"Absolutely," he said with a nod. "You didn't hear the story of how she and Lara became friends. She was a foster kid, and she aged out of the system without anyone wanting to adopt her. Lara befriended her in high school and they've been extremely close ever since. They're like sisters, and if Cora says Lara's in danger...well, I'm starting to believe her."

"You're right, I *didn't* hear that story. But I didn't need to. The concern and love for her friend is easy to see. Besides, after what almost happened to Alaska, the thought of anyone else going through that...it turns my stomach."

Pipe nodded, his lips pulling down in a frown.

"All right. I'll let you tell her what's up. Let me know if you run into any snags, otherwise I'll see you in the morning," Owl said.

"Copy," Pipe said, reverting to military speak. Up until now, everything had been somewhat casual. He'd started the evening just hoping to satisfy his curiosity about why Cora wanted to win that auction so badly. Now that he and Owl had decided to check into Lara's situation officially, things felt more formal and urgent.

He nodded at Owl and didn't wait for him to head toward the elevators before walking over to Cora.

She turned as he got close. Her arms were still around her waist protectively, but she lifted her chin as if preparing for him to tell her bad news.

"We're leaving in the morning. Owl and I will meet with our friends at The Refuge and make a plan for going to Arizona to potentially talk to your friend."

Cora's eyes widened, then her shoulders sagged in what Pipe could only assume was relief. "You believe me?" she whispered.

Pipe stared at her for a long, intense moment before nodding.

She closed her eyes briefly before looking back up at him. "No one else has," she said in a tortured tone.

"You know your friend better than anyone. If you say she's in trouble, why shouldn't I believe you?"

"Because there's no evidence? Because she told me that she's fine? Because what woman *wouldn't* want some rich man to sweep her off her feet and whisk her away to a life of luxury?" Her tone was a bit bitter, but Pipe didn't take offense.

"I've relied on my gut more times than I can count. And it's never let me down. If you say she's in trouble, she's in trouble," he said with a shrug. "Any chance you'll wait here in DC while I go find Lara?"

Cora looked aghast. "What? No! I'm going with you!"

Pipe couldn't stop the small smile from forming on his lips.

"What's so funny?" she asked a little belligerently.

"Sorry, nothing. I had a feeling you'd want to come with us."

"Of *course* I'm coming with you! My best friend may or

may not have been kidnapped by her asshole boyfriend. There's no way I'm staying here while you go and see her."

Pipe nodded. Anticipation churned in his gut. He couldn't be upset that she was coming back to New Mexico with them. He was looking forward to spending more time with the woman. Getting to know her better. Not that anything would come of it...she lived in DC, and he wasn't going to leave The Refuge. But it had been a long time since he'd been drawn to a woman the way he was to Cora.

"All right," he told her. "I'll escort you back to your apartment so you can pack a bag. I've got two beds in my room here at the hotel. It'd be easier if you came back and stayed here, but if you don't feel comfortable with that, I can pick you up at your place in the morning, then we can meet up with Owl and head to the airport."

Cora nodded, even as she turned toward the restaurant's exit. "You don't have to take me home. I'm a big girl, and I've been riding the Metro my entire life without any issues."

"I know I don't, but if you think I'm going to let you walk off into the dark by yourself, you didn't do as much research into me as I thought."

Her lips twitched, then she sobered. "I just don't want you to think I'm some wilting flower who can't take care of myself. I've never had anyone to lean on before, other than Lara, and with the way I'm feeling right now—pissed off and frustrated about this whole situation—I can more than handle anyone stupid enough to come at me tonight."

"You've got someone to lean on now," Pipe said quietly as he gestured toward the exit. "Come on, let's get out of here."

She stared at him for a moment, and Pipe had no idea

what she was thinking. She was very good at hiding her emotions when she wanted to.

Finally, she nodded and walked past him.

As she did, he heard her whisper, "Thank you."

Those two words, spoken so softly, so earnestly, did something to Pipe. He'd been thanked before, many times, but never had an expression of gratitude sounded so heartfelt.

# CHAPTER SIX

Cora sat next to Pipe on the Metro, his thigh against her own, and couldn't remember when she'd felt so safe. Usually when she used public transportation, especially this late, she was on edge and fully alert. But with Pipe next to her, looking badass and wearing a scowl on his face, people gave them a wide berth.

She would've laughed if she wasn't so concerned about Lara.

It was hard to believe things had worked out so well. When she'd left her place earlier that evening to head to the auction, she had no idea what would happen. If she won the bid for Pipe, she didn't know when they might go to dinner. She didn't know if he'd believe her, or if he'd think she was just some paranoid, desperate, on-the-brink-of-bankruptcy nutcase.

She hated to think anything good about Eleanor fucking Vanlandingham, but the woman had actually done her a favor tonight by being her usual horrible self.

They rode the Metro in silence until they neared her stop.

"This next one is me," she told Pipe. He nodded and stood, holding his hand out to her.

Cora must've stared at his ink-covered fingers for a beat too long, because before she could take his hand, he shoved it into his pocket as if embarrassed.

She wanted to apologize. Tell him it wasn't that she didn't *want* to take his hand, just that she wasn't used to people helping her. She wasn't the kind of woman for whom others, men especially, went out of their way to assist. She wasn't flirty or coy, and she definitely didn't come across as helpless. She dressed for comfort, didn't wear makeup, didn't care about using womanly wiles to get her way...not that she had any. In this city in particular, her attitude didn't go over well. People were always trying to impress others, and if you didn't play the game, you were overlooked.

But this man didn't seem to care that she'd come to a fancy event in a dress from a big box store and cheap heels. In fact, he hadn't looked at her any differently after she'd changed into her jeans and sweatshirt.

Making a split-second decision, Cora reached up and took hold of Pipe's arm and used it to help her stand in the still-swaying Metro car. He immediately tightened his muscles, using his core strength to assist her.

"Thanks," she muttered.

They stepped off the subway into the mostly deserted station near her apartment, heading for the stairs. Cora stopped when she saw Milton, the homeless man she'd known for years. He usually spent the colder nights here in the station. She stopped beside him, and could feel Pipe's gaze boring into her as she crouched near the other man.

"Hey, Milt," she said softly.

The man, who couldn't be that much older than her,

rolled over. At seeing her, he grinned and sat up. "Cora. It's good to see you. What are you doing out so late, you shouldn't—" Whatever he was going to say abruptly cut off when he caught sight of Pipe behind her.

"This is Pipe. He's my friend," she told Milton. "He's escorting me home."

Milton turned back to Cora and said suspiciously, "Haven't seen him before."

"I know. He's going to help me find Lara," she said in a low tone. She'd talked to Milton about Lara on a couple of occasions, usually when she brought Milton some food. He knew that Cora was worried, that she thought Lara had been kidnapped. Milton might be homeless, and smelly, and drunk a lot of the time, but he was a good man and she considered him a friend. She didn't know his story, about how he'd ended up living on the streets, but since she'd felt as if she was days away from being right where he was at times, she never judged him.

Milton stared up at Pipe and narrowed his eyes. "You take care of her," he said in a menacing growl.

Instead of laughing or rolling his eyes at the empty threat obvious in Milton's voice, Pipe nodded once. Respect filled Cora. Not many people looked twice at homeless men and women, whose population seemed to be growing year after year in DC. The difference between the haves and the have-nots in this city, and many cities across the country, was becoming more and more obvious.

Cora shrugged a shoulder and brought her backpack around so she could unzip it. She reached in and fingered the white envelope under the dress and shoes she'd worn earlier that night. She took out a few bills and held them out to Milton. "Here."

He looked down at her hand and blinked in surprise.

"Nope," he said with a shake of his head, not reaching for the money.

"Please, Milton. Take it. I'll be gone for a while, and I'm worried about you with the weather getting colder."

"That's too much," he insisted. "I know you can't afford it."

"I can," Cora lied.

"No."

"*Yes.*"

They glared at each other for a heated moment before Milton sighed. "You aren't going to let this go, are you?"

"No. Please take it. If you don't, I'll be stressed out. Then I'll stop eating and fade away into nothing," she teased.

Milton rolled his eyes but reached for the money. "Wouldn't want that," he mumbled.

"Thank you," Cora said, then leaned forward and kissed him on his cheek. He smelled pretty horrible, and his face was dirty, but she didn't care. He was a decent man deserving of care and affection. They'd met when he'd intervened while she was being harassed by two other homeless guys. He'd saved her that day, and they'd been friends ever since.

"Be careful," Milton said solemnly.

"I will." Cora stood and smiled at Milton, then turned to Pipe. "Ready?"

She couldn't read the expression on his face. He nodded.

They walked toward the stairs once more.

When they reached the street, Pipe asked, "How much did you give him?"

"Two hundred bucks. He'll probably spend it all on alcohol in the next few days, but I don't mind."

"How much do you usually give him?" Pipe asked.

Cora glanced at him. "How do you know I've even given him *any* money before?"

He raised a brow in response.

She sighed. "Maybe five dollars or so. Enough that he can get some coffee and a sandwich at a place around the corner," she mumbled.

"Hmmmm."

Cora didn't know what that noise meant. If he thought it was too little, or if he didn't think Milton deserved to be given any money. But she wasn't sorry. All it took was a few life crises and anyone could be in his shoes, at any given time.

She led the way to her apartment building, and when they entered, she turned to Pipe. "It'll only take me a few minutes to pack."

He stared at her with another look she couldn't inter-pret. Then said, "I'll walk you up."

Cora shook her head. "No, it's okay. I'll be all right."

But he wasn't budging. "It's one in the morning and nothing good ever happens after midnight. I'll walk you up, Cora."

Her chest got tight. "Seriously. Just wait here in the lobby for me."

"No."

They glared at each other, even as panic tickled in. Pipe couldn't come upstairs. He couldn't see her apart-ment. Despite barely knowing the man, she knew he wouldn't be happy if he did.

"What are you afraid of?"

Her back straightened. "Nothing," she said too quickly.

Pipe's gaze bore into her own. "You're lying."

If anyone else talked to her like this, Cora would've lost

it. Not only had he accused her of being a scaredy-cat, but a liar as well. But the truth was, he was dead-on correct— on both counts. She *really* didn't want this man to see her apartment.

As she and Pipe engaged in a stare-down, she realized he wasn't going to relent. He was determined to protect her, which was a weird feeling in and of itself, and he wouldn't let anything she said deter him. That very stubbornness was one of the things that would help her get to Lara. But she was beginning to understand it wasn't good for her own peace of mind.

She finally broke the eye contact, turning toward the elevators. "Fine," she said belligerently.

To Pipe's credit, he didn't crow over her acquiescence. He simply stood next to her as they waited for the elevator to arrive. They rode up to her floor in silence. She appreciated that he didn't comment on the many lights that were out in her hallway, or the nasty smell of the carpet, or the general lack of maintenance in the place.

It wasn't the Taj Mahal, that was for sure, but it was a roof over her head, and Cora was content with that. After all the ups and downs she'd had over the years, and the many times she'd had to sleep on Lara's couch, she'd finally felt as if she was getting ahead when she was able to afford a place of her own again.

And then Ridge fucking Michaels happened.

Taking a deep breath, she turned to Pipe when they reached her door. "Will you wait here for me?" she asked, hoping against hope he'd agree.

He studied her face for a moment before asking, "What don't you want me to see in your apartment, Cora?"

"Nothing...I just...I don't really know you," she finished lamely, lying yet again.

"You think I'm gonna hurt you? Force you to do something you don't want to do?" Pipe asked, taking a step backward, giving her more space.

Now she felt guilty. "*No.*"

Pipe stared at her for a few seconds, then nodded stiffly and looked away. "I'll wait out here."

Cora sighed. She didn't want him to feel as if she didn't trust him. "No. It's okay. You can come in." She turned toward the door, every muscle tense. He wasn't going to be happy when he saw her apartment, but it didn't matter. As long as he and his friends would help her, it didn't matter if her living situation was embarrassing. She wouldn't change anything about what she'd done, not if it meant helping Lara.

She unlocked the dead bolt and took a deep breath before pushing open her door. She didn't have to look behind her to see if Pipe followed or not. She heard his footsteps and the click of the door shutting. "I'll be right back," she told him as she made her way toward the one bedroom.

Her cheeks felt warm, and she knew she was blushing in pure mortification. But she went to her closet and knelt down and opened her backpack. She grabbed the envelope of cash and ignored the dress and shoes. It wasn't as if she'd need those in New Mexico or Arizona. She rifled through the stacks of T-shirts, pants, and long-sleeve shirts on the floor of her closet and packed them into a larger duffle bag. She grabbed a handful of underwear from another stack, as well as socks and a few extra bras.

She headed out into the hallway with the bag, into the bathroom, refusing to look in the direction where she could see Pipe standing near the galley kitchen. She reached into the shower and got her shampoo and conditioner and a shower pouf. Then collected some toiletries on the counter.

True to her word, she was finished packing in less than five minutes. She went back out into the main room and finally met Pipe's eyes. "I'm ready," she told him.

As she'd thought, he didn't look happy. But he also looked thoroughly confused as well.

"Where the fuck is your furniture?" he asked between clenched teeth.

Looking around, Cora tried to see the apartment from his point of view. The only furniture in the room was a battered bookshelf against one of the walls, with pictures of her and Lara and a few well-read paperbacks. That was it. She had a moment to be glad he hadn't gone into her kitchen and opened the cabinets. He would've found them just as empty of dishes, cookware, and even silverware.

Following Pipe's gaze, she looked back into her bedroom, and the lack of furniture in there as well. She had a blow-up mattress on the floor, one that she'd borrowed from Lara a while back, and that was about it.

"Cora? Seriously—what the hell? You *live* here?"

Straightening her shoulders and feeling defensive, she nodded. "Yes. I sold my stuff to get the money for the auction," she explained, voice steady.

"You sold your stuff," Pipe repeated.

Cora had never felt as humiliated as she did right now. But it didn't last long before she mentally shook her head. She had nothing to be ashamed of. She'd done what she'd done to help the only person who'd ever treated her as if she was more than a piece of trash.

"Yes," she said, her chin inching up.

Pipe ran a hand through his hair as he stared at her almost empty apartment.

"I would've invited you to stay the night here, rather than taking the Metro all the way back to your hotel, but... well..." She lamely gestured to the empty room.

In response, Pipe surprised her by walking into the kitchen.

Cora stiffened as she watched him open her fridge and several of her cabinets. She waited for his judgement. For comments about her lack of food, and anything to cook or eat it with.

But he surprised her again by simply turning back to her and saying, "You got everything you need?"

"Yeah."

"Good. Let's go." He reached out and grabbed her bag, swinging it over his shoulder and gestured toward her front door.

Cora narrowed her eyes, fully expecting him to lay into her. Tell her that she was stupid for selling literally all her belongings for a ridiculous bachelor auction. For just a *chance* to talk to him, not even a guarantee. But he didn't. He simply waited quietly while she locked her door behind her. Then he put his hand on the small of her back as they walked toward the elevator.

The trip back across town was quiet. Neither said a word. But Cora didn't miss the way Pipe's gaze never stopped scanning their surroundings. They'd arrived back at his hotel before he finally spoke again. "I can get you a room of your own."

She looked up at him. "It's okay. I mean, if it's still all right that I stay in your room."

"I'd prefer it," he said simply.

With his fingers lightly resting on her back again, they walked toward the bank of elevators.

Cora felt edgy. Unsettled. Her skin under her sweatshirt tingled where his hand rested. She was keenly aware of Pipe standing so close. She inhaled deeply and realized the piney scent she'd gotten whiffs of throughout the evening were coming from him.

The urge to rest her head on his shoulder was suddenly hard to resist.

They walked down a hallway to the very end, to a room next to a stairwell.

"Owl's across the hall," Pipe said, pointing to the door to their left. "We always choose rooms close to the stairs. It's safer."

Cora's lips twitched. She actually wasn't surprised in the least. Anticipating danger was practically bred into these men. It was one of the reasons she'd thought the guys from The Refuge would be perfect for helping her rescue Lara.

Pipe hadn't been wrong, she *was* kind of a stalker. She'd read everything she could get her hands on about each of the men. She didn't know any of the specifics about the missions they'd been on while in the military, because they were obviously classified or top secret or whatever it was called, but she felt as if she'd gotten enough of an insight into their characters by reading the news reports of Alaska Stein's rescue from Russia, and the subsequent incident at The Refuge itself. Then when Reese Woodall was stolen away by Colombian cartel members and almost taken across the border. And from what residents of Los Alamos were quoted as saying about the men when Jasna McClure disappeared, how desperately they'd helped search for her.

Yeah, it was safe to say she was impressed by Pipe and his friends. The level of commitment toward ensuring the safety of the women who lived on the ranch had made Cora suspect they'd be willing to help her as well.

And she hadn't been wrong.

Pipe held the plastic key card up to the sensor on the door and it clicked open. He pushed open the door and held it for her. Taking a deep breath, and praying she hadn't been mistaken in her evaluation of Pipe, Cora walked into the room.

It was nothing fancy. Just two queen beds like he'd said, a dresser with a TV, a small, uncomfortable-looking chair in the corner, and a typical hotel bathroom. Pipe shut the door, threw the dead bolt and the little thingy above it that would prevent the door from being opened, then walked past her to the bed by the window and put her duffle bag on the surface. "You want the bathroom first?" he asked almost nonchalantly.

Cora shook her head. Pipe nodded and headed for the small room without another word.

When he'd shut the door, Cora wandered over to the bed that was obviously going to be hers for the night, and sat on the side. She should be doing something, planning, thinking of things to tell Pipe and the others that would help them get Lara away from Ridge...but suddenly she was exhausted. She hadn't been sleeping well because of her worry for her friend, and the stress of trying to make as much money as she could before the auction.

She flopped to her back, and her eyes closed as she waited for Pipe to be finished in the bathroom—then jerked awake when she felt someone touch her arm.

Cora threw herself to the side out of reflex, immediately embarrassed at her over-the-top reaction when she saw Pipe backing away from her with his hands up, as if showing her that he wouldn't hurt her.

"Sorry," she mumbled, running a hand over the back of

her neck. "I'm not a fan of people touching me to wake me up. Bad memories."

She wasn't scared of Pipe when he scowled at her words, and actually made a growling sound in the back of his throat. Instead, she was...turned on?

No, that couldn't be right.

But it was. It had been a long time since someone had been pissed off on her behalf. And this man didn't even know the half of it.

"Someone hurt you when you were sleeping?" he bit out.

"Well, not when I was sleeping, but...after they woke me up. Yeah," Cora said, not meeting his gaze. "It was a long time ago. And no, he didn't get to do what he wanted. I didn't...cooperate."

"Good for you," Pipe said, though still not sounding happy.

"Right. But as a result, I was kicked out of that house the next day, after the asshole made up a story about me stealing money out of his wife's purse."

"Wanker," Pipe said under his breath.

For some reason, Cora smiled.

"What? This isn't funny."

"I know, it's just...wanker?"

His lips twitched. "I've been here in the States a while, but sometimes my Britishisms come out."

"Yeah."

"Anyway, I'm sorry I touched you without your permission. I'll remember next time. I'm done in the bathroom."

For the first time, Cora noticed that Pipe had changed out of the black slacks and white dress shirt he'd been wearing all night. Lord help her, he had on a pair of gray sweatpants and a black tank top that showed off the tattoos on his arms and upper chest.

But it wasn't his tattoos that had her attention. The outline of his cock was prominent in the sweatpants, and she swallowed hard at seeing his size. She tried not to stare, but it was difficult.

She'd had her share of sex, but she'd never instantly craved a man like she craved Pipe at this moment. It wasn't just the fact that his dick was above-average in size, it wasn't the tattoos...it was the entire package that was Bryson Clark.

He'd been pissed on her behalf when he'd heard Eleanor talking shit about her, open about listening to what she had to say, empathetic, protective, understanding...and generous. It wasn't exactly surprising for Cora to realize she wanted him. And not just sexually. She wanted to know everything about him. Why he'd chosen the tattoos he had. What put the shadows she'd seen in his eyes. Why he'd left his country and moved to the US. How he'd gotten involved with The Refuge. All of it.

"Cora?" Pipe asked, his brows furrowing as he looked at her. "You can trust me."

She hated that he thought her silence meant she was second-guessing staying in the room with him.

"I know," she said, forcing herself to tear her gaze away from his crotch. "I'll just go and do my thing now..." she said a little lamely, picking up her bag.

Pipe stepped into the space between the two beds, giving her room to pass without having to worry about brushing against him.

When Cora shut the bathroom door behind her, she leaned against it and sighed. "Get a hold of yourself," she scolded softly. "He's helping you find Lara. That's it."

She quickly did her business, changed into a pair of boy shorts and an oversized T-shirt, and brushed her teeth before heading out of the bathroom. She left her duffle inside because it wasn't as if she'd need anything for the—she looked at her wristwatch—next four hours or so that she'd be sleeping.

The room was dark, except for a sliver of light coming through the curtains that hadn't been shut all the way. Cora pulled the covers back and crawled under the sheet. She fluffed up the pillows behind her and sighed in contentment as she finally relaxed.

The blow-up mattress had been fine, better than the hard floor, but it felt heavenly to be on an actual bed at the moment.

"Pipe? Are you asleep?" she whispered.

"No. What's wrong?"

"Nothing. I just...thank you."

"Don't thank me until we find your friend," he countered.

"No, seriously. No one else would listen to me. Or they'd listen to me, then quote me an exorbitant price to do nothing more than some searches on the Internet. Even if you guys can't find her. If she's...if Ridge has...you know. I'm grateful for your help. I know this isn't normal for you guys, and I don't want to get anyone in any trouble. But I'm so relieved you gave me a chance to tell you my story."

She heard the covers in the bed next to her rustle, and she looked over at where she knew Pipe was lying. She could barely see his shape in the darkness of the room, but she could feel him looking at her. "I promise that I'm gonna see this through. I don't know what the outcome will be, but I give you my word that we'll find out what happened to your friend."

Tears sprang to Cora's eyes. She wasn't a crier. Ever since a kid in one of her foster homes called her a crybaby and made fun of her, she'd done her best to keep any tears to herself. But she couldn't help but hear the sincerity in Pipe's voice, and it felt like the gentlest and warmest of hugs. "Thank you," she whispered.

"Go to sleep. Tomorrow will be a long day," he said.

Cora nodded. It was hard to believe she was actually going to The Refuge. She'd read so much about it, she was actually excited about getting to meet Melba and Scarlet Pimpernickel, and the squirrel with the missing legs, and the other guys, and even the women. Cora had a hard time making friends, but she'd gotten the feeling Alaska and the others were pretty down to earth.

She expected to lie awake thinking about her evening, and Lara, and worrying about what was to come, but because she felt down to her bones that she was safe with Pipe in the other bed, within moments of her closing her eyes, she fell into a dreamless sleep.

# CHAPTER SEVEN

Pipe stared blankly at the back of the seat in front of him on the plane and scowled. He didn't get much sleep the night before. He'd been too keyed up. Now his mind was going in a thousand different directions. He was as amped as he used to get before a mission. He had so many questions rolling around in his head.

He'd been shocked at the condition of Cora's apartment. Of all the reasons why she didn't want him to see inside, he never would've guessed it was because she was embarrassed that she'd sold every single one of her belongings that she could get any kind of money for, in order to raise enough money to "buy" him. And even winning a date with him wouldn't have guaranteed that he'd listen to her, or agree to help. Yet, she'd done it anyway.

If anything could convince him that Lara Osler really was in danger, it was that. Most people wouldn't go to such extremes to convince someone else that they thought their friend was in danger if they honestly, down to their soul, didn't believe it themselves.

But that brought up the question of what exactly

they were going to do. Yeah, they could go to Arizona, knock on this Ridge guy's door...but what then? Special forces or not, it wasn't as if they could kidnap Lara a second time if she didn't want to leave. Would Cora accept that she wanted to stay and simply walk away? He doubted it.

Cora shifted in the seat next to him, and he turned to look at her. Her brown hair was mussed around her shoulders. He couldn't shake the memory of it spread out on the pillow this morning. He felt like a creeper as he lay in his own bed and watched her sleep, but he couldn't *not* look at her. He was both pleased and disconcerted that she'd trusted him so quickly last night. He could've done anything to her while she was sleeping. Could've seriously hurt her. And yet, she fell asleep seemingly without a second thought.

As if she could feel him looking at her, Cora turned her head and met his gaze.

"What?" she asked a little self-consciously.

"Nothing. I'm just having a hard time wrapping my head around the fact that this is really happening."

She chuckled. "I think that's my line," she told him with a small smile. "And for the record...last night wasn't smart on your part."

Pipe blinked in confusion. "Why?"

"You don't know me, and yet you let me stay with you. I could've taken your wallet and all your other stuff while you were sleeping. I could've hurt you."

Pipe burst out laughing. He couldn't help it. "I was just thinking the exact same thing about you," he told her honestly.

They shared a smile. Then Cora's faded.

"What was that thought?" Pipe asked.

"Lara is probably scared and maybe being abused, and I'm sitting here enjoying myself, and it feels so wrong."

"If Lara's truly the kind of friend you described, she isn't going to want you to be miserable, even if she is. And we're going to find her and get to the bottom of what's going on," Pipe promised, reaching out and covering her hand with his own.

Cora gave him a sad smile. "I hope so."

"I know so. You stalked us, so you know what we can do," he teased.

"I still can't believe my crazy scheme worked. I mean, it didn't, but Eleanor actually did me a favor. Maybe I should send her some flowers or something," Cora said with a small grin.

"The one thing I don't understand is why you went to all the trouble. I mean, I get that you're doing it for Lara, but why didn't you just contact us directly?" Pipe asked. He'd been wondering that for a while now and was glad he had a chance to ask.

Cora shrugged. "I did."

"What? When?"

"I sent several emails. They all went unanswered. I even called. Left a message, but no one ever got back to me."

Pipe frowned. Alaska was in charge of the administrative duties for The Refuge, and he honestly couldn't see her ignoring a cry for help.

"It's okay," Cora said, leaning toward him. "I mean, it's not like you guys are obligated to help every damsel in distress who contacts you. I'm sure you get a lot of requests for help because of your skills."

Honestly, Pipe had no idea. He'd kept his head down over the last five years and hadn't even thought about using what he'd learned in the SAS in his civilian life. He wondered if his friends had. They all had special skill sets that could come in handy in certain situations. They definitely had with Alaska and Reese.

"I'll talk to Alaska," he told Cora.

Her eyes widened, and she shook her head almost frantically. "No! Don't! I mean, it's fine. I'm sure she had her reasons for not responding."

Pipe's lips pressed together. He couldn't make that promise. Now that he knew Cora had contacted The Refuge for help, but hadn't received a response, he wanted to know why.

"Great. Alaska's gonna hate me now," she said, staring out the window.

"No, she's not. She's very welcoming."

She didn't turn back to him.

"Cora?" Pipe asked.

When she finally looked at him, he was appalled to see tears in her eyes. This tough-as-nails woman was sincerely upset by the idea that Alaska might be in trouble, or might dislike Cora for ratting her out.

"I'm fine," she said, sitting up straighter.

Pipe could practically see her donning a set of armor to protect herself from the outside world. And he hated it. He'd seen her with her guard down and was attracted to that woman. Cora hadn't had an easy life, and he wanted to do whatever he could to fix that.

She looked out the window again, and Pipe reached for her without thought. He put his fingers under her chin, turning her face toward him. "You want to know what I thought the first time I saw you?" he asked.

Her eyes widened but she didn't pull out of his loose grip. "No. I don't think so."

He ignored her and went on. "I was on that stage, a place I didn't want to be. I was wearing clothes that made me feel uncomfortable and out of place. I wasn't anything like the men who'd come before me, strutting all over the stage, playing to the audience. I just wanted the entire thing to be over with. It's a weird thing...I'd felt as if I was a lad again, waiting to be picked on a futbol team at primary, and knowing I wouldn't because I was crap at futbol and everyone knew it. As much as I tried to tell myself I'd be happy if no one bid on me so I could go home, deep down, I would've been mortified if I was the only guy to *not* get any bids.

"Then *you* were there. At the front, looking at me, calling out a bid. That first thousand-dollar bid was a relief."

"Yeah, the short, chunky, anything-but-sophisticated chick in the Walmart dress bid on you. I'm sure you felt *soooo* relieved," she told him with an eye roll.

"That's not what I saw. Last night, I saw a determined woman who looked beyond the tuxedo, the pomp and circumstance. You were looking at *me*—Pipe. Not Bryson Clark."

Pipe was pretty sure he was mucking this up, but from that first glimpse of Cora, he'd felt a jolt of...recognition. That he'd found someone who would understand him.

It made no sense. Most people would say he was being ridiculous. But when she'd been outbid, a feeling of despair had swamped him. It was why he'd gone looking for her in the crowd. She might not have won a date with him, but he'd wanted to talk to her anyway. Wanted to know her name.

"Eleanor was right," Cora said softly. "I didn't belong there. If I had won, I would've embarrassed you at that fancy restaurant. I didn't even understand most of what was on that menu you read off. I'm more of a pizza-and-burger kind of girl. My shoes were from Payless. Do you know what that is?"

"Yeah," Pipe said.

A sheen of pink crossed her cheeks, but she didn't drop her gaze. "I was wearing an outfit that cost me fifty bucks, when every other person there probably spent that a hundred times over. That's always been who I am. On the outskirts looking in."

"You might feel that way, but I think when others look at you, they see someone who's comfortable in her own skin. Who doesn't feel like she has to conform to society's norms. They're jealous, Cora. They want to be like you. Free to be who they've always *wanted* to be, but don't feel as if they *can* be."

"That's not true," Cora said softly.

"It is. Why do you think that bitch Eleanor is still treating you as if you're in high school? It's because she's stuck. Meanwhile, you're free to do what you want, without concern for the opinions of people who just don't matter."

She stared up at him, looking unconvinced.

"The woman I saw from that stage intrigued me. You weren't afraid to look me in the eye. You were going after what you wanted, and that came through loud and clear. I can appreciate a beautiful woman, much as I'd appreciate a piece of art or a pretty sunset. But your loyalty to your friend sets you apart. The hoops you were willing to jump through make you unique. And I'll tell you this, and I'm not lying—I'd much rather have someone like you at my side as I went through life, than a woman who would ditch me in a heartbeat for someone they thought could give them money or fame or prestige.

"Many women have bought into the scam that men have been perpetuating for thousands of years...that beauty is more important than anything more meaningful. But not you. Your loyalty is more attractive than the most expensive dress or shoes anyone could parade themselves in while in front of me."

Pipe didn't know where the words were coming from, just that he felt a bone-deep compulsion to say them. To make this woman know her own worth.

"Pipe," she whispered.

"And you don't have to take my word for it. You can ask Lara when we find her. Or Milton. Most people probably look through him simply because his circumstances make them uncomfortable. But not you. You gave him money you earned by selling your belongings, even knowing he'll probably spend it on alcohol instead of food or a warm place to sleep for a couple nights."

"He saved me one night from two guys who were drunk and looking to score," Cora whispered.

"See? Loyalty," Pipe said.

She bit her lip. "I've spent a lot of time researching The Refuge, and the people who live and work there. I read all the stories I could find on what happened to Alaska. She seems like someone I could really like. And if you get on her case about the emails, she'll think I just want to use you and your friends. And I do...but that's not why I ultimately decided to go to that auction."

"Why did you?" Pipe asked.

"Because deep down, you all have a core of goodness. You wouldn't have started The Refuge if you didn't. You could've started some sort of high-end luxury camping retreat. One that catered to the richest people in the world, and you probably would've made a lot more money. Don't get me wrong, I think it's great that you can make a living doing what you're doing now, and helping people while doing so, but I've learned to read people. To see their true intentions. And in watching the interviews with you and your friends, and reading the articles, I can tell that you're all good people. That if anyone could help me find Lara, at the price I could pay, which honestly isn't a lot, it would be you guys."

She wasn't wrong. Pipe was glad that she could read them so well. "Alaska isn't going to think you're there just to use us," he told Cora.

She wrinkled her nose.

"She isn't," Pipe insisted.

"If I was married to the man I'd loved my entire life, and living on The Refuge, and feeling as if my life was beginning for the first time—that's a direct quote from her, by the way; I saw it in an article online—I wouldn't want *anyone* coming in who might get my boyfriend into a situation where he could get into trouble or hurt. I'd want to protect him, and the rest of the people who worked at The Refuge."

Pipe hadn't dropped his hand from under her chin, and he wanted to keep it there, keep feeling her soft skin, but he forced himself to cover her hand instead, which was sitting in her lap.

"I give you my word that Alaska, Henley, Reese, and everyone else who works at The Refuge will not only embrace you, but completely champion the reason why you're there. In fact, we'll probably have to make it perfectly clear that they aren't going to be allowed to come with us to Arizona to get your friend."

Pipe could see the skepticism in her eyes. But she'd see for herself. She was right about one thing though...the reason Alaska had probably ignored her emails and phone calls *was* probably about protecting Brick and the rest of the men. He had no idea how many requests for assistance for one thing or another came in through their website. For all he knew, there were dozens a day. It wouldn't be hard to ignore them as a collective whole. The more he thought about it, the more he was sure he was right. He wasn't upset with Alaska, not in the least, but it would probably be a good idea for one of them to look through any similar requests. To take that burden off Alaska's shoulders.

Feeling the need to lighten the conversation, and wanting to see the stress fade from Cora's eyes, if only for a little while, Pipe asked, "You ever been to New Mexico before?"

She shook her head. "No. I've barely been out of DC."

"Really?"

"Not many people want to take a foster kid on vacation, and since then..." She shrugged. "I haven't really had the money to go anywhere. Lara and I did go up to Gettysburg and Antietam once. It really wasn't her thing, but she humored me. I find history fascinating, and being at the battlefields, standing where thousands of men and women fought...it was amazing."

Pipe smiled. "Well, I think you're going to like our little slice of the world. The Refuge is nestled in the mountains of northern New Mexico, and the air smells so clean that I swear sometimes I'm on a different planet than where I grew up around London, instead of just a different country."

"I can't wait to see it. Honestly, after reading so much

about it, I feel as if I've already been there. But I know the reality will blow the pictures in my head and what I saw online out of the water."

She wasn't wrong. The first time Pipe had seen the land where they were going to build the cabins, he'd known it would be an amazing place. And he hadn't been wrong.

They made small talk for the rest of the plane ride and when they got on their connecting flight to Santa Fe, they weren't able to sit together. It gave Pipe a chance to figure out what his next steps should be.

Cora needed to tell her story again, this time to all the guys. They'd need to decide on a plan of action...how to get to Arizona and make contact with hopefully Lara, and if not, this Michaels guy. What happened after that would depend on what they found when they got there...and what intel Tex gave them about Ridge Michaels. For some reason, Pipe had a feeling this wasn't going to be as easy as knocking on the door, getting Lara, and leaving.

Owl had talked to Stone last night and filled him in on what was happening, who Cora was, and when they'd be back at The Refuge. Pipe was planning on asking Cora if she wanted to stay in his cabin. She'd been comfortable enough sharing a hotel room the night before, and because there were no available cabins anytime soon, he figured she'd jump at the chance to save money on a motel by bunking with him.

Pipe couldn't help but smile at the idea. He'd thought Spike was crazy for letting Reese stay with him when she'd come to The Refuge, but he understood it now. The thought of being separated from Cora was unsettling...and not just because he had a feeling if left to her own devices, she'd be on her way to Arizona to get Lara back with or without help.

Her loyalty was attractive, there was no doubt, but it also meant she'd set aside her own safety to help her friend. Which wasn't acceptable for Pipe. Or any of *his* friends. They wouldn't allow anyone to get hurt while under their watch.

The plane landed in Santa Fe on time, and they picked up Pipe's Challenger in long-term parking and were on their way to The Refuge without any delays. Cora was quiet, most likely nervous. She sat in the back seat and let him and Owl talk about nothing in particular as they drove.

In contrast, the closer they got to The Refuge, the more settled Pipe felt. He couldn't wait for Cora to meet his friends. He had no doubt whatsoever that she'd fit in perfectly.

# CHAPTER EIGHT

This was a disaster.

Cora stood in the lobby of the huge main lodge at The Refuge as Pipe had an intense conversation with his friends across the room. Alaska, Henley, and Reese sat at a table off to the side after meeting her, and even though they'd invited her to sit with them, it felt to Cora as if they were merely being polite.

So here she stood. Awkwardly, in the middle of the room, waiting to see what would happen next.

The front door of the lodge opened and a woman walked in, someone Cora didn't recognize from her research. She had straight black, shoulder-length hair and wore black pants and a T-shirt that said *The Refuge*. She waved at the three women sitting at one of the tables, then frowned when she saw Cora standing by herself.

To Cora's surprise, she walked toward her.

"Hi. I'm Ryan. I work here. Can I help you with something?"

"No, I'm good. Thanks."

But Ryan didn't nod and back off as Cora thought she would.

"What's happening?" she asked instead, looking from her to the guys, then to the table with the women.

"I came here with Pipe and Owl. They're talking to their friends about me. About why I'm here."

Ryan's brows furrowed. "You came with Pipe and Owl?"

"Yeah," she said with a nod.

"They were in Washington, DC, at a thing," she went on.

Cora did her best to hide her amusement. "They were."

"And you came from DC with them?"

"Yup."

"Okay, I'm missing something, but whatever. I'm new here and not always included in all the ins and outs of running this place...which is fine. I mean, I don't *want* to know. I'm just a maid. Are you hungry? I had a hunch that Robert is making his world-famous chocolate chip cookies. That's why I'm here, to grab a couple while they're warm. Come on, we'll go check it out." Ryan hooked her arm with Cora's as if they'd been friends forever, instead of just meeting a minute ago, and started pulling her toward a door on the far end of the lodge.

"Ryan." The man Cora recognized as "Tiny" called out to them from where he stood, huddled with Pipe and the others.

Cora felt the woman stiffen a moment before she turned, without letting go of her arm. "What?" she called back.

"Where are you going? We need to talk to Cora."

"Kitchen. Cookies," she said, gesturing impatiently, and without waiting for a response, turned them both back toward where they were headed in the first place.

"Um, maybe I should stay here if they want to talk to me," Cora said hesitantly.

But Ryan didn't pause or even indicate that she'd heard her. She stayed on her path to what Cora assumed was the kitchen.

She pushed open a door and the smell of freshly baked cookies was strong enough to make Cora's stomach growl. Loudly.

Ryan beamed. "I know. I swear Robert puts some sort of narcotic in his cookies to keep us coming back for more. I've only been here a few months, but I think I've put on at least ten pounds."

"You needed to put some meat on your bones," an older man said with a grin, entering the kitchen from what she could only assume was a pantry or something. Cora guessed he was in his fifties or sixties.

"Robert." Ryan smiled wider as she walked toward him. She gave him a hug, then stepped back. "This is Cora," she said, gesturing as she spoke.

"I know. She tried to win Pipe in that bachelor auction but someone outbid her. Pipe found out why she wanted to win so badly, so he brought her back home to figure out how he and the others could help get her friend away from some asshole who took her to Arizona and won't let her leave."

Cora's mouth fell open as she stared at the chef in disbelief. How the hell did he know all that? She'd only been here about two-point-three seconds.

Ryan nodded, as if she wasn't surprised in the least. She glanced at Cora and chuckled. "You have to understand, this place is like the smallest small town you've ever been in or read about. There aren't any secrets. Well, hardly any. Anyway, the guys'll figure things out. You did good in hooking up with Pipe. Robert...are you gonna give us some cookies or what?"

The man smirked. "You want the ones from earlier, or the ones I just took out of the oven?"

"Is that even a question?" Ryan asked.

"Of course it is." But Robert made no move to show them where the hopefully still-warm cookies were.

Ryan narrowed her eyes and put her hands on her hips. She studied Robert shrewdly. "Did I tell you that I have an inside line to get those Little Debbie Christmas Tree cakes that you like so much...like, all year? I can get them in July if I want them."

Robert's eyes widened. "Really? You aren't just pulling my leg to get the warm cookies, are you?"

Cora's gaze went back and forth between Ryan and Robert as they bantered.

"I would never lie about Christmas Tree cakes," Ryan said with a straight face.

"I want in on that," he demanded.

"And *I* want warm chocolate chip cookies," she countered.

Robert moved quickly toward a box on one of the counters. He opened it, and Cora realized it must be a warmer of some sort. He pulled out a tray of cookies and set them on the counter, then scooted them toward where Ryan and Cora were standing.

"Mmmmmm, cookies," Ryan said in delight as she leaned over to inhale the scent of the gooey treat.

"I'm in, right?" Robert asked with a smirk.

"Oh, you're in," she agreed as she reached for a cookie. "You're *so* in."

Robert did a weird little dance, then grinned at Cora.

"Go on. Since you're friends with Ryan, you get warm cookies whenever you want too."

Grinning, Cora picked up a cookie and moaned when she bit into it. Ryan was right, there had to be more than eggs, flour, and chocolate in this cookie, because the second she swallowed, she couldn't wait to take another bite.

"I'll set things up so you get a box of Christmas Tree Cakes every week," Ryan told the chef.

He beamed. "Make it two."

Ryan's brow lifted. "Two?"

"Well, I was gonna make it four, but compromised."

They all burst into laughter—and that was when the kitchen door opened and Alaska, Henley, and Reese entered.

"What's going on in here? Wait—is that a new batch of cookies?" Alaska asked.

Ryan hunched over the tray on the counter and growled as she did her best to protect them. Cora couldn't help but giggle at the over-the-top antics of her new acquaintance. Eventually, Ryan stood and slid the tray toward the other women.

"I don't know how you always seem to know when Robert's made a new batch of cookies," Henley mumbled between bites.

"Right? I mean, we were here and *still* didn't know," Reese agreed.

Ryan took a large bite of cookie and pantomimed zipping her lips closed.

Everyone chuckled.

Cora could feel Alaska staring at her, but she refused to look at the woman. Suddenly, once again, she felt like an outsider. It wasn't until she could sense Alaska approaching that she turned. Her chin came up and she refused to cower. She'd done nothing wrong.

"Are you okay?" Alaska asked gently.

Cora hid her surprise. She'd been ready to defend her actions, to explain why she'd asked Pipe for help. She hadn't expected Alaska to sound concerned.

"I'm fine," she said.

Henley stepped forward. "We don't know what's going on. Tonka just said that Pipe wanted to talk to them about helping you and your friend. Can we do anything for you?"

"How long are you going to be here? Do you want a tour of the place?"

For some reason, their...niceness...was almost too much to take at the moment. "I don't know. Not long, I hope. Not because I don't want to get to know you guys or see The Refuge, but I'm worried about my friend and want to get to her as soon as I can."

She wasn't planning on saying much more than that, but Alaska reached for her hand, gripped it tightly, then towed her toward a small table off to the side of the kitchen. "Sit," she invited as she pulled out a chair. The other women—and surprisingly, Robert too—all joined them. It was crowded with everyone huddled around the small table, but it also felt comfortable.

"I'm sorry about our behavior out there," Alaska started. "We didn't mean to seem standoffish, we just didn't know what was going on, and we didn't want to force you to sit with us if you didn't want to. And Pipe doesn't...he's not...he...Shoot," she sighed. "He's not the kind of guy to bring women here. We weren't sure what the nature of your relationship was...beyond your friend's situation...so we were just trying to respect your privacy. But when Ryan brought you in here, and we heard you guys laughing, we couldn't stay away," Alaska said with a sheepish smile.

"I'm not here *with* Pipe," Cora said. "Not in the way you think. I did try to buy a date with him at that auction, just for a chance to talk, but an old high school nemesis outbid me. Afterward, Pipe heard her talking to me, took exception to what she said. Then I talked to him, then to him and Owl together, and the next thing I know, we're on our way here and he said he'd help me find my friend."

She was talking too fast, telling these strangers way too much, but truthfully, they didn't really seem like strangers. Not after all the info she'd dug up about them. And she kind of felt the need to fill any silence.

Taking a deep breath, Cora turned to Reese first. "I'm glad you're okay. I don't know what I would've done if I'd been in your situation. Probably freaked out. I can't swim at all, so actually I'd probably be dead. And, Henley, I can't imagine what you went through when your daughter was missing. I don't have any kids, but if I did, I'm sure I would've been a basket case. And Alaska...God. You're so brave. You've been to so many places, seen so many things, there's no way I could've done what you did, exploring other countries all by yourself.

"I admire all of you so much. I just want you to know that. And I'm not here to put anyone in danger. I need the expertise of Pipe and his friends, but I honestly think as soon as Ridge Michaels sees that I'm not going to stop, that I now have help in my quest to figure out what's going on with my friend, that he'll give her back without much trouble."

"Holy crap," Alaska said, sitting back in her chair with an astonished look on her face.

Henley's mouth opened and closed, as if she was trying to think of something to say.

Reese simply blinked at her.

It was Ryan who actually spoke first. She had a huge smile on her face as she said, "I knew you'd fit right in the second I saw you. Small-town Refuge gossip doesn't have anything on you, apparently."

Cora felt herself blushing. Shoot, she shouldn't have been quite so gung-ho about making these women understand she wasn't there to cause trouble. She always seemed to say the wrong thing at the wrong time. Social niceties weren't exactly her thing. Lara was way better at that than she was, and it was why she usually left the introductions and small talk to her friend.

"I swear I'm not a stalker," Cora blurted. "I mean, Pipe jokingly accused me of being one, but I had to know for certain that selling my stuff would be worth hiring him and his friends to kidnap Lara back. And I just did lots of Internet searches. There are tons of articles about the men who started this place. And after all the stuff that happened to you guys, there were even more articles. I didn't hack into any databases or anything, I wouldn't even know how to do that. I just used Google to search."

She turned to Robert and Ryan. "I'm sorry, I didn't find any information about you guys. But, Robert, if everything else you make is half as good as your cookies, I might never leave. I might move into the barn with Melba and sneak over here in the middle of the night to gorge myself. Maybe I could clean the dishes like some kind of dish fairy and earn my keep. And, Ryan..." Cora shrugged. "Well...I don't know you at all. Sorry again."

"Wait, wait, wait—I feel as if we're missing a huge chunk of info here," Henley protested. "Selling your stuff?"

"You hired our guys?" Alaska asked.

"*Kidnap* your friend back?" Reese threw in.

"I can't believe you three haven't heard from your men about Cora and her friend," Ryan said with a shake of her head.

"And *you're* in the know?" Alaska countered.

Ryan sobered. "Her lifelong friend Lara was dating a guy named Ridge Michaels, and is now in Arizona with him. They left abruptly, and they're not talking to Cora anymore, which has Cora freaked out. She heard about Pipe being in that auction and researched all she could about him and The Refuge. As she said, she didn't win, but Pipe was intrigued enough to track her down, talk to her. Now here she is, and Pipe and the others are out there talking about their next steps, how to go about figuring out once and for all if Lara's okay, or if she's being held against her will."

Cora would've laughed at the shocked looks on the other women's faces if she wasn't so surprised herself.

"It's the quiet ones you have to watch out for," Robert said with a chuckle.

"Right? How the hell do you know all that? Pipe, Owl, and Cora have only been here for like twenty minutes!" Henley protested.

"Owl called Stone last night. I was cleaning the lodge and heard them talking in the admin office. I didn't mean to eavesdrop, but I couldn't exactly shut my ears off. Stone had the phone on speaker, and you know how he tends to talk rather loudly when he's on the phone."

"Right, okay, so our sneakster friend here has the deets, but we don't. If there's anything we can do to help, we're more than willing," Alaska told Cora.

"You sold your *stuff*?" Henley asked again, obviously

still stuck on that part of her random word vomit from moments ago.

Cora shrugged. "It was just stuff. I had to get money to be able to bid on Pipe."

"Like, your electronics and other expensive things?" Reese asked.

She bit her lip. "No. All of it. My furniture, TV, dishes and cutlery, pots and pans, linens...*all* of it."

Everyone was silent for a long moment.

"Holy shit, seriously?" Henley asked.

"It still wasn't enough to win though," Cora said, staring at the table.

"Tell us about your friend," Alaska said firmly.

This was a topic Cora was more comfortable with. She told them everything. Not leaving anything out. How she was a foster kid with no family. How Lara took her under her wing. How she'd bailed her out more than once when she needed a place to live. How her parents were nice but distant. How they were disappointed in Lara when she'd become a preschool teacher instead of trying for a better, more prestigious job.

"She's everything to me," Cora said, still studying the table as if it was the most interesting thing ever. "My best friend and my family all rolled into one. When she met Ridge, I was skeptical about how perfect he sounded. I told her to be careful, but Lara's a romantic. She's dreamed about being swept off her feet all her life. I think she was starting to feel as if she'd missed out. Like she was too old to find someone to love her the way she wanted to be loved. So when Ridge showed up and acted like the man she'd always dreamed of, she was overwhelmed and all in pretty much immediately.

"We had a fight about him. Two days later, she didn't

show up for work and wasn't answering my calls. She sent an email to the school about taking a leave of absence. The next thing I knew, I got a text from her saying she's staying in Arizona for a while. A *text*. After over two decades as best friends.

"I tried to call her immediately, but she never picked up. And the few texts I got didn't sound like her at all. They were…unemotional. And as I told Pipe, there wasn't any punctuation in them, and Lara *always* uses periods and commas and stuff. She's always worn her heart on her sleeve, so she also uses lots of emojis and exclamation points and gifs. But the texts I got were brief. Not one emoji. The one time Ridge allowed me to see her on a video call, she told me she loved Arizona and wasn't coming back to DC, ever. But she also gave me a signal. She's in trouble. Even if I'm the only who believes that with all my heart, I *know* she is."

"The guys are going to help though, right?" Reese asked.

Cora shrugged. "I don't know. That's what Pipe is doing now. Discussing the situation with them."

"They'll help," Alaska said without a shred of doubt in her voice.

"Have they called their techie friend?" Henley asked.

Everyone looked at her.

"You know, the one who tried to help when Jasna was missing and when Reese was taken?"

"The one who actually *didn't* help?" Alaska asked. "I mean, he tried, but it was that mysterious unknown person who thought of using Reese's tile to track her car. And they also told the guys where to find Jasna."

"When Owl was talking to Stone, he said something about how he'd already contacted Tex—that's the techie guy's name," she said to Cora, "and he was researching Lara's boyfriend," Ryan explained.

"Good. Okay, so I'm guessing you won't be leaving today. That means we need to figure out where you'll be staying," Alaska said matter-of-factly.

"Are there any cabins open?" Henley asked.

Alaska huffed out a breath and shook her head. "No. We don't have any openings for months. Unless someone cancels, but then I can usually fill that spot pretty easily."

"She can stay with Gus and me," Reese offered.

"Didn't I hear you say you were having morning sickness really bad, and that you get up in the middle of the night to puke?" Henley asked.

Reese blushed. "Yeah, but—"

"She can stay with us," Henley said firmly.

Alaska laughed. "As if staying with you and your preteen is any better."

"Pipe said I could stay with him," Cora cut in.

Everyone's head swiveled to stare at her.

Then Alaska smiled. "Right. Then...that's that."

Henley tilted her head. "You're not what I expected for Pipe."

Cora did her best not to be offended by that.

"And please don't take that the wrong way," she added quickly. "I know it probably sounded bad, it's just that Pipe is...rough around the edges. And he's kind of quiet."

"We aren't together like that," Cora said quickly, wanting to clear that up. "He's just helping me find Lara."

"Uh-huh, you go on telling yourself that," Reese said. "I was only staying with Gus while my brother was here healing. And now I'm married, pregnant, and happier than I've ever been in my life."

"We're embarrassing her," Alaska said. "Whatever's

between her and Pipe is just that, between the two of them."

"I like his tattoos," Cora mumbled, picking at one of her fingernails. "They make him seem tough...untouchable. Even though from what I've gotten to know of him so far, that's not who he is."

"You're right, it's not. He's a teddy bear," Henley agreed.

Robert burst out laughing. "No, he's not," he said.

This time, everyone turned to look at the cook.

"He's not," Robert insisted. "Just the other day, one of the guests was talking shit about a woman he saw in town. You know, doing what a lot of guys do...talking about her tits and how he'd like to 'tap that.' Pipe overheard and got all up in his face, told him he was being disrespectful and he needed to pack his shit and leave. Immediately."

"Oh my God, is *that* why that guy checked out early?" Alaska asked. "I tried to figure out if something was wrong, but he was all tight-lipped and wouldn't say much."

"Because Pipe scared the shit out of him," Robert said with satisfaction. "That man isn't someone I'd ever want on my bad side. You ladies might think he's a teddy bear because he's all nice to you and everything, but he's actually a powder keg that's two seconds from exploding...all it'll take is the right spark."

"Should I talk to him?" Henley asked, her brow furrowing.

"Lord, no!" Robert exclaimed. "If he wanted someone messing around with his brain, he'd have already talked with you."

"I don't mess with people's brains," Henley huffed, sounding offended.

"She's our resident psychologist," Reese said in a loud whisper to Cora.

She nodded, her attention stuck on the fascinating conversation around her.

"I'm just saying, if he's on the edge as much as you seem to think, that's not good," Henley added with concern.

"Why do you think this place is here?" Robert asked. "We're *all* dealing with the demons in our heads. Love you, Henley, but when I'm ready for you to root around inside my brain, I'll let you know. I'm sure Pipe's the same way."

"You're right. I'm sorry," Henley said, reaching across the table to put her hand on Robert's arm. He patted it and smiled at the other woman.

The door to the kitchen opened, and Pipe stuck his head in. "Cora? You good?"

His concern was surprising. Glancing around, she saw Alaska was trying to hide a smile, Henley was looking at Pipe in concern, Reese was looking at Cora, probably trying to see if she was indeed all right, as Pipe was asking. Ryan was looking down at her phone, typing rapidly, and Robert had stood and was already halfway across the kitchen.

"Yeah," Cora told him.

"Okay. We'd like a word with you, if that's all right."

Cora wasn't sure why it *wouldn't* be all right. The whole reason she was here was to try to convince these men that she wasn't losing her mind, that Lara really was in danger. She nodded and stood.

"Be nice," Alaska told Pipe.

"We like her," Reese added.

"And we want to help if we can," Henley said.

"Yeah, if there's anything we can do, let us know," Ryan agreed.

Pipe's lips twitched. "She's been here for like fifteen minutes and you guys are already claiming her?"

Alaska grinned. "Yup. And her friend too."

"Right. Cora, you ready?" Pipe said.

She couldn't read what he was thinking. Didn't know if he was upset that the other women had offered their help and seemed to like her so quickly. It was confusing to Cora too. This kind of thing didn't happen to her. She had a hard time making friends, so she was just as baffled as to why these women were so willing to help her and Lara… people they didn't even know.

She nodded but before joining Pipe, she walked over to where Robert was standing by the sink, putting dishes into the industrial-sized dishwasher. "Thank you," she said softly. "For the cookies, and for…well…for sticking up for Pipe."

"No matter how tough the packaging, everyone needs propping up now and then," he replied in a low rumble. "Now get. Go figure out how to rescue your friend. Does she like chocolate chip cookies?"

Cora nodded. "Yeah. But you know what her favorite thing ever is?"

"What?"

She somehow suspected even if she named the most difficult dish ever, if he had a chance to meet Lara, this man would find a way to master it. So she grinned widely as she said, "Little Debbie Christmas Tree cakes. I buy boxes and boxes for her for Christmas every year, for her to freeze, and she always runs out by June anyway."

Robert shared her smile. "A woman after my own heart.

When you bring her back here, I'll make sure she has a box waiting."

"Thanks," Cora whispered. Then she surprised herself by going up on her tiptoes and kissing Robert's beard-covered cheek. She squeezed his arm, took a deep breath, and finally walked toward Pipe, who hadn't moved from the doorway.

When she neared, he reached for her elbow. The second the kitchen door closed behind them, he asked, "What was that about? Are you really okay?"

Again, his concern for her felt good. Even the scowl on his face didn't scare her. "Yeah. Robert's cookies are to die for. You guys should put *that* on the website."

Pipe's lips twitched. "Can't have all our secrets on the web for stalkers like you to find."

She returned his smile. Then it faded. "Are they going to help?"

"They want more intel."

His answer made Cora stiffen. She knew she'd gotten lucky just with Pipe agreeing to talk to his friends, with him bringing her here to The Refuge. She'd held out hope that maybe he'd be able to convince his friends to help her too. But that hope was already waning.

"They didn't say no, they're just concerned. As am I," Pipe said as he stared at her.

Briefly, Cora wanted to give in to despair, but she steeled her nerves instead. If they weren't willing to help, she'd go to Arizona from here. Figure out a way to see Lara when Ridge wasn't around. Get her away from him. Even if she had to flee with Lara to Mexico, she would.

Her mind spun with possibilities. Lara could be brainwashed by now. Maybe she wouldn't *want* to leave. Cora might have to convince her, maybe even stoop to Ridge's level and kidnap her friend.

"Breathe, Cora," Pipe ordered.

She looked up at him in surprise. She'd been so lost in making alternate plans in her head that she'd actually forgotten where she was for a moment.

"When they hear what's going on from your own mouth, they'll agree."

"And if they don't?" she couldn't help but ask.

"Then we'll head to Arizona and see what we can do."

Cora stared at Pipe. "What?"

"If they don't agree, we'll go to Phoenix and see if we can't get in to see Lara."

"We?" she asked. "You'd go against your friends' wishes and help me?"

Pipe's gaze bore into hers. "I said I'd help when we were in DC, and I won't go back on my word. Remember what I said about loyalty?"

Cora nodded.

"I could no sooner turn you away and ignore your cry for help than I could one of my friends in there," he said, gesturing toward what looked to be some sort of conference room on the other side of the lodge. "I'm immune to a lot of things women use to get what they want. But like I said before, the kind of loyalty you have for Lara? It's precious. And so damn rare. I'm going to help you, Cora. I give you my word."

She wanted to cry. Wanted to go to her knees right there in the lobby of this amazing place. Cora had never met men and women like the ones she'd encountered here. The staff at The Refuge was kind. Generous. Accepting. And so open to those who needed help. She liked it, but it was also overwhelming.

"Come on, let's go talk to the others."

Cora nodded. And the urge to cry dissipated and determination rose within her. She knew she was right. Knew Lara was in trouble. And she needed to be smart, convincing. Needed to give the facts as she knew them to the other men. They'd either believe her or not, but one way or another, she would get to Lara and talk to her in person. Would find out if she was in Arizona of her own free will, or if she needed help getting home.

# CHAPTER NINE

Pipe had no idea what had gone down in the kitchen while he'd been bringing his friends up to speed, therefore he couldn't decide if it was good or bad. He hadn't liked how emotional Cora looked, especially when she'd spoken with Robert, but the other women looked fairly relaxed. Seemed as if they were glad to have met Cora. He could've told her that would happen. *Had* told her, in fact. But with her history, he wasn't surprised she needed to see for herself that the other women wouldn't turn their backs on a stranger.

Admittedly, he'd been a little worried at first, because Alaska had spoken to Cora, then seemed to leave her standing in the middle of the room alone while she went and sat with Henley and Reese, but after Ryan brought Cora into the kitchen, they'd followed soon after.

He'd wanted to go check on her, to make sure all was well, but he'd needed to convince his friends to help. They'd gone into the conference room, and it hadn't taken Pipe long to realize Cora needed to share the details herself. His friends would be able to hear and see her concern for Lara. He hadn't been able to deny Cora his assistance, and Pipe knew without a doubt that the others wouldn't be able to either, once they heard her side of the story.

Pipe and his friends weren't mercenaries. They hadn't started The Refuge as a cover for continuing to do what they'd done while in the military. But it couldn't be denied they had certain skills. They'd used them when they were searching for Jasna, and when they'd raced after Reese. Hell, Owl and Stone had climbed into a helicopter—something they hadn't done in years—to prevent Reese from being taken across the border.

And to be honest, using his skills to rescue an innocent woman from an abusive situation was something he found he was itching to do. It had an appeal he hadn't expected. If he could use what he'd learned from years of hunting down and killing bad guys, to help a civilian, it made what he'd done in the service feel...more worth it.

Pipe followed Cora into the conference room and gestured to a chair. She sat, and Pipe took the seat next to her.

Brick cleared his throat. "It's good to meet you, Cora, although I wish it wasn't under these circumstances."

She nodded. "Same. Before we start, can I just say that I'm very impressed by what you've all done here. The world needs more places like The Refuge. Places where people can go and not worry that they'll be looked down on if they have flashbacks. Where they can be around others who can relate to what they've gone through."

"Thanks. And I agree. So...you think your friend Lara is being held against her will?" Brick asked, not beating around the bush.

Pipe mentally winced. The way his friend had phrased

his question made it clear that Cora had an uphill battle to get the others to believe her.

Instead of intimidating her, though, Brick's question seemed to make her even more determined to convince them. She sat up straighter and once again her shoulders tensed.

"I don't think. I *know* she is," Cora said. "Look, I get it. Lara's an adult. She's allowed to move across the country with whoever she wants. And if I truly believed she was safe and happy, I wouldn't say a word. But she's not. I know that without a doubt."

"How?" Tiny asked.

To Pipe's surprise, instead of directly answering the question, Cora began to tell a story.

"When I was seventeen, I was kicked out of yet another foster home. It wasn't because of anything I did. There was a twenty-eight-year-old son who needed to move back home because he was fired from his job and wanted his old room back. The couple who fostered me didn't think twice. One day I was there, and the next I was back at social services with my stuff in a tattered old suitcase. I was embarrassed and frustrated. I didn't tell anyone at school about my situation, but Lara could tell something was wrong.

"She eventually got me to admit that once again, I didn't have a place to live. And since I was about to age out of the system, the situation was even worse. It wasn't as if anyone was lining up to take me in for five months. I was ready to quit school. I'd lost all respect for adults in general. I wasn't a very happy person, held a lot of resentment and bitterness inside. But Lara talked to her parents, and they agreed to let me stay at their house until I graduated from high school.

"She saved my life. I'm fully convinced of that. And it wasn't the last time either. Every time I've been down on my luck, needed a place to stay, needed a friend, she was there without hesitation."

"She sounds like a great friend...but that's not what we're questioning here," Spike said gently.

Cora took a deep breath. "Sorry, I know. I'm just trying to illustrate how close we are. Lara and I share everything. *Everything.* I know when she's sad, when she's happy, when she's pissed off—which isn't often. I know what that woman has for *dinner* every night. She's also unbelievably dependable and conscientious. There is zero possibility that she decided to move to Arizona without notifying her job weeks in advance, and without talking to me about it first. She would've made a list of the pros and cons, given at least a month's notice at her job, and she probably would have asked me to move with her. Because that's the kind of person she is. That's how close we are.

"We talked on the phone every day. She called me on her way to work, and then we'd text throughout the day, and usually talk when we got home in the evenings too. We haven't gone a day without talking practically since we've met. And now it's been *weeks*, and I've gotten just a few texts and one video chat that was basically moderated by her boyfriend.

"I woke up one day and she was just gone. Yes, we had a fight before she left, but Lara doesn't hold grudges. I fully expected to have a text from her when I woke up the next morning, apologizing. She left without one word to me. Without a word to *anyone.* Some people have said it's possible she fell head over heels in love and decided on the spur of the moment to move across the country without a word to even her parents, but those people don't know

Lara like I do. Something is terribly wrong. And every day that goes by, and I don't talk to her, I'm more sure of it."

Pipe wanted to comfort Cora, but he was afraid she'd break down if he touched her. She was breathing fast and glaring at his friends so ferociously at this point, it was somewhat alarming.

No one said a word, the only sound in the room was Cora's harsh breathing. Then she took a deep breath and cleared the emotion from her voice.

"Before she disappeared, we'd had a few conversations about Ridge. I told her about some of my concerns. He didn't want to meet any of her friends, didn't seem interested in her job. He was also possessive, and not in a good way. She wasn't happy with me, and said I was just jealous and bitter. Then she disappeared. He took her away from DC, away from her friends, her family. That's what abusers do, right? They take away a person's support system. Isolate them."

"We had a friend who's very good with computers look into Ridge Michaels," Stone told her.

Cora nodded. "I hope he was able to find more than I did."

"Ridge is actually his middle name, he uses it casually, for social media and apparently for his personal life. For professional purposes, he goes by his first name...Peter. He's the CEO of a bitcoin company. He has a sister who lives in France, who's a successful model, and his parents are well respected in California. He's thirty years old, never been married, no children. His company gives hundreds of thousands of dollars to charities every year, and he's a regular attendee at political gatherings at the White House. Well...his father donates money, and as a result, Michaels gets invited to the political shindigs."

Cora stared at Stone, then sat back in her chair with a disbelieving huff of breath. "How the hell did I not find that out when I did my research?" she asked under her breath.

"Apparently he keeps his professional life very separate from his personal one," Brick told her. "From what we were able to find, there's nothing that says this guy is an undercover kidnapper. He's seemingly an upstanding businessman who's apparently invested in starting a life with your friend. The Michaels family has a large estate in the Phoenix area, and they employ a dozen or so people who work in the house every day. It's highly unlikely all those people—maids, cooks, landscapers, drivers, and bodyguards—are all in on some nefarious plan to keep Lara hostage."

"There's also no reason why he would do something like that," Tonka added. "He's had several girlfriends over the years, and none have claimed he's been abusive or done anything to harm them."

Pipe kept his attention on Cora. Her bottom lip trembled for a moment, before she shook her head slowly. "I don't believe it," she whispered.

"Maybe Lara has found her prince charming," Owl suggested gently. "You said yourself that she was a romantic."

Cora let out a little growl as she stood so fast, the chair she was sitting in flew backward and hit the floor with a loud crack. "No!" she exclaimed, her hands in fists by her sides.

Then she closed her eyes and took a deep breath, struggling to regain her composure.

When she opened her eyes a moment later, Pipe could see she was still upset, but had gotten control of her emotions. "You're wrong. You're *all* wrong," she said, disappointment easy to hear in her voice.

"About what? About the information we found online?" Brick asked.

"No, that's probably true. You're wrong about thinking Lara is with this Ridge guy because she thinks it's true love. I don't disagree that she probably *thought* she was in love, but she's not the kind of woman to up and leave without a word to anyone. Lara's in trouble. I don't care what your friend might've found online about him being an upstanding businessman. Peter Ridge Michaels is holding her hostage for some reason. And if I'm the only person who believes that, so be it. I appreciate your hospitality, and I think you're doing great work here. I'll get out of your hair and you guys can keep doing what you do. Thank you for your service to our country...and yours too," she added, looking at Pipe.

Her eyes were full of tears she refused to shed, and she was breaking Pipe's heart.

"Sit down," Brick said. It wasn't a request.

Snapping her head to look at him, Cora didn't move for a long moment. Then she slowly bent over, picked up the chair, and sat. She didn't scoot up to the table though, and perched on the edge of the seat as if prepared to bolt at any second.

"Like I said, nothing we were able to find indicates he's holding your friend against her will...but it's been my experience that no one is as squeaky clean as Michaels seems to be," Brick finished.

Pipe looked at his friend in surprise. In the short conversation he'd had with the others, no one had hinted they might not be buying the good-guy image Tex had found.

"I understand from Pipe that you've looked into us?" Brick asked Cora.

She nodded.

"So you know what happened to Alaska."

She nodded again.

"If she hadn't managed to call me while she was in Russia, if she hadn't been able to trick the asshole who'd taken her, she wouldn't be here today. *I* wouldn't be the man I am today. So...what exactly is it that you want us to do?"

Cora swallowed hard. "Help me find her. Make sure she's okay."

"We have the address of the property the Michaels family owns in Arizona. So finding her shouldn't be an issue," Brick said.

"We aren't mercenaries for hire," Spike added. "Or bodyguards."

"We're just a bunch of former military guys who own a retreat in the woods," Tiny explained. "We can't exactly cross state lines with AK47s and RPGs and storm his house," he finished with a small smile.

Cora looked down at her hands, and her shoulders slumped. "Yeah, I know."

"This is a tricky situation," Brick went on. "But for what it's worth...we believe that things don't seem quite right."

She glanced at Brick, and Pipe could see the hope in her eyes.

"You seem to have made an impression on Pipe, and trust me, that's a hard thing to do. It's because of my loyalty to and trust in my friend that I'm agreeing to help you."

"Thank you," Cora whispered.

"Don't thank me yet. I'm willing to give you the benefit of the doubt, and I believe you probably know your friend better than anyone…but like Spike said, we're not body-guards or mercenaries or security specialists. We aren't going to Arizona in any official capacity. We'll do what we can to help you see Lara, but if *she* says she's okay, that's all we can do. Understand?"

Cora nodded.

"Any volunteers to go with Ms. Rooney?" Brick asked with a small grin.

"I'll go," Pipe said without hesitation.

Brick's smile grew. "Duh."

"Me too," Owl said.

"Hell, if Owl's going, I will too," Stone said with a shrug.

Pipe wasn't surprised. The two men were very close. Almost dying in a helicopter crash, and then being held hostage and tortured together, forged an unbreakable bond.

"Right. Stone, I'm putting you in charge," Brick said.

Pipe frowned. It wasn't as if they were a special forces team, and Brick wasn't their team leader. Then again, he was basically the driving force behind the reason they were all in New Mexico in the first place.

"You're not as close to the situation as Pipe and Owl, since they met Cora in DC. I expect you to be the voice of reason here, to not get emotionally involved. If you think things are hinky, then you report back to us and we'll decide on a next course of action. And you," Brick pinned his gaze on Cora, "do *not* do anything to put my friends in danger. Or yourself. Or Lara, for that matter. You want to know if she's okay? Then that's the plan. Talk to her, alone if possible, and see what she's really thinking. If she loves this Michaels guy, you're going to have to learn how to deal with the fact that she now lives on the other side of the country. Okay?"

"But what if she isn't? And what if Ridge won't let her leave?" Cora asked.

Brick frowned and sighed. "Then we'll figure out how to extract her at that point."

Cora looked relieved. "All right. But if I can make a suggestion..."

Spike laughed. "Sure."

"Maybe it would be good if you guys started thinking of some sort of plan to get her out while we're gone...you know...just in case."

Most of the men around the table chuckled.

"Don't worry, we will. Has anyone told you that you're really stubborn?" Brick asked.

She smiled. "Yeah. Lara."

Brick nodded. "Right. I'm thinking you guys can leave the day after tomorrow."

"Wait—what? Why not *now*?" Cora asked, the humor wiped off her face.

"Because we need to plan," Stone told her. "We need the layout of the estate, we need to figure out our best course of action. We need more intel."

Cora sighed in frustration. It was obvious she wasn't happy with the delay, but she seemed to understand that she'd gotten what she wanted—namely, their help—and if she pushed her luck, she might lose that.

"We'll see if Tex can get us some satellite images of the estate and some sort of schedule of the comings and goings of the people who work there. Maybe we'll get lucky and figure out Michaels's routine, or actually see

Lara out and about," Tonka said. He'd been mostly quiet, but that wasn't unusual for the man.

"I'd love to find out if Lara goes for coffee, or to a gym, or to do yoga every morning or something, so we could catch her away from the estate," Stone agreed.

Cora snorted. "She hates coffee and is allergic to working out."

"Right. Of course she is." Stone grinned.

Pipe hadn't said much during the discussion, but he couldn't keep quiet anymore. "We're going to get to the bottom of this, Cora," he told her.

She turned to look at him. He could see the worry in her eyes, but she simply nodded. His respect for her rose. What they were doing wasn't exactly dangerous, at least he didn't think it would be, but she'd need to control her emotions if she wanted Lara to talk to her. That would be Cora's biggest struggle. He knew that without a doubt.

"Okay, so...Cora, are you okay with staying with Pipe?" Tiny asked. "He mentioned he's volunteered the spare room in his place while you're here. We'd offer you one of the cabins, but we're completely booked."

"That's fine. I can't afford your prices anyway," she said with a small smile.

"That's not what I hear," Spike said, grinning. "Heard you had six K at your disposal."

"Oh, but that's to pay you guys," she said with a straight face. "It's in my bag, which I left in the car. I can go get it now and—"

"No," Brick interrupted her. "Did you not hear Spike when he said we weren't paid mercenaries or bodyguards?"

"Yeah, but—"

"No buts. We aren't taking your money," he said firmly.

"Especially not after we heard you sold all your stuff to raise it," Tonka added.

"Any chance you can get everything back?" Spike asked.

"Or maybe you can buy better stuff," Stone said. Then he actually blushed. "I mean, I don't know what you *had*, so that might've been a stupid thing to say."

"Wait. Is it cash? You shouldn't be carrying that much money around," Owl interjected.

"We can exchange it for a cashier's check," Brick offered.

Cora looked from guy to guy, seeming a little shell-shocked at the concern being shown to her—and it pissed Pipe off. No one should have cause to be that surprised when people were being nice.

"I...I'll need it to get Lara and I back to DC, when I get her away from that prick," Cora finally said.

Pipe couldn't help but smile. She was so sure she'd be able to convince her friend to return to DC. He just hoped it would be as easy as Cora wanted it to be.

"No, you won't," Pipe blurted. "I'll take care of it."

"You can't do that," she told him.

"I can, and I will. Consider it part of the deal of winning me at the auction, since you never got your fancy dinner."

"But I *didn't* win you," Cora said with a frown.

"Didn't you?" Pipe asked, raising a brow.

She stared at him for a long moment, and Pipe felt like they were the only two people in the world at that moment. He would've given anything to know what she was thinking right then.

He was ninety-nine percent sure that she wasn't playing him and his friends...but what if she was? What if showing him an empty apartment, the cheap dress and shoes she'd worn to the auction, even the nasty confrontation with Eleanor that he'd overheard...what if it was all part of some elaborate plan?

But as soon as he had the thought, Pipe dismissed it. Cora's emotions were too real. No matter how good an actress she might be, there was no way she could fake everything. Besides, he couldn't come up with a single good reason why she might lie about her friend. If she wanted to get to Arizona for some reason, there were a hundred easier ways to go about it.

"I'm *so* sending those flowers to Eleanor," Cora finally whispered.

Brick cleared his throat. "So...Pipe, if you want to take Cora and show her around the place, explain how things work around here, Stone can get back in touch with Tex and see what else he's found for us."

"Can I...can I see Melba? And Chuck and his girl-friend?" Cora asked Tonka. "I mean, since I'm going to be here for a day or so..."

Tonka smiled, and Pipe was glad to see it. The difference Henley had made in his friend was amazing. Instead of hiding out in the barn all day and night, Tonka had made a concerted effort to be more involved in the running of The Refuge.

"Of course. I'm pretty sure Wally and Beauty will be in the barn too," Tonka said.

"Wally and Beauty?" Cora asked.

"You mean your stalker research didn't go that far?" Pipe teased.

Cora turned appalled eyes his way. "Pipe! Your friends just agreed to help Lara, I don't want them to change their minds."

"I already told them that you stalked us," he said without a hint of remorse.

"Great. Just great," Cora said with a sigh.

"Come on," he said, finding that he was actually enjoying himself. He couldn't remember the last time he'd bantered with a woman. Usually they were either too nervous around him to talk at all, or they wanted the bad boy his physical appearance projected.

Cora stood once more and turned to Brick. "Thank you," she said fervently. "I mean it. I was planning on going to Phoenix myself if the auction didn't work out. But I know with you guys at my side, I have a much better chance of actually being able to talk to Lara and getting her out of there."

"If she wants out," Stone reminded her.

Cora simply rolled her eyes. "She does."

"You're welcome," Brick said. "But again, we aren't planning on storming his home as if he was a terrorist planning the assassination of the president or something."

"I know," she assured him.

Pipe wasn't sure if she was agreeing simply to be amenable, or if she truly thought Ridge Michaels was up to something sinister behind the walls of his estate. Either way, he supposed they'd find out in a few days. In the meantime, he was looking forward to showing Cora around The Refuge. He was as proud of it as the rest of his friends. They'd worked hard to make it what it was today.

Cora headed for the exit with Pipe at her heels. They left the room and found Alaska sitting behind the front desk, checking in a guest. She looked over and smiled at Cora and Pipe before turning her attention back to the woman in front of her.

Pipe made a mental note to talk to Brick about the fact

that Cora had emailed and called, and had gotten no response. But first he had a tour to give.

"I'll bring her bag to your cabin," Owl told them as he passed.

"Thanks," Pipe replied.

"Can we see the barn first?" Cora asked, and for the first time, Pipe saw the woman Cora probably was on a daily basis. The fact that he and his friends had said they'd help made her seem relaxed in a way she hadn't been in the short time he'd known her. And he had to admit that he liked laid-back Cora a lot. Not that he didn't like the other Cora. No, her stubbornness, her loyalty to her friend, the front she showed the world of the fierce woman who didn't care what others thought of her…it all added up to someone Pipe wanted to get to know better.

While he was anxious to get to Phoenix and check on Lara, he couldn't deny he was looking forward to the day or so he'd have to get to know Cora before leaving. "Far be it from me to stand between a woman and the cow she wants to meet. One of these days, people will want to come to The Refuge for more than the animals."

Cora giggled, and the sound shot straight to Pipe's heart. It was a carefree sound, one that he had a feeling she didn't make often.

He held open the door to the lodge for her, and when they started walking toward the barn, Pipe was shocked when Cora reached out and took hold of his hand. Looking down, he saw his tattooed fingers intertwined with hers, and once again, his heart jolted in his chest.

"Thank you," Cora whispered as she squeezed his fingers.

It hit Pipe then. In this moment, Cora was just as worried about Lara as she'd been in the middle of the discussion in that conference room. But she was letting her guard down, allowing her vulnerability to peek through again—which felt damn good. It was another show of trust.

"We're going to get to the bottom of what's going on," he reassured her.

"I know. I just hope that you and the others won't have to use your super-secret military skills in the process."

Pipe hoped the same thing. But he was beginning to realize that if he had to bust out some of the things he'd learned over the years to keep this woman and her friend safe, he'd have absolutely no regrets.

Spike was right, they weren't mercenaries, weren't hired guns or bodyguards, but when it came to keeping Cora safe, Pipe suspected he would do whatever it took... and damn the consequences.

# CHAPTER TEN

It was frustrating not to be leaving immediately for Phoenix, but Cora understood the men's need to get as much information as possible before heading into what she thought of in her mind as a battle. They might not think Lara was in danger, or that Ridge Michaels was holding her against her will, but she knew differently. She just hoped they were ready for whatever waited for them behind the doors of the jail where Lara was being held. It might be a fancy estate with a dozen paid employees waiting on Ridge hand and foot, but it was still a prison.

In the meantime, she was excited to get to see the place she'd read about and researched so extensively. Meeting Melba earlier had been a highlight. And the goats were just as hysterical as many guests said they were. After meeting them, they'd immediately started trying to chew on her pants.

Tonka's dogs, Wally and Beauty, were well-mannered, if not spoiled rotten. It was amusing to see big bad Tonka carrying Beauty around as if she was a little princess...

which she kind of was. The barn cats were friendly, and she'd even gotten to meet Mutt…Brick's three-legged dog.

But it was Chuck who delighted her the most. The squirrel was missing two feet, and he lived with his squirrel girlfriend in a little condo Tonka had built against a tree behind the barn. To her surprise, after she'd sat down with a handful of peanuts, the little guy had come right up and sat in front of her as he chowed down.

"He likes you," Pipe said quietly from her right. He hadn't said much while she'd met The Refuge's other animals. Now, he sat beside her and simply watched as she remained entranced by the little guy.

"I tend to get along better with animals than people," Cora told him, as Chuck nudged her hand for more peanuts. It was adorable how he'd stuff one into his mouth, then take one into the little wooden hut Tonka had made him. Cora mused that it was kind of sad this little squirrel took better care of his mate than anyone had ever taken care of her.

"It's because they know you're not going to hurt them."

"They can't know that," she protested, looking over at him.

Pipe was sitting with his feet flat on the ground, his arms looped around his updrawn knees, and instead of looking at Chuck, he was staring at her.

Feeling self-conscious, Cora turned back to the squirrel.

"They can sense it," Pipe told her.

They were quiet for a few seconds, before Cora blurted, "Your friends don't really believe me."

She winced at the blunt statement. Even if it was true, she probably shouldn't have brought it up.

Pipe simply shrugged. "This is unfamiliar territory for us. I mean, when Alaska was in trouble, Jasna and Reese too, it was a no-brainer that we'd do whatever it took to help them. No one messes with our loved ones. But we don't know Lara. It's harder to get a read on a situation when you're dealing with strangers."

Cora nodded. She understood that. Completely. And she respected Pipe all the more for being honest with her.

"And things could get weird really quickly if we rush in to help your friend...and it turns out she doesn't need helping."

"She does," Cora couldn't help but say as she turned to look at him once more.

Pipe's lips twitched.

"Look, I know this situation is messed up. You and your friends are trusting me when I say that she's not there of her own free will. You don't know me, you don't know Lara, and like you said, you're risking a lot to go to Arizona with me. Your reputations, at the very best, are at risk, and getting hurt in the process at worst."

Pipe snorted, and Cora couldn't stop the smile from forming on her lips at the disgruntled sound.

"No one's getting hurt," he told her.

"You can't know that," she said with a shrug.

Pipe's gaze bore into hers with an intensity that she thought was a little out of place for the situation. "No one's getting hurt," he insisted. "You stalked us. Did you miss the parts where it listed all our accomplishments and the medals we've earned?"

Cora frowned. "You've earned medals?" she asked.

Pipe chuckled. "Can't tell you. That shit's top secret. All I'm sayin' is that when you set your sights on me and my friends, you chose well. It's not going to be hard for us to figure out if Lara is there of her own free will or not."

"Really?" Cora asked.

"Really," Pipe said confidently.

"He's not going to be happy," she told him.

"Nope."

Cora turned her attention back to Chuck, who'd stuffed four peanuts into his mouth and was desperately trying to add a fifth. "I don't know what I expected when I went to that auction, but it wasn't this."

"This?" Pipe asked.

"Sitting here at The Refuge, feeding Chuck, and feeling so damn grateful that you were willing to listen to me that I can't even put it into words."

"I want to say something, but I'm not sure if I should or not," Pipe said.

Cora looked over at him. His gaze was still locked on her. "Please do."

He licked his lips, and Cora's attention was distracted for a moment. He really was a good-looking man. She'd never been with a guy with a beard as full as Pipe's, but she had a sudden longing to know what it felt like to kiss him. To feel that beard on her face. She'd been impressed with all the things she'd read about him, but to meet him in person? To see for herself that he was polite, protective, attentive, and committed to helping her, a stranger, her esteem for him had only gone up.

"I don't want your gratitude," Pipe said.

Cora blinked. "You don't?" she asked.

"When I stood in that ballroom and listened to that bitch say those horrible things to you, I wasn't happy. I decided to walk you home to assuage my guilt for somehow letting her win the auction, instead of you.

Which I know makes absolutely no sense. I had no control over that. But I still felt bad. And somehow, between the short time when we left the auction and reached that diner, my feelings about walking you home had changed."

Cora held her breath as she stared at Pipe.

"You're the most down-to-earth and open woman I've ever met. You didn't blink at my physical appearance. And don't think I missed the way you stepped closer to me when we entered that diner back in DC, as if you were trying to protect me from the suspicious looks the hostess was giving me. You respond to me like no other woman has, in fact. Others either flirt with me because they think I'm a bad boy and they want a walk on the wild side, or they cringe away and cross the street so they don't have to pass me on the sidewalk."

"I've learned over the years that someone's outward appearance means nothing when it comes to what kind of person they are. Look at Eleanor. She's gorgeous. She could be a model, and probably *has* modeled before. She's close to what society deems to be the ideal image of beauty. But she's rotten to the core. All she cares about is herself, and she'll walk on whoever it takes to get attention and to be in the limelight."

"I agree. And you are so far from that, it's not even funny."

Cora winced.

"I didn't mean that in a bad way. And if you think I'm saying you aren't pretty, you're wrong."

Cora couldn't help it. She laughed.

"I'm serious," Pipe insisted.

"Pipe, I'm short and dumpy. I have boring brown hair and equally boring brown eyes. There's nothing remarkable about me."

"You're wrong. Anyone who takes the time to look twice at you would see the same thing I have. You have an inner light that's so damn bright, it burns. You've got walls, tall ones, but I've seen what happens when someone gets beyond them. People like Lara. You'd do anything for her. That kind of love and devotion is something people rarely experience. Your friend is damn lucky to have you, Cora. And in my eyes, that doesn't just make you pretty, it makes you fucking *beautiful*."

To her surprise, tears welled up in her eyes. Damn, she wasn't usually this quick to cry, but more than once since meeting Pipe, it had felt like she was two seconds away from bawling. She blinked, trying to clear the wetness, and looked away from Pipe's piercing gaze.

"Too much?" he asked.

She heard the humor in his voice. Cora nodded.

"I'll stop then. You sure about staying with me tonight? I can get you a hotel in Los Alamos if you aren't comfortable staying with anyone here."

Cora stared at him incredulously. "And give up a chance to stay at *The* Refuge? No way!"

Pipe chuckled. "Right."

"You might not want my gratitude," Cora said. "But you've got it anyway. I've had to work my ass off for everything good I've ever had in my life, and for some reason, you didn't make me work for your help. I don't really understand why, but I'm so thankful you're helping me find Lara."

"If you could have anything in the entire world...money being no object...what would it be?" Pipe asked.

Frowning, not sure what his question had to do with her thanking him, but willing to go along with his change of subject, Cora thought about it for a moment. Then said softly, "A family."

Pipe made a noise in the back of his throat, encouraging her to continue.

"That's all I've ever wanted. As a kid, I thought if I was prettier, cuter, nicer, quieter, more outgoing, less outgoing, neater...you name the adjective, I tried to be it, thinking maybe it would get me adopted. It never worked. Family after family returned me to the state. No one wanted to keep me, and I never understood why. The more I was rejected, the more I tried...for a long while. Until I eventually stopped trying altogether.

"When I aged out of the system, I began trying to find a guy who would give me what I wanted...and that was an even bigger epic fail. Again, I'm not sure why. I guess I'm too...me. Not into using clothes and makeup to appear as something I'm not. Not willing to lie to stroke a man's ego. Too outspoken, too brash.

"So, what do I want? A family of my own. Kids I can love, who will never go even one day without knowing that they're the most important thing in my life. I want to have a biological kid, if possible, which is becoming more and more of a crapshoot because of my age, but I also definitely want to adopt. Maybe find an older kid who's been returned again and again, and give him or her a forever home."

"I'm not judging...but is there a reason you haven't adopted already?" Pipe asked.

Cora snorted. "I've had a hard enough time taking care of myself. I ended up on Lara's couch too many times to count. If I had a kid with me? That would've been awful. Besides...do you know how hard it is to adopt in this country?"

"No."

Cora turned to look at Pipe to see if he was messing with her, but when she saw the expression on his face, she realized he was completely serious.

"Incredibly hard," she answered. "Adopting an infant would be completely out of the question for me. Too expensive, and as a single woman with a low income, I wouldn't get chosen anyway. It's a little easier to adopt an older kid, but even still, it takes a lot of money, and I'm still on the bottom of the list of people who the state would want to give a child to." She sighed.

A minute or two went by before Pipe spoke again. "That's it? If money was no object, that's what you'd pick? A family? Not a mansion, a yacht, a million dollars in the bank?"

Cora shook her head. "That stuff doesn't last. But if I could give a child a home? Let them know every day that they're loved, safe, and free to be who they are, no matter what? That's what I want."

In response, Pipe reached out and took her free hand, the one that wasn't holding peanuts for Chuck.

Surprisingly, Cora felt fairly calm. Talking about her lack of a family, her lack of *anyone* in her life other than Lara, usually depressed her. Made her sink into a pit of despair that was hard to shake. But somehow, talking with Pipe, feeling as if he was truly listening, didn't send her spiraling downward. The Refuge truly was a magical place.

"What about you?" Cora asked after a minute of silence. "What would you want if money was no object?"

When he didn't answer right away, Cora wondered if she'd overstepped. They weren't really friends...were they? And maybe he wasn't comfortable answering his own question.

Just when she thought maybe she *should* take him up on his offer to stay in town, he spoke.

"My dad was in the British Armed Forces. He was deployed a lot...by his own choice. My mum was loving, but she didn't deal well with my father being gone. She kind of fell apart, actually. I learned as a young lad that if I wanted to eat while my dad was away, that I'd need to make supper myself. I did our laundry, cleaned the house, took care of the garden, even went shopping. When Dad returned, Mum went back to normal, pretending she hadn't been leaning on her ten-year-old son to keep the household running.

"She loved me, as did my dad, but I didn't feel as if I could have friends round to the house, because I wasn't sure what kind of mood Mum would be in. I joined the service as soon as I could and never looked back."

"Do you talk to your parents?" Cora asked gently.

"Of course. On holidays and their birthdays," Pipe said.

"How'd you meet Brick and the others?" Cora asked.

"You know the guy who's finding out information on Michaels?"

"Yeah. Tex, right?"

"Right. He connected us. I'd gotten to know him after a mission went completely sideways. He was helping a team of Navy SEALs, and he took my unit under his wing until we were able to get out of the country. We kept in touch and when I decided to get out...he introduced me to Brick. The rest is history."

"I want to ask something, but I don't know if I'll offend you or not," Cora admitted.

"You want to know why I left," Pipe said.

Cora squeezed his hand. "Yeah, but if you don't want to talk about it I understand."

"It's not something I usually share, but for some reason, I feel comfortable talking to you about it."

Cora's heart flipped in her chest. She wasn't usually the kind of woman who people confided in. Maybe because she never let anyone get close, or they didn't *want* to get close. But she found that she really wanted to get to know Pipe better.

"My team and I were ambushed on what should've been a routine intel-gathering mission. There were six of us. We were picked off one by one. When I called for backup, I was told that because of the sensitive balance of the relationship between the locals and the Armed Forces, they couldn't intervene. I watched my team members being slaughtered in front of my eyes. My own country threw them away like trash, because of politics."

Cora inhaled deeply and turned so she was facing Pipe. He was staring into the distance, eyes unseeing. She held his hand even tighter.

"I was shot, and I must've passed out. When I came to, the locals were stripping me and my teammates of all our gear. I pretended to be dead, knowing if they discovered I was still alive it wouldn't go well for me. They took all our gear and clothes, except for our underwear, and left us in the rubble of the rundown building where we'd taken refuge.

"I waited until darkness fell, then I crawled out of there, aware that any second I could be discovered and finished off with a bullet to my brain. By some bloody miracle, I made it to the outskirts of the town and into the forest. I crawled, stumbled, and walked back to our base, which was over five kilometers away. When I told my superior office what happened, he clapped me on the back, said he was sorry for the loss of my men, then reminded me that my missions were top secret. Basically, he was warning me that if I told anyone what happened, my career was over.

"But what he didn't understand was that it was *already* over. I was done. How could I go back to being the man I was before? A man who'd believed that those he worked for had his best interests in mind? They left me and my men to die and didn't think twice about it. And for what? Because the town was between our temporary base and the airfield we used to bring in supplies."

"I'm so sorry," Cora said, at a loss for anything else to say.

"I was up for reenlistment that year and declined. I had a hard time acclimating to civilian life," Pipe admitted. "I started getting tattoos shortly after. The pain of the needle seemed to be the only thing that turned off the noise in my head. If Tex hadn't hooked me up with Brick and the others, I don't know what would've happened to me."

Cora shifted and rested her head on Pipe's shoulder. With no idea what to say, she decided to support him nonverbally instead.

"Intellectually, I know it wasn't my country's fault... what happened to my teammates. It was a decision made by one man, or maybe a group of them. What they did that day doesn't reflect on an entire country. But I can't help but feel as if England deserted me. I was happy to move to the States. Don't get me wrong, there are just as many or more issues with the United States government, but still...being here in New Mexico lets me breathe. I haven't felt the urge to get more ink since relocating.

"You asked me what I would want if money was no object, and to finally answer your question...nothing. I've got everything I could ask for. A group of friends I know without a shred of a doubt will have my back if things go to shit. A cabin in the woods where I wake up every morning and breathe the clean air. A purpose in helping others deal with the demons in their head. I'd be selfish to ask for anything more."

Cora lifted her head, and he turned to meet her gaze. "You don't want a family?"

Pipe shrugged. "I feel as if that would be asking for too much. Tipping the scales into the greedy category."

Cora smiled at him. "I don't think that's how the world works."

"Don't want to chance it. But I'll tell you this, if I ever found a woman who loved me exactly as I am—slightly damaged, scary as hell to little kids and old women—and who could live out here in the middle of nowhere without blinking? I'd bend over backward to give her whatever she wanted. Jewelry, designer clothes, kids. It wouldn't matter. I'd give her everything."

"And if all she wanted was someone to love her without strings and with no reservations?" Cora whispered.

"Any woman of mine would know down to her soul that I'd die for her," Pipe said simply.

Goose bumps rose on Cora's arms. They were having a philosophical and hypothetical conversation...weren't they? Somehow, it felt like more.

It was almost scary how in tune with Pipe she felt. They were two people from opposite ends of the world. Raised completely differently, with contrasting experiences...and yet, she'd never felt as close to anyone as she did Pipe right that moment. Even Lara.

"I think she'd rather you *lived* for her," Cora whispered.

"Yeah," Pipe said before taking a deep breath. "You want to continue the tour?"

"Sure," she said. She was looking forward to seeing the rest of The Refuge, but mostly she wanted to spend more time with Pipe.

He stood while still holding her hand, helping her to her feet. Then he moved his hand to the small of her back as he led her back through the barn. He did that a lot, and while Cora had never liked when people she didn't know touched her, she found that she actually felt safer when Pipe had his hand on her.

She peeked up at him while they were walking and noticed how alert he was. His eyes constantly scanned his surroundings, as if he expected someone to jump out from around a bale of hay or something. But now that he'd opened up, and told her about why he'd left the military, she understood a little better.

And instead of making her feel wary that he was a little bit paranoid, it felt...reassuring. She remembered how he'd done the same thing in DC, his head constantly on a swivel, looking for trouble. It was something she did all the time herself, but it felt good to have him on alert as well. With him on guard, Cora felt as if she could let down the shield she always had up. With Pipe near, nothing and no one would hurt her. She had no doubt about that.

"Come on, I'll show you the guest cabins, where our owner cabins are, and if you're up to it, maybe take you on a little hike."

"Ooooh, will you show me Table Rock?"

Pipe chuckled as he looked down at her. "Stalker," he teased.

Cora grinned. "Yup," she retorted. She'd seen the beautiful pictures former guests had posted of the sites around the property, always tagging The Refuge. And she couldn't wait to see Table Rock for herself.

A small part of her still felt guilty that she was enjoying herself while Lara was enduring whatever she was going through, but the time would come soon enough to rescue her friend. In the meantime, Cora was going to soak up every bit of good karma this place could offer.

# CHAPTER ELEVEN

Cora sat around the table with The Refuge staff and guests at dinner that evening, enjoying Robert's delicious food and reflecting on her day. She was even more impressed with this place than she'd been before, and that was saying something, because she'd already been enthralled by what she'd seen online.

The Refuge truly was a place where people could come to relax. To get away from whatever demons they had in their heads and lives. Table Rock had exceeded all her expectations. She could imagine what it would look like when there were leaves on the trees in either the summer or fall. But even with the bare trees, the view had taken her breath away.

She'd stood on the rock looking out over the vista for at least ten minutes, feeling...small. She'd never been much of a nature girl. Growing up in the city and having lived there all her life, she hadn't really spent time camping or hiking in the woods. Standing on the edge of that rock and looking out at the miles and miles of forest suddenly made the things she experienced on an everyday basis, annoyances that could put her in a bad mood for hours, seem so petty.

"You feel it," Pipe had whispered from next to her.

Cora could only nod.

"I come out here when things get to be too much. Being out here reminds me that we're here for such a short time. That my life is fleeting. It grounds me."

Cora understood perfectly.

"You're lucky," she said softly. "To live here, I mean. This is...it's so beautiful I can't put it into words."

"Yeah," Pipe had agreed. Then he'd taken a step closer to her, close enough that she could feel the warmth of his body seep into hers, and they gazed out at the beauty that was all around them in silence. His hand moved, tentatively touching the small of her back once more, and Cora hadn't been able to stop herself from leaning into him.

How long they'd stood there, she had no idea, but even now she could feel the echo of his hand on her back. Every minute she spent around this man, the more she *wanted* to be near him. It was as if she'd found a missing part of her soul. It was corny. Unbelievable. Ridiculous.

And yet, she couldn't shake the feeling that Pipe was hers.

Lara would be eating it up. She'd be encouraging Cora to go for it. To not be scared of what she felt. She was the romantic of the two of them. The one who always saw the best in people. Who fell in love at the drop of a hat.

Just thinking about it made her frown. As the others continued to eat, Cora's concern for her friend filled her yet again. Lara was in her current situation because of her naiveté. Cora had tried to warn her that something about Ridge made her nervous, but Lara had disagreed, and they'd gotten into that big fight as a result.

Eventually, Pipe noticed her silence. "You okay?" he asked quietly from next to her.

Cora blinked and realized she'd been inside her head and completely oblivious as to what was going on around her for who knew how long.

"Yeah. Just worried about Lara."

"Tomorrow we're going to talk plans," Pipe told her. "Tex is supposed to get back to us with any new intel he was able to find, and we'll figure out how to get in touch with Lara and find out what's going on."

It wasn't going to be that easy, Cora knew that. She wasn't going to be able to walk up to Ridge's door, knock, and leave arm-in-arm with Lara for an ice cream run or something. Ridge had gone to a lot of trouble to make Lara fall so quickly. Quick enough to agree to move to Arizona without warning...if she'd even agreed at all. Since Cora hadn't been able to talk to her friend to find out exactly how the move happened, she wasn't sure of anything at this point.

"Okay," she said belatedly. "I appreciate you keeping me in the loop, but it doesn't make my worry for my friend go away. Lara is...she's not like me. She grew up sheltered. Her family is loaded, Pipe. She never understood what it was like to go to bed so hungry it feels as if your stomach is eating itself. Or to go to sleep knowing the second you do, someone might come into your room and touch you inappropriately. Didn't have to wonder when her next shower would come or if she'd be living in an entirely new house from day to day. And I *never* wanted her to experience that stuff. Ever. Now I'm afraid that's exactly what's happening. That she's suffering some of the things I endured as a kid...and she's completely unprepared for it."

Instead of responding, Pipe stood up, then reached

down and grabbed her hand, pulling Cora to her feet as well. "We're done. We'll see you guys in the morning," he told his friends.

"I'll be here early, if you wake up and want some company," Alaska said. "I need to work on the website a bit and do some scheduling."

"And I'm always up early too," Henley said. "I take Jasna to school and then head to my job in Los Alamos. If you need anything in town, let me know and I can grab it before I head back here around lunchtime."

"I'll be sleeping," Reese said with a sheepish grin. "I'm not a morning person, unlike these weirdos." She grinned. "And this kid in my belly is making me extra tired."

"Yeah, sure, it's the kid who's keeping you up at night and making you tired," Henley quipped.

Everyone laughed, and Cora smiled weakly. These women were being so nice to her. They were essentially strangers, and yet they'd offered their help without hesitation. It was a little disconcerting, and she felt as if she was waiting for the other shoe to drop. Like they'd discover something about her they didn't like, and figure out she wasn't worthy of befriending.

Pipe shook his head as if amused by the women, then began to pull her toward the door. "Tell Robert thank you for me!" Cora called as she was towed away.

"No thanks needed," Robert said as he came into the large room from another door on the other side of the room.

Cora wanted to protest, tell him that he definitely needed to be thanked for the amazing food he'd made for dinner, but Pipe didn't give her a chance. He was walking fast, holding her hand in his with a firm grip. Though Cora had a feeling that if she gave him any indication she wanted him to let go, he'd immediately loosen his fingers.

But she had no desire to let go of his hand. Even though he was walking fast, he was making sure she was right by his side. That he wasn't taking steps so big, she couldn't keep up. He was considerate, observant. And even though it was dark outside, and she knew there were critters big and small in the forest around them that would completely freak her out if she came face-to-face with any, she felt as safe with Pipe as always. He wouldn't let any bear, moose, or Chupacabra eat her.

A grin formed on her face at her thoughts. It was hard to believe that with everything going on, with how worried she was about Lara, she could still smile.

Pipe led them to his cabin, which he'd pointed out earlier. But instead of going to the door, he led her around the side of the structure. To Cora's surprise, when they got to the back, instead of the deck she'd assumed would be there, like she'd seen on some of the other cabins, she saw only a tiny little stoop off the back door.

More interesting was the sturdy-looking spiral staircase near the rear corner of the cabin.

"Pipe?" Cora asked as he led her toward it.

"Up," he said in response.

Again, Cora's lips twitched. But she did as ordered and stepped onto the first step.

The staircase was narrow, and she concentrated on not tripping as she headed upward. When she reached the top, all Cora could do was gasp.

There was a rooftop deck.

From the front, the structure looked like any other cabin she'd ever seen. But this deck was...it was literally breathtaking.

It wasn't huge, maybe ten feet by ten feet, but it had a sturdy railing all around it, and Pipe had put two Adiron-dack chairs in the space. There was a low table between the chairs, and a circular rug that she assumed was waterproof.

While she was checking out the space, Pipe headed to the left side of the deck and flipped a switch. Colorful fairy lights came on, illuminating the space, but with a soft light that wouldn't ruin her night vision.

"Sit," Pipe ordered. "I'll be right back."

Cora turned to ask him where he was going, but he was already stepping onto the staircase and heading back down.

Too enchanted to sit, she wandered over to the railing and looked up. There were trees all around the cabin, but the space directly over her head was completely clear. The night was crisp—and she gasped, literally *gasped*, at a sight she'd never seen before.

She stared at what seemed like millions of stars shining overhead.

She'd heard of light pollution, and intellectually, she knew that looking at the night sky from an apartment in the city couldn't compare to what it might look like in the wilderness, but she'd had no idea the difference would be so profound.

The stars seemed brighter. Closer. More awe-inspiring. Cora didn't even want to blink, afraid she'd miss something.

She must've been staring at the stars for longer than she thought, because she jerked in surprise when she felt a touch on her back.

"Sorry. It's just me," Pipe said in a low, rumbly voice,

even as he took a step away from her, giving her space after scaring her.

Cora turned and smiled at him. "This is...it's amazing, Pipe."

"Yeah," he agreed. "The chairs are perfect for star gazing if you want to sit. I brought up some blankets since it's a little chilly out."

It was more than a little chilly, it was actually kind of cold, but Cora didn't care. She nodded and headed for one of the chairs, lowering herself and leaning back. Pipe was right, it was a great star-gazing chair because when her head rested on the back, it was at the perfect angle to look upward without craning her neck.

He shook out a blanket and draped it over her before sitting in the other chair. They didn't speak for a while, until Cora turned her head. The small lights around them let her see the man at her side.

To her surprise, instead of looking up at the sky, Pipe was staring at her.

"What?" she asked with a small frown.

"You like?" he asked.

"Duh," Cora said. "What's not to like?"

"Hard chair, it's cold, it's dark, and it's not like the sky is as entertaining as a TV show would be."

Cora snorted. Honest-to-God snorted. She would've been embarrassed at the sound, but was feeling too awed at the moment. "You know, if someone had asked me what I expected to get out of winning a dinner at that auction, I never in a million years would've said ending up here at The Refuge, sitting in the dark, staring at a night sky I've literally never seen before in my entire life, snuggled in a warm blanket, with a man who has more layers than I ever would've thought."

His lips twitched, and it was only then that he turned his attention upward. "When I feel my thoughts overwhelming me, I come out here and look up at the sky. I was on a mission once. It was in the desert in Iran. We'd entered the country stealthily and were waiting for the next phase of the mission to start. It was absolutely silent, only the sound of our breathing and the occasional shifting of someone on the sand. I was focused on what was to come when I happened to look up. I literally gasped when I saw the stars. Out there, with absolutely no light pollution, I'd never seen anything so bloody beautiful in my life.

"When I got here, before our houses were built, I camped out a lot. I felt more comfortable outside, without four walls around me. I've gotten much better with that trapped feeling, but I knew I wanted to build a rooftop deck. Somewhere I could go to see the stars when my PTSD flared and I needed space. I've slept up here more times than I can count. Being able to look up and see the stars, to know the world is so much bigger than my problems are...it helps."

Cora sighed and turned her gaze upward again. She thought about what he'd said for a moment, then nodded. "Yeah, it does help."

In the ensuing silence, she argued with herself for a few minutes...before mentally shrugging. She'd always been impulsive. Saying things she probably shouldn't. Doing stupid crap. Why would tonight be any different?

Cora stood with the blanket still wrapped around her and took the few steps over to Pipe's chair. She felt more than saw his gaze locked on her. Without a word, she turned sideways and sat on his lap.

To her relief, he didn't ask her what she was doing.

Didn't throw her off his lap. His arms encircled her as she lay her head on his shoulder and snuggled close. Her legs were hanging over the arm of the chair, and to be honest, it wasn't exactly the most comfortable position, but Pipe was warm, and she was content.

"Is this okay?" she whispered after a moment.

"It's perfect," Pipe reassured her.

Smiling, she relaxed into him.

As far back as she could remember, Cora had kept her emotions to herself. She'd found that it never helped to cry as a child. She was still removed from one home and placed in another. If she acted out, she was labeled "difficult" and, once again, moved to a different home. If she admitted she was depressed, she was taken to the hospital and given pills. She'd learned it was easier to keep what she was feeling to herself. And while it had been a very long time since she was in the foster care system, much of what she'd learned during that time had become a lifelong habit.

She was able to talk to Lara about what she was feeling, but that was literally the only person she'd opened up to in years. Until now.

"I'm scared," she admitted in a barely there whisper.

Instead of immediately telling her that everything would be fine, Pipe asked, "Of what?"

Cora snorted. "Everything."

"Break it down for me."

She sighed. "That Lara's already gone. I know the statistics...when women disappear for so long, it's unlikely they're found alive."

"I'm not saying that's not a possibility," Pipe started... and while Cora didn't like what he was saying, she appreciated that he was being honest, wasn't trying to sugarcoat the situation. "But this doesn't feel like a normal kind of kidnapping. Michaels didn't keep it a secret that he was in Arizona, and that Lara was with him. If he did want to hurt or kill her, I'd think he would've just done it in DC. What else?"

"I don't want you or your friends to get hurt. I convinced you to help me and if anything happens to any of you, I'm not sure I could live with the guilt."

"What happens from here on out is not your responsibility," Pipe said sternly.

Cora merely shrugged. "You can say that, but it doesn't mean I won't still feel as if it is."

"We're going into this with our eyes open," Pipe told her. "We aren't thinking we can just walk up to the door of this guy's mansion and ask to speak to Lara and that will be that. We know it's likely to be much more of a bloody mess."

Unbelievably, Cora smiled.

"What's that smile for?" Pipe asked.

"I thought the exact same thing earlier, about walking up and knocking on Ridge's door and asking to see Lara."

Pipe tightened his arms around her for a moment. The hug felt good. "What else are you scared about?"

Cora debated for a second whether to say what was on her mind, but since it was dark out, and she was feeling braver than usual, she blurted it out. "You."

Every muscle under her stiffened. "Me? You're *scared* of me?" Pipe asked, sounding completely shocked.

"Yes."

"Stand up, Cora," he said in a strangled tone.

But she refused. She burrowed into him deeper. He was strong enough to stand with her still in his lap and physically put her away from him, but she hoped against hope that he wouldn't.

"You make me feel things I never have. Never thought I would," she said quickly. "Lara's the romantic. She's always seeing Prince Charming around every corner. Every man she meets could potentially be 'The One' for her. Me? I'm the exact opposite. I see a monster in a man's body when I meet most guys. I've learned the hard way that people aren't who they seem to be on the surface. But the more I'm around you, the more it feels as if you're exactly who you portray to the world."

"A fucked-up freak covered in tattoos because it was the only way he could feel anything other than a detached kind of fog?" Pipe asked a little harshly.

"See? Most men wouldn't even admit that was why they'd gotten tattoos. They'd probably just say they looked badass, or they liked the designs or something. But not you. You're more genuine than anyone I've ever met. And...around you, I feel...safe," Cora said softly. "And it's my *feelings* for you that scare me."

Little by little, the muscles under her relaxed, and she went on. "I like the way you look. I liked that at the auction, people were a little scared of you. I totally would've won my bid if bitchface Eleanor hadn't done what she always does, try to put me in what she sees as my place...beneath her, simply because she's pretty and has money."

"You're safe with me," Pipe told her.

"I know. I wouldn't be here if I didn't think so. Can I admit something else?"

"Of course."

"I know I'm not supposed to want a protector. I'm a modern woman, and I don't *need* a man. But traveling here opened my eyes a lot. Usually when I'm going about my business, some men stare. They think it's their right to say whatever they want, no matter how inappropriate, or to undress me with their eyes. Or they dismiss me completely. They look through me, as if I'm not important enough for them to notice. But when I'm with you, no one treats me disrespectfully. I felt as if I could relax for the first time in public. It's…I know that's not a popular thing for women to want, or think, but I can't help it."

"No one will even *think* to look at you with disrespect when I'm around."

"I know," Cora said with a small nod. "That's what I'm saying."

"I think most women are probably a happy medium between you and your friend Lara. They don't think every person they meet could be their other half, but they don't think they're out to get them either," Pipe said after a comfortable few minutes of silence.

"I agree."

"You don't have to be afraid of me, Cora," Pipe said in a tone she couldn't interpret. "You're in no danger from me. Physically, emotionally, or in any other way. There's something about you that I…" His voice trailed off.

"Yeah," Cora agreed.

"You feel it too." It wasn't a question.

She nodded against his shoulder.

"The timing's not great," Pipe said, and she could clearly hear the humor in his tone now.

"Right? Like…thanks, universe, for putting a guy I think I might actually be able to trust and who I want to get to know better in my path, right when the shit's hitting the fan."

Pipe chuckled, and the sound vibrated through her. One of his hands moved from around her to clasp the back of her neck gently. Cora tilted her head so she could see his face. He was so close. She could feel his warm breath against her cheek. Smell the coffee on his breath that he'd drank with dinner. Her body began to tingle under the blanket. She'd never felt this close to a man before. As if she wanted to melt into him.

"One thing I've learned over the years," Pipe said, "is that you have to grab hold of opportunities when they present themselves. I can't tell you how many times we've been in the middle of an intense op, and suddenly something utterly unexpected happens. Kids start a pick-up game of futbol, we come across a choir practicing and singing the most beautiful songs ever, someone randomly gives up intel that turns out to be vital to getting out of a particular situation alive. In every case, when I've gone with the flow...kicked around that soccer ball, stopped to listen to a song, took information we were given seriously... things turned out all right in the end."

"And when you didn't? When you stayed the course? Focused on what you were there to do?" Cora asked.

"Things went to shit," Pipe said flatly.

"So...you're saying we shouldn't ignore what we're feeling," she said with a small smile.

Her core clenched when he smiled down at her. "Exactly."

"So if we get the urge, we should drop down on Ridge's front lawn and have wild monkey sex?" she teased.

Pipe burst into laughter. His head flew back and he chuckled, long and heartily. And Cora had never been as turned on in her life as she was right at that moment. His head tilted back down, and she could've sworn his blue eyes twinkled as brightly as the stars over their heads.

"I'm not sure I'd go that far. But maybe we could start with a kiss." His thumb on the back of her neck caressed her as he spoke, making goose bumps break out on her arms. "You know, test the waters."

"You think?" Cora asked breathily.

"Oh, yeah. And for the record...you're the only woman I've brought up here. This is *my* place. Where I go when I need to relax, to get away from the world. My safe space."

Cora's heart turned over in her chest. She knew how big of a deal that was, that he was sharing it with her.

"Now it's your safe space too," he added.

"No," Cora said with a shake of her head. "*You're* my safe space. I have a feeling it doesn't matter if we're here, on a plane, in a coffee shop, or in a dungeon in some terrorist's hideaway...I'm safe with you."

"Bloody hell," Pipe sighed. "I'm going to kiss you now," he warned.

Cora smiled up at him. "Okay."

But he didn't move. Simply stared down at her.

"Pipe? I thought you were going to kiss me."

"I am. I'm memorizing this moment first. It's not every day that a man meets the woman he wants to marry."

It was Cora's turn to be shocked. "What?"

"I know. Too fast. But I'm not a stupid man. I know when I've been given a gift. Just as I knew I could take the time to play with those kids, or listen to a couple of songs. I'm forty-two years old. Too old to think with my dick. But old enough to listen to fate when she knocks me upside my head."

"I don't know—"

"Not today. And not tomorrow. I don't care how long it takes, I'm gonna show you that you can be yourself with me, Cora. You can let down your guard, tell me all the things you're feeling, good and bad. I'll be your protector. I'll be anything you need me to be."

Cora knew she should be freaking out. Things like this didn't happen to her. This was the kind of situation that Lara should be in. A man declaring that he wanted to marry her after only knowing her a single day? Before sharing even one kiss? Yeah, that was totally something that would happen to Lara, not her.

And yet, here she was. And surprisingly, the more she digested what he said, the more she was excited by the idea. "Okay. But I want it here. On your deck. At night. With the fairy lights on. Only us....and whoever's marrying us. Everyone else can be down in the yard, cheering us on. And I'm not wearing a white dress."

Where all this was coming from, Cora had no idea, but it felt right.

Pipe grinned. "Agreed."

She smiled back. "Good Lord, did we just decide on how we wanted our marriage ceremony to go when we haven't even kissed yet? We might not click. Might not have any chemistry."

"Oh, we'll click all right," Pipe growled. Then his fingers tightened on her neck and his head lowered.

He kissed her as if he'd been doing it all his life. No hesitation, no tentative fumbling.

Cora immediately opened for him and wrapped an arm around his neck, urging him closer.

And he was right. They had serious chemistry. More than she'd ever experienced with anyone. The moment his lips touched hers, sparks flew.

Cora tilted her head, wanting to get closer. His tongue stroked hers as they spoke without words. His other hand came up and he palmed her face as he worshiped her mouth. She couldn't describe it any other way. She held on to him for dear life, afraid she'd fly into a million pieces if she didn't have him to cling to.

When he finally lifted his head, Cora almost felt bereft. She opened her eyes and found that he was staring at her as if he'd never seen her before. He still cradled her face in his hands, and the look in his eyes made her feel strong and weak at the same time...and so feminine.

"Pipe?" she breathed.

"Bloody hell," he swore.

Cora giggled.

"Seriously, woman. That was...I don't know what that was."

"I think it's safe to say we definitely have chemistry," Cora told him.

"Yeah," Pipe agreed before lowering his head again. This time, the kiss was sweet and slow, not quite as passionate as the previous one, but no less life-altering.

Cora's nipples were hard and tight under her shirt, and she could feel how wet she'd gotten between her legs. From kissing, of all things. That had never really happened to her before.

And she hadn't missed Pipe's erection under her ass. She had the sudden thought that if she moved, she could straddle his lap and all it would take was a little shimmy and shake and he could be inside her.

But as soon as she had the thought, Pipe lifted his lips from hers, cradling her against his chest once again. One arm went around her back and the other draped heavily across her lap as he clasped her to him.

"I was kidding about going at it on Ridge's lawn, but now I'm thinking that's not too far outside the realm of possibilities," Cora said with a small laugh.

"We're gonna find Lara, find out what the hell's going

on, then I'm bringing you back to The Refuge and making love to you up here on our deck. With the stars shining over our heads," Pipe told her.

Cora squirmed. She wanted that. Badly. "Can we maybe bring up a space heater or something? Because the thought of getting naked in the cold isn't very romantic."

She felt more than heard his chuckle. "Yeah, love, we can do that."

Intellectually, Cora realized that Pipe wasn't declaring his love for her with the pet name, it was just something that British people called others, she'd heard it often enough on TV shows and read it in books. But still, something deep down preened and basked in the nickname. All her life, that was all she'd wanted. To be loved. And to hear that word from Pipe's lips made her yearn for it to be true all the more.

They sat cuddled together for at least another thirty minutes before the chill in the air got to Cora. She shivered, despite being plastered against Pipe and under a blanket.

"Time to go in," he announced.

Cora pouted. "But I'm comfortable."

"Liar," he said without heat. "You're freezing."

"I'm a little chilly."

He snorted and sat up with her in his arms. Just as she'd thought earlier, he could totally stand while she was in his lap. But instead of standing right away, Pipe stared down at her with a look she couldn't interpret.

Then he said, "Luckiest day of my life was when I pulled the short straw to be in that auction and met my stalker."

Without giving her time to respond, Pipe stood and put Cora on her feet. He pulled the blanket away and turned her toward the stairs. "I'll give the blanket back when you're on the ground. I don't want you to trip on your way down the stairs."

Another shiver went through her, but it wasn't from the cold. It was because he was being protective again. She carefully made her way down the spiral staircase as Pipe turned off the fairy lights and started down behind her. She looked up once more and gasped as a shooting star streaked across the sky.

"Holy crap, did you see that?" she asked as Pipe stepped up next to her.

"Yeah."

"It was...I have no words. Amazing. Beautiful. Breathtaking."

"Sounds like you have plenty of words to me," he teased.

Cora smacked his chest as she turned to him. "Don't make fun of me. I've never seen a shooting star before. Wait, it *was* a star, right, not a meteor coming down to explode and decimate earth?"

He chuckled, and Cora decided she loved the sound of his laugh. She wanted to hear it a lot more. "It was a star," he reassured her. "Come on, let's get you inside and warm. It's later than I thought, and we have to get up to talk to the guys in the morning."

"Pipe?" Cora said, looking up at him.

"Yeah?"

"The way you make me feel when I'm around you has nothing to do with gratitude, but you're going to have to let me thank you. Lara's the only family I've ever known."

"Until now."

"What?" she asked with a tilt of her head.

"The only family you've had...until now. You've got me,

the rest of the guys, their women, and don't think I missed how you've already got Robert wrapped around your finger. And Ryan too. I'm sure as soon as you meet Jess, Jason, Hudson, Luna, Carly, and Savannah, you'll make them like you just as much."

Cora pressed her lips together, trying not to cry again. "You don't understand. This isn't me. I don't make friends this easily. I'm the weird chick, the one people don't get and don't click with."

"Wrong. This *is* you. You've just had the misfortune to not have found your people yet. Here, we accept everyone just as they are. We're all weird, love. Embrace it, and be exactly who you were meant to be. Now, I can see you shivering. Inside, woman."

Cora let him push her toward the back door to the cabin. She felt off-kilter, but more optimistic than she'd been in her entire life.

She was going to find Lara, get her away from Ridge— because she knew deep down he wasn't a good guy—come back to The Refuge, have that wild monkey sex with Pipe, and figure out the rest of her life after that.

She had no illusions that things would be quite so easy, but she truly believed that maybe, just maybe, she could finally be happy.

# CHAPTER TWELVE

Pipe wasn't happy.

Nothing about the upcoming situation was making him feel all warm and fuzzy. It wasn't as if he hadn't believed Cora when she'd insisted Ridge Michaels had kidnapped her friend, though without proof, he couldn't make any hard and fast decisions.

But now that they were listening to the new information Tex had dug up, he knew without a doubt that going to Arizona and getting Lara back, if she was still alive, wouldn't be easy.

Peter Ridge Michaels was the son of John Michaels, a man who'd made his money inventing a new painkiller and who now lived in California. Pipe didn't understand all the ins and outs of the drug, but apparently it was very strong, and he'd done a lot of lobbying to get it into the mainstream doctor and drug networks.

But a decade after the drug was approved by the FDA, and subsequently prescribed to millions of people, questions were being raised about the ethical responsibility of doctors who prescribed the drug to their patients because of its highly addictive nature.

All of that was practically a moot point, because John Michaels had long-since ridden the wave of his drug's popularity, making millions of dollars before selling the formula—which *really* made him some serious cash. Despite the price of the drug plummeting, and anyone who prescribed it now being raked over the coals, the Michaels family was enjoying the benefits of the painkiller's early successful years.

"What does Ridge have to do with the drug?" Owl asked. They'd decided to use the name Lara and Cora knew the man as, because it was less confusing for everyone.

"Nothing, as far as I can tell," Tex said through the phone in the middle of the table. "He benefited from his dad being the creator and has more money than most people know what to do with at his disposal."

"So why would he risk all that by kidnapping Lara?" Cora asked.

"Don't take this the wrong way...but we don't know that he did," Tex said.

Pipe felt Cora stiffen next to him.

"I hear what you guys are saying," she said quietly. "I'm willing to concede that maybe Lara did move to Arizona with Ridge voluntarily. She *is* a romantic. She could've been so enamored with the idea of love and marriage that she went with him. Maybe she expected it to be a short leave of absence, as she told our workplace. Maybe she actually found her prince charming. But I still want to hear from her own lips that she's there of her own free will."

Pipe's admiration for Cora rose. She'd been insisting over and over that her friend had been kidnapped, but she was still at least willing to consider that maybe she was wrong.

"The Michaels family has a twenty-four-room mansion in the Phoenix area. Michaels Senior employs a dozen people who are regularly in and out of the house, day and night. Ridge has two bodyguards, one of whom is with him at all times. He was seen at a charity fundraiser in the last week, by himself, and nothing seems amiss with his schedule," Tex went on.

"Has anyone seen Lara?" Stone asked.

"Yes. Ridge took her out to eat a couple weeks ago... rented out the entire restaurant so they could have privacy."

"That doesn't prove she's there of her own free will," Cora said. "He could've rented out that restaurant so she couldn't make a scene or ask anyone for help. He's isolated her completely, both in his home and now seemingly even in public."

"Which is a good point," Tex conceded. "I've uncovered satellite images of her in the gardens on the estate, always with Michaels at her side. Granted, those pictures were from when they first arrived."

"Has she made any phone calls? Talked to anyone outside Ridge's bubble?" Brick asked.

"Not that I've been able to find."

Pipe looked over at Cora and found her staring at her hands, which were clenched together in her lap. He hated this for her.

"Is she using any of her credit cards?" Tiny asked.

"Actually, yes. Quite regularly. The Osler family is also very well off. Lara has a trust fund that's quite generous, and she'll be the sole inheritor of their estate when her parents pass, currently estimated at around twenty million dollars."

Cora's head came up and her brows furrowed as she stared at the phone.

"What are you thinking, Cora?" Tonka asked.

She glanced at him. "I knew Lara's parents had money, but she's the last person you'd ever think was rich. She works hard, but doesn't make a ton of money as the executive director of a preschool. She's also very frugal. Doesn't like to go out to eat a lot, doesn't buy a lot of stuff. So it's weird that she's using her credit cards so much. Every now and then she'll go to a function with her parents, but she's always been more of a jeans-and-T-shirt kind of girl."

"Where's she been spending money? And how much?" Spike asked Tex.

They heard the other man clicking on a keyboard before he spoke once more. "Looks like in the last three weeks, she's spent almost a hundred thousand. Ralph Lauren, Saks Fifth Avenue, a couple jewelry stores, lots of high-end restaurants, and...Oh. Well, shit."

"What? What's wrong?" Brick asked.

"A large chunk of the money went to the Blue Moon," Tex answered.

"What's that?" Owl asked.

"A high-end gentlemen's club."

Cora abruptly stood and began to pace the length of the conference room. Pipe kept his eye on her as the others erupted into conversation.

"So he's either taking Lara with him, or he's using her credit cards."

"Why bring Lara to Arizona if he's indulging in strippers?"

"More importantly, why would he be using her credit card when he's loaded himself?"

"Is there a pattern to when he goes to the Blue Moon?" Stone asked.

Pipe turned his attention back to his friends.

"Sort of, but only due to frequency," Tex said. "There are expenditures just about every night."

"Which is good," Stone said. "We can go to the Blue Moon, see what's what. And we also know he's out of the house every night."

"Which also means we can head there while he's gone and see if we can talk to Lara," Owl agreed.

Pipe turned back to Cora and was surprised to see her crouched down with the wall at her back, hugging her legs. He pushed away from the table and went over to her. "Cora?" he asked, kneeling beside her and putting a hand on her shoulder.

She shook her head. "He's using her for *money*," she said in a tone that was so defeated, so full of bitterness, it made Pipe want to take Cora in his arms and simply rock her. "It's the one thing she dreaded most. It's part of the reason she didn't date much. I figured she thought Ridge was ideal because he's just as rich. Lara might assume having money means she can trust that he likes her for who she is, not because of her bank account."

"Let's go back to the important question. Why would Michaels need her money if his family is so rich?" Tiny asked.

"Tex?" Brick said. "Any ideas?"

More clicking came from the phone on the table, but Pipe's attention was on Cora. He felt powerless to do anything for her. It was obvious she was devastated by this latest news, and he couldn't do anything to help other than remain by her side.

"Not really," Tex said. "His family is loaded, and like Ms. Osler, Michaels has a trust that doles out money every month."

"Something's fucked up here," Brick mumbled.

"Agreed," Stone said with a nod.

"Wait a second," Tex said. "Hmmmm...for years, it looks like he was getting twenty thousand a month from his trust. But before he started dating Lara, it dropped to three thousand."

"That's a huge drop," Brick said.

"It is," Tex agreed.

"Daddy took away most of his money before he met Lara. That seems like a good motive to me," Tiny said.

"Right. So we know he's using Lara's money, and he goes out a lot, which is good for us," Owl said with a nod. "Maybe going right up to the door and knocking isn't actually a bad plan."

"Or we can talk to the ladies at the Blue Moon," Stone said. "Do some recon and learn who his favorites are, see what kind of information they can give us."

"Cora?" Pipe asked. "What do you think we should do?"

Her head came up, and she met Pipe's gaze head on. "Find where he's holding Lara and get her the hell out of there," she said firmly.

"I'm thinking we shouldn't start out with a B&E," Spike said with a wry grin. "We've got good connections here, but the last thing I want is to have to bail all of you out of an Arizona prison."

"Wait, isn't Arizona where that one guy made the inmates wear pink underwear?" Brick asked.

Pipe tuned out his friends' chatter, his focus fully on Cora. "We're going to find out what's going on," he told her.

She shook her head. "All she wanted was to find someone who loved her for who she was, not for her money."

"You knew about her trust fund?"

Cora rolled her eyes. "Of course. We're best friends. I know everything about her. But she doesn't care about the money. I mean, she's grateful for it because it means she can have an apartment in a safe part of the city, and she can do what she loves rather than having to find something that pays better. But she's not the kind of person who wants designer handbags and expensive jewelry. She's generous to a fault, always giving money to the homeless, and she buys every one of the kids at the preschool a present during the holidays. She makes sure all the lower-income families have a turkey at Thanksgiving, and if any of her kids come to school with dirty clothes or looking rough, she personally reaches out to their families to check in. And she does it in a way that no one feels as if they're accepting charity. She's truly amazing. And to find out that Ridge only wanted her *money*?" She shook her head sadly.

"We'll get her out of there," Pipe reassured her.

"Which I'm grateful for...but you don't understand. Finding out the truth about Ridge probably broke her," Cora said, putting her forehead on her updrawn knees.

Pipe didn't like seeing her so devastated. He stood, then leaned over and put his hand under her elbow. He gently helped Cora to her feet and led her back to the table, helping her sit. Then he pulled his chair right up against hers and put a hand on her thigh. He didn't care if his friends saw his open affection toward her. He couldn't *not* touch her right now.

"We'll leave in the morning," Pipe said. "Fly to Phoenix, go to Michaels's house, see if we get lucky and he lets us in. If not, we do surveillance on the house, then go to the Blue Moon. Depending on the intel we get, we'll go from there. Yeah?"

"I'll email the satellite pics of the property and the addresses of the places where Lara's credit cards have been used. Maybe you can go to the stores with pictures of both Lara and Michaels and see if anyone recognizes them," Tex said.

"Yeah, that's a good plan," Stone agreed.

"Can you get us the addresses of the employees who work at the estate? Maybe we can approach some of them away from the house. See if they'll talk to us about what's going on inside," Owl added.

"Of course," Tex said. "I'll send you a list of names and see what I can find out about each of them on my end."

"Thanks for the intel," Brick told him.

"Don't thank me," Tex said grumpily.

"Sorry, forgot you hate that shit," Brick said with a small laugh.

"I'll be in touch. Cora?"

Her head came up. "Yeah?"

"If your friend is being held against her will, the men around that table will figure out how to get her out of there," Tex reassured her.

"She is," Cora said firmly. "And I hope you're right."

"I am. I'm out."

Silence descended around the room for a moment. Then Owl said quietly, "I don't like this."

"Agreed," Stone said. "This situation stinks to high

heaven. Would Michaels really kidnap Lara simply to use her money because his dad essentially cut him off?"

"There's no telling. But I'm sure Tex will do some more digging and figure it out," Spike said.

"You guys will need to get to the airport a little early, so you can check your sidearms," Tiny told Owl, Stone, and Pipe.

Cora's gaze flicked to Pipe upon hearing that. "You're bringing weapons?" she asked.

Pipe nodded. "Of course we are. That bother you?"

"No," she replied. "I mean, I'm glad. I just...I read that weapons weren't allowed here on The Refuge, and with all the uncertainties, with you guys not really thinking that Lara was kidnapped, I wasn't sure..." Her voice trailed off.

"Stalker," Pipe accused tenderly.

He was rewarded with a small smile. He couldn't wait for the day he could make her smile wholeheartedly. When her friend was safe, and she wasn't so stressed out and could let herself completely relax.

"While we don't allow guests to bring weapons onto the property, for obvious reasons, that doesn't mean we aren't prepared to protect ourselves. And there's no way I'm going to Arizona to try to figure out what happened to Lara without some way to protect you in the process," Pipe told her.

"Were you...did you have a weapon on you when we were in DC? I mean, I don't remember you doing anything special when we flew here," Cora said.

"I never go anywhere unarmed," Pipe told her.

Her head tilted as she studied him.

"As if Pipe actually needs a knife or gun to protect himself. Or anyone else," Tiny added.

Cora flinched slightly, as if she'd forgotten they weren't

alone. Pipe felt the same way. When he was with her, he wanted to give her his undivided attention. And here with his friends, he could do so. Could let down his guard and not be on alert so much.

She turned to Tiny. "Really?"

"Yup. I mean, we're all fairly good at hand-to-hand combat. But Pipe? He's the master."

Cora studied him once again. "Huh."

He grinned. "That's all you have to say?"

"Yup. Oh, wait, no. Can you teach me?"

"Teach you what?"

"How to protect myself if I'm attacked? I mean, I've learned some stuff over the years, kind of had to, but I'd love to be trained by a professional."

"Absolutely," Pipe said without hesitation. "The main thing you need to remember is to go for the weak spots."

"Like a guy's dick?" Cora asked.

Pipe's friends laughed, but he kept his gaze glued to Cora's. "Yup. Although honestly, guys are used to people aiming there. I was talking about the soft-tissue spots. Eyes, especially."

Cora wrinkled her nose.

"I know, it's gross. But I guarantee someone will let go of you immediately if you stick your finger in their eye. That gives you time to get the hell away from him or her and get help. That should be your goal—not standing and fighting, but getting away."

She nodded, not offended in the least. "Do you teach a class on this kind of thing here?"

"No, why?"

"You should. I mean, if people are here because of some traumatic experience, they might want to know more about how to defend themselves if they're ever in that kind of situation again."

"She's right," Brick said with a nod. "That's a great idea, and I can't believe we haven't already thought of it. Thanks, Cora. I'll talk to Alaska and see where we can fit it into the schedule. Maybe we can offer a class twice a week or something, to maximize the number of guests who can attend."

"I'm not as good as Pipe with hand-to-hand, but I'm happy to help," Spike volunteered.

"Same," Tiny said.

"I'm in too," Brick said.

"Don't look at me," Owl said with a self-deprecating chuckle. "I had some instruction in Basic Training, but the Army was more interested in teaching me to fly a helicopter than meeting the enemy head on."

"Right?" Stone said with a shake of his head. "Maybe if they'd trained us more extensively in hand-to-hand combat, we might've fared better when our chopper went down."

Pipe frowned. His friends were still dealing with the aftermath of their time in captivity, it was obvious, and it sucked that they hadn't been given the tools they needed to maybe evade capture in the first place. They might be some of the best helicopter pilots in the world, but that wouldn't help them if they fell into enemy hands...something they'd learned the hard way.

"I'll let you guys know if I hear anything back from Tex that might affect what happens in Phoenix. In the meantime, make sure you have everything you need for the trip, and if not, let me know and we'll scrounge it up," Brick said.

Pipe nodded. "Appreciate it."

His friend sighed. "I'm beginning to understand why Tex doesn't like to be thanked. When I needed you guys the most, when that asshole came to The Refuge to get Alaska, you were all there for me, no questions asked. So if you get to Arizona and find the situation is more fucked up than you expected, you'd better call us. We'll be there in a heartbeat. The women can keep things running here without us. And you don't ever have to thank me for doing what needs to be done for you and yours," Brick said, staring intently at Pipe.

He nodded, gratitude swelling inside him. His friends didn't ask what was up between him and Cora. They simply accepted what they could see with their own eyes, that she meant more to him than some random person he was doing a favor for.

Brick addressed Cora next. "You okay?"

"No. I'm overwhelmed. Angry at that asshole, Ridge. Scared to death for Lara. But also wondering what I've ever done in my life to be lucky enough to have you all on my side. And Lara's."

"I have a question...how hard would it have been for you to access Lara's account to borrow money to use for the auction?" Brick asked, leaning forward and studying Cora carefully. "I'm only asking because I assume after everything you've said about your friend, about how generous she is and how close you are, she might've given you access to her money."

Cora's cheeks pinkened. Suddenly, Pipe wanted to hear her answer just as much as Brick.

She shrugged, staring at the table, gaze only occasionally flicking up to Brick. "I'm listed on her bank account... for emergencies. She marched me down to her bank the last time I lost my apartment and had to move in with her.

Said she didn't want me to be homeless ever again, and made me promise to use her money if I needed it for rent or to pay my electric bill or something," Cora said. After a beat, she raised her chin enough to look Brick in the eye. "I never have though. I think knowing she was so willing to give it made me more determined *not* to use her money."

"Wait," Pipe said in confusion. "You sold all your furniture, every last dish and mug in your cupboards, *all* of your belongings to raise six thousand dollars to use at the auction...when you could've simply gone to the bank and taken what you needed? Enough to outbid that cow, Eleanor?"

"It's not my money," Cora insisted. "And I know that sounds stupid because I needed it to help Lara, and it's her money in the first place, but I just couldn't."

"It doesn't sound stupid," Tonka reassured her. "It sounds like you're the kind of person anyone would want to have at their back."

Pipe was astonished by this woman once more. If it had been anyone else—literally *anyone*—they would've used the money at their disposal without a second thought. Especially in a dire situation. But not Cora. She probably hadn't even considered it. She simply did what she'd always done...relied on herself to solve a problem.

Well, never again. She had a complete tribe of people to support her now. Whether she knew it or not.

"Right. So...I heard Alaska asking Robert to make his famous taco bar tonight for dinner. Trust me when I say that you'll roll yourself out of the lodge afterward. Whatever he uses to spice up the meat is so damn addictive. She also mentioned something about wanting to get to know you better. Just a heads-up," Brick told Cora, giving her a wink.

That reminded Pipe of something. "Before we go... Cora said she emailed several times asking for help, before hearing about the auction and learning one of us would be there. But she never got a reply. She also left a phone message, again with no reply. Can you ask Alaska about that?"

Cora stiffened next to him. "It's not a big deal," she said quickly.

"You emailed?" Brick asked, his tone surprised.

"Yeah, but again, it's fine. I'm sure you guys get a ton of emails asking for help," Cora told him.

"I'll talk to Alaska," he told Pipe with a nod.

"No, please don't! I don't want to get anyone in trouble. I mean, it was a stupid thing to do on my part. It's not like you guys would just read an email and believe me and jump on a plane or something. Don't be mad at her, Brick. Please."

"You think I'm mad?" he asked.

"Aren't you?"

"No. Not at all. Alaska works her ass off for this place. I have no idea how we survived without her all those years. It's a miracle we're still in business, if I'm being honest. She's in charge of all the admin stuff, and I'm thinking it's time we hired someone else to help out. You're right, we wouldn't have immediately gotten on a plane and agreed to help a stranger, but things like that probably need a second pair of eyes to sort through."

Cora didn't look appeased.

"It's fine, love," Pipe said, wanting only to take away the worry he saw in her eyes.

"She's gonna be upset that I got her in trouble," Cora said softly.

Tonka laughed, and Pipe shot him a glare.

His friend ignored the warning look. "Alaska's not going to be upset. Not at you, at least. She'll probably beat *herself* up about not responding to you, once she realizes that you emailed. I'm guessing she'll bend over backward to make it up to you. Probably insist on taking you shopping, buying you some of the best chocolate you've ever eaten, show you all the best places to get deals...She's got a huge heart. You have nothing to worry about."

"Tonka's right," Spike said with a nod. "She's the heart and soul of this place, and she's not going to be happy that she overlooked your emails."

"All the more reason not to tell her," Cora mumbled, making the men all around smile.

"You're good people, Cora Rooney," Tiny said after a moment.

"Agreed. And on that note, I need to go pack," Stone said, pushing back from the table.

Everyone else stood as well, each of them reassuring Cora that they'd do whatever they could to help Lara, and that she was in good hands with Owl, Stone, and Pipe.

Then it was only Pipe and Cora left in the room. He stepped into her personal space and reached for her, tilting her head up and holding her face gently, like he had last night. "We're going to get her back. I give you my word."

She swallowed hard and reached up to grip his wrists. She held on tightly, as if she was a moment away from flying into a million pieces. "I'm even more scared now. I can't believe Ridge kidnapped her for her money. And everyone knows money often makes people do desperate or stupid things. What if he's already hurt or killed her?"

"I don't think he has. She was seen at that restaurant, remember?"

"Yeah," she muttered. "But I still don't understand what he's doing. It doesn't make sense, and that worries me too."

It worried Pipe too. "You're going to go crazy if you try to understand everything right this second. Put it aside, if only for a few hours. Tomorrow, we'll head straight to his estate and see what we can find out."

"And if he won't let us see her?"

"Then we'll go to Plan B. And then Plan C, Plan D, and Plan E."

"We *have* all those plans?" she asked.

"Nope, but we will. One thing you should know, us special forces guys are used to changing things up on the fly."

"Okay."

"Okay," Pipe agreed. "You hungry?"

Cora shook her head.

"Right. You want to go see Chuck and the others at the barn?"

She shook her head again.

"What do you want to do?"

"Stress. Wonder what Lara might be going through. Figure out how to get her home."

Pipe couldn't help but smile down at her. He'd hoped she'd stop worrying, but like the true friend she was, she simply couldn't do it. "All right, how about this...we'll go back to my cabin, I'll make us some lunch, we'll sit on the roof and you can tell me more about Lara. About what you guys like to do back in DC. About your job and the kids you work with. Yeah?"

She looked up at him. "You'd do that for me? Let me

bore you to tears by telling you yet again how awesome Lara is?"

"I think I'd do anything for you," Pipe told her honestly.

"We don't really know each other," she replied.

"We know each other," Pipe countered. "We know the stuff that counts."

He didn't think she was going to respond, but she finally nodded. "Yeah."

"Yeah," he agreed, satisfaction coursing through his veins.

"Maybe we can do some more of that kissing thing?" Cora asked with a small smile.

"I think that can be arranged," he said.

"Pipe?"

"Yeah?"

"When this is all said and done, I want to get a tattoo. Will you go with me?"

"I'd be honored." And just like that, a new design began niggling at his brain, despite years of no interest in getting another tattoo.

A skeleton key...because keys open things, and it felt as if Cora was slowly entrusting him with the key to understanding who she was, deep down. Not only that, but she was working her way through his shields, as well.

He envisioned barbed wire around the key, symbolizing how he'd guard it with his life and wouldn't take advantage of her trust. He wanted to incorporate a wolf somehow too, as the animal was known for its loyalty. Maybe the key would be around the wolf's neck, or clenched in his teeth.

"What are you thinking about?" she asked.

Pipe dropped his hands from her face and pulled her

against his side as he walked them toward the door. "What I want to get for my next tattoo."

She giggled. "Why am I not surprised?" she asked.

"Because you know me," he said simply.

He felt Cora's gaze as they walked. "I'm beginning to think I do," she said, more to herself than him.

Her words made him smile. He wasn't exactly an open book, but he'd opened up more to this woman than he had with anyone in a very long time. He never talked about the reasons he'd left the military and the UK. And yet she hadn't judged him. Had simply listened. Which was what he needed.

No, what he needed was this woman. He'd never met anyone like her, and he had a feeling he never would again. She felt familiar, as if they'd been together for years instead of less than two days. He connected with her on a level he hadn't clicked with anyone else.

He'd be an idiot to let her go, and one thing Pipe wasn't, was an idiot. They needed to figure out how to help Lara, and then he'd make it very clear, if he hadn't already, that he didn't want Cora out of his life.

She'd probably want to go back to DC with her friend, and he'd never ask her to leave the city where she'd lived her entire life. He'd need to talk to Brick and see if he could continue as an owner of The Refuge while living across the country. If he could, great; if not, then he'd sell his share.

He looked around as they walked...and was surprised to find the thought of leaving everything he knew in this country for a woman didn't freak him out, even after just meeting her. He'd miss it, but he'd also do whatever it took to earn Cora's loyalty, because he knew deep in his heart that it would be the best thing he'd ever done in his life. Hands down.

They continued toward his cabin, and somehow Pipe felt lighter than he had in a very long time. He had a plan. One that included making Cora understand without a shred of doubt that he was in this for the long haul. She wanted a family? He'd happily give her one. She'd never be alone again. Not if he could help it.

# CHAPTER THIRTEEN

"I'm so sorry!" Alaska said mournfully when Cora walked into the lodge later that evening.

Cora frowned at the angst in the woman's voice. She didn't like it. Not at all.

She'd actually been able to relax with Pipe earlier. They'd done just what he'd suggested...gone back to his cabin and sat on the rooftop deck, eating sandwiches he'd made and talking about Lara. Eventually, that conversation had morphed into talking about herself. What she liked to do in her free time, her job at the preschool, the best dive restaurants in DC.

They'd sat in the comfortable chairs, but Pipe had moved the table that sat between them and pulled his chair right next to hers. After they'd eaten, he'd held her hand, and Cora swore she could still feel the weight of his thumb moving over the back of her hand even now. It wasn't until they'd stood up to head back down the stairs that Pipe had taken her into his arms and kissed her. It had been a tender kiss, one that made Cora long for more.

By dinnertime, she'd been looking forward to heading

up to the lodge for the taco bar Robert was putting together for the guests and staff. It was hard to believe how...*nice* everyone was. In her experience, she never really fit in with groups of people, and women rarely seemed interested in getting to know her.

But Alaska, Henley, Ryan, and Reese, along with the others she'd met so far, were the opposite. They seemed happy to get to know her. In some ways, Cora felt as if she was in an alternate dimension. Like any moment the bubble would burst and everyone would see the "real" Cora and turn up their noses at her.

As soon as she'd walked into the lodge, Alaska had made a beeline for her and immediately apologized.

"You have nothing to be sorry about," Cora told her.

"I do! I shouldn't have ignored your emails and your phone message."

"It's okay."

"In my defense, we get several emails a week from people who want to hire the guys. And they don't do that. I mean, they *could*, because they're damn good at it. I should know. But I've never even thought about showing any of the emails to Drake because it wasn't something the men were considering. I just skim them quickly and delete." She looked miserable at that admission. "But if I'd taken the time to read your emails more carefully, maybe I would've mentioned it to Drake and the others."

"I get it, I do," Cora told her, hating that Alaska seemed so upset.

"I talked to Drake about it, and while it doesn't help your situation, we agreed that I'd put any emails of that kind, from people wanting to hire the guys because of their backgrounds, in a separate folder, and Drake or someone else would review them and decide how to proceed."

"Are you...Never mind," Cora said, changing her mind about asking the question that was on the tip of her tongue.

"Am I what?" Alaska asked.

Cora sighed. "Are *you* okay with that? I mean, having your boyfriend—ugh, that word doesn't seem to fit Brick at *all*—doing something potentially dangerous to help someone else?"

The two women were standing alone in a corner of the great room. Pipe was talking with Owl and Stone off to one side, the guests were laughing and mingling, and Henley, Jasna, and Reese were going through the line at the buffet.

"Honestly? Yes," Alaska said. "Drake and his friends were excellent at their previous jobs. I experienced it first-hand when they rescued me. Will I worry about him? Absolutely. But the thought of someone else out there desperately needing the kind of help I did, and not getting it, would haunt me. I don't know how this is going to work. I mean, the logistics of it all. But we'll see what happens. If it's not something they ultimately want to do, they have some friends they can refer people to, or they can ask Tex for recommendations.

"And as for Drake being my boyfriend..." Alaska smiled and glanced across the room, at the man in question. "I think I'm ready for him to be my husband."

Cora's eyes widened. "Wow, cool."

"Yeah. I mean, we're already engaged, and I know he wants to get married, but I've been putting it off. I think it's because I was waiting for the other shoe to drop, you know? For Drake to come to his senses and realize that

I'm the same dork I was back when we knew each other in high school. But I swear with every day that goes by, we get closer. I can't imagine not living the rest of my life with him."

"That's awesome," Cora said with a huge smile. She was truly happy for the woman.

"I think so too. And I suspect Tonka and Henley are thinking about a civil ceremony, though I know Jasna wants to throw a huge thing, with all the animals involved, and have it in the barn." The women laughed. "I don't think Tonka is all that thrilled about it, but he'll do whatever makes his girls happy. I don't think The Refuge will become wedding-central, because that's not what this place was created for, but knowing my best friends started their married lives here makes me feel warm and fuzzy inside."

Cora smiled. "The whole vibe of this place is very serene and laid-back."

"It is," Alaska agreed. "Come on, my stomach is yelling at me. Robert's tacos are the absolute best. But then, everything he makes is awesome."

Alaska dragged Cora over to the end of the line, and while they were waiting for their turn to pile their plates high, Pipe, Owl, and Stone joined them.

"You two plotting world domination?" Pipe teased, wrapping an arm around her waist and crowding her from behind.

Cora tilted her head back and smiled at him. "Of course," she retorted.

"Did Brick tell you about the self-defense lessons we want to start?" Owl asked Alaska. "Pipe said he'd lead them, and Stone and I are gonna attend each and every one."

"Yes!" Alaska said, her eyes widening in excitement. "I think it's such a good idea. I've already looked at the schedule to see where we can fit them in. I think in the afternoons, after lunch, but not *right* after, so everyone's food has time to settle. In the summer, it'll be good for the people who might not want to go hiking in the heat, and in the winter, it'll give the guests one more option for something to do indoors. Oh, and I've talked to Ryan, Jess, Luna, Savannah, and Carly, and they're all excited about them too." She made a karate chop move and grinned up at Pipe.

He chuckled, and Cora felt the rumble against her back. Once again, a burst of desire shot through her body. It was such a foreign feeling. This wasn't like her, but she didn't hate it. How could she when it was because of Pipe?

"Easy there, ninja warrior," he told Alaska.

She giggled and turned back to the buffet line to grab a plate.

"You good?" Pipe asked. He'd leaned down and whispered into her ear, making Cora shudder as his warm breath tickled her skin.

"Yeah." She looked up at Pipe. "She doesn't hate me," she whispered.

"Of course she doesn't," he said, his brows furrowing.

"You don't understand. Other women don't usually get along with me."

"That's because they sense that shield you carry around, keeping them at arm's length," Pipe said matter-of-factly. "But Alaska doesn't care. Neither do any of the others here. Probably because they used to have similar shields and they recognize a kindred spirit."

Cora blinked at him. Was he right? Did she have

trouble making friends because of some sort of vibe *she* was putting off?

"Your turn, love. Grab a plate."

Turning, Cora saw there was a large gap in the line between her and Alaska. She felt a little dazed as she picked up a plate.

Pipe stepped even closer, tightening the arm around her waist. "This place'll heal you...if you let it," he told her. He kissed her temple and straightened.

Her skin tingled where his lips had touched her. She had a feeling he was right. She'd felt at home here from the second she'd arrived. Granted, she hadn't been here all that long, but with every minute that went by, she felt more... normal. Not that she really knew what normal was.

She'd spent her life being rejected by everyone. Her own mother and father, countless foster families, bosses at the many jobs she'd had over the years, men and women she'd met along the way...but from the second she'd looked up and made eye contact with Pipe while he'd been on that stage during the auction, she'd felt a shift. In herself? In time? In the universe? She wasn't sure. All she knew was that she'd felt more comfortable in her own skin from the minute she first spoke to Pipe.

Because she was busy frantically trying to blink away her tears, Cora piled food on her plate blindly. It didn't matter what she grabbed; everything smelled and looked delicious. When she sat at a table next to Henley, who greeted her as enthusiastically as if she hadn't seen her in months, rather than a few hours, Cora realized with a sudden flash of insight that everything she'd been searching for her entire life was right here.

In the middle of nowhere, New Mexico. In this homey, peaceful setting that Cora never in a million years thought she'd enjoy. She was a city girl, had lived there all her life, but sitting on Pipe's rooftop, smelling the crisp winter air, seeing how everyone at the lodge interacted with respect for each other...a longing hit her, deep and visceral.

She wanted this.

Wanted to belong to a group of people like this.

No. She wanted to belong to *this* group of people.

But she was essentially a stranger. And there was a good chance, because of *her*, that Pipe, Owl, and Stone could be in danger when they went to Arizona.

Cora clenched her teeth together. Hard.

She couldn't let that happen.

She wanted their help, yes. But not at the risk of anyone getting hurt or in trouble. She couldn't do that to these people who'd accepted her so willingly. Couldn't do anything that might cause their loved ones grief or despair.

She made a mental vow that if Ridge called the police, or if something crazy happened, she'd do whatever was necessary for the men of The Refuge to stay clear of trouble. Spike had joked about everyone being arrested for breaking and entering, but if push came to shove, she'd do what needed to be done without involving them.

"What's that thought?" Pipe asked as he sat.

"Nothing."

"Doesn't look like nothing to me," he muttered.

"I just...I appreciate all you guys are doing to help Lara. When I started researching The Refuge, I never expected all of this," Cora said, helplessly gesturing around the room, trying to encompass everything she was feeling.

Pipe studied her for a long, intense moment. Finally, he said, "Eat."

Cora blinked, then chuckled.

"What?" he asked.

"I just thought you were going to say something profound."

He smiled. "Something like how you find the people you're meant to find, when you're meant to find them? When you need them the most?"

Cora stared at him. "Yeah. Just like that."

Pipe nudged her elbow. "Eat, Cora. Tomorrow's going to be stressful."

"And eating will make it less stressful?" she asked dryly.

"No. But it'll give you the fuel you need to push through it. To do what needs to be done. To be there for Lara, to be strong. And...Robert's tacos are the best."

This man. Cora truly enjoyed being around him. Which was quite the revelation, because there had only ever been one other person she actually liked spending time with—Lara.

But now, she found she was looking forward to hearing what Henley had done all day. And how school was for Jasna. And what the goats might've eaten today that they shouldn't have. And how Chuck was doing.

There was so much she wanted to know...small, everyday things...and suddenly it felt as if she didn't have enough time to learn it all.

"Hey, Cora, is the Vietnam Veterans Memorial in DC as cool as it looks in pictures?" Jasna asked.

"Don't talk with your mouth full," Henley scolded her daughter.

"Sorry," she said with a smile, running an arm across her lips. "But is it? I've seen pictures of all the monuments and stuff there and it all looks *so* neat!"

"It *is* neat, but you know what my favorite place is?" Cora asked the girl.

"What?"

DESERVING CORA

"Arlington National Cemetery. It's solemn, and sad, but so beautiful at the same time. One thing everyone should see in their lifetime is the changing of the guard at the Tomb of the Unknown Soldier. I cried the first time I watched it."

Jasna's head tilted. "Really?"

"Really," she said with a nod.

"Do you think I can find a video of it online?" Jasna asked her mom.

"I'm sure you can...*after* dinner," Henley said sternly.

"Okay," Jasna agreed readily, then turned her attention back to her plate.

As Cora ate the most delicious tacos she'd ever had in her life—the others were right; Robert must put some sort of drug in the meat to make them so addictive, just like he did with the cookies—she found herself fully participating in the conversations going on around her. That usually didn't happen. She either stayed silent, not knowing what to contribute, or she was ignored.

She got to meet Luna, Robert's daughter, who came out to help him when she could. A student at the college in Los Alamos, Luna was beautiful, with long brown hair and intelligent brown eyes. She was also just as welcoming as everyone else had been.

All too soon, it was time to head back to Pipe's cabin. Almost reluctantly, Cora said goodbye to everyone. She hated that this might be the last time she saw them. Which was yet another revelation.

"Be careful," Alaska said as she hugged Cora.

"I will."

"I hope you find your friend," sweet Jasna said, before running out the door, presumably to surf the Internet for videos of the changing of the guard.

185

"Don't underestimate this guy," Henley said with a small frown. "I don't know everything about what's happening, but if someone kidnapped your friend, he had to have done so for a pretty big reason. And he's not going to want to admit it...or let her go."

"I know," Cora said. And she did. She'd already come to that conclusion, even before she'd heard about him using Lara's credit cards at a strip club.

"Bring her back here," Reese said when she hugged Cora. "Before you go back home, I mean."

Cora wasn't sure what to say to that. First, she was more pleased than she could put into words that Reese seemed to have no doubts that they'd find Lara and be able to get her away from Ridge. And she *wanted* to come back here, more than anything. But there was still the issue of the cabins being booked for months, and she didn't know what Lara would want. "We'll see," she ended up saying.

Reese nodded, then stepped back.

Ryan approached her next, giving her a long, tight hug. In the process, she whispered in her ear, "Stay smart. Guys like the one who took your friend aren't as smart as they think they are. They always screw up. Wait until the moment he does just that and take advantage of it."

Cora nodded when Ryan pulled back. She stared into her eyes for a few seconds, and in that moment, Cora suspected Ryan hid a lot from the world. She saw the same shields in the other woman that Cora herself employed. But the moment quickly disappeared when Ryan smirked. "And if this rich asshole has a helicopter or something sitting around, Owl and Stone can fly that baby...I think you should steal it, just like he stole your friend."

Everyone around them laughed, but Cora simply smiled. There had been...something...in Ryan's expression that made her think she wasn't exactly kidding. She wondered if she had knowledge the other women didn't, if she'd overheard something else the guys had discussed. But she didn't have time to ask any questions because suddenly Robert was there.

He hugged her and told her that he'd have a batch of cookies waiting in the morning for her to take with them. She said her goodbyes to Jess, Carly, and Jason, two of the housekeepers and the maintenance man, respectively. Then she was getting chin lifts from Pipe's friends, with promises to see them bright and early in the morning, before she was being whisked out the door toward Pipe's cabin.

They were quiet as they walked, but it wasn't an uncomfortable silence. Pipe unlocked his door and held it open for her. He immediately locked it behind them and said, "I'm thinking we should forgo the roof deck tonight. We have to get up early. If you need anything, just let me know."

Cora nodded and immediately headed for the guest room, where she'd stayed the night before. She needed some time and space to think. It felt as if her entire world had been turned upside down in the last two days, everything she thought she knew upended. She'd always thought she was weird, too strange for people to feel comfortable around. That she had some sort of neon sign that only others could see, announcing to the world that she wasn't worthy. That since she'd been rejected by everyone who should've loved and cared about her, she shouldn't even bother letting others get close.

But being at The Refuge for just two days had changed her fundamentally. Most people would roll their eyes and say she was being ridiculous. That there was no way visiting a place could change her feelings about the world so quickly. But they'd be wrong.

Pipe and his friends had proven to her that maybe, just maybe, she *was* worthy of having friends. That rejection by those in her past wasn't about her, but more about *them*. The epiphany was unsettling. Especially now that Cora realized a lot of her issues with making friends were because of her attitude. Because she *expected* people not to like her.

She used the restroom, brushed her teeth, and changed into an oversized T-shirt before crawling under the covers of the bed. Staring up at the ceiling, Cora wondered for the first time in a few hours what Lara was doing right that moment. Was she hurting? Was she okay? Maybe she *had* gone to Arizona with Ridge of her own free will...but did she know about him spending her money? About the strip club?

She had too many questions and no answers, but thanks to Pipe and his friends, hopefully she'd get those answers soon enough.

Closing her eyes, Cora let out a long breath. She needed to get some rest so she'd be able to outsmart Ridge tomorrow. It took a while, but she finally fell into a restless sleep.

\* \* \*

*"No!"*

Pipe jerked awake and was on his feet before he'd even registered Cora's panicked exclamation. He'd left his bedroom door open, just in case, and was glad he did. He moved silently down the hall, on alert for any dangers that might be lurking in the dark. He got to the door of the guest room without incident, only to hear Cora cry out once more.

"I'll be good! Please let me stay!"

His heart broke at her plea. From the outside looking in, she seemed confident and brash. But from what she'd said about wanting a family of her own, and after hearing what she'd been through as a child in the foster care system, it was obvious she was still struggling with her past.

Pipe clicked on the hall light and opened the guest room door. In the light from the hall, he could see Cora tossing and turning on the double bed. He immediately went to her side, his only thought to calm her.

"Cora," he said in a low tone, so as not to startle her. "Wake up."

His words didn't seem to penetrate through her nightmare.

"I promise I won't cause any trouble. Don't send me back!"

Pipe's heart couldn't take another moment. He sat on the edge of the mattress and put his hands on her shoulders, gently shaking her as he tried to wake her again. "Cora, love, wake up. You're okay, you're having a nightmare."

In response, her eyes popped open and she stared at him blankly for a moment...before she took a huge shuddering breath that turned into a sob.

Pipe reclined next to her and pulled her into his embrace. If he'd thought about it, he might not have acted so boldly. But he was too desperate to soothe her. "Shhhh," he murmured as he felt her curl into his chest. "You're okay. It was only a dream. You're safe."

His hands smoothed up and down her back as he held

her against his bare chest. He just now realized that he'd come to her wearing only a pair of boxers. He usually slept naked, but in deference to her being in his house, he'd put on underwear. Cora didn't seem to notice or care what he was or wasn't wearing. She shoved her nose into his chest and he could feel her trembling against him.

"It wasn't a dream," she said after she got her breathing under control. "It was a memory. One of many. I'd get to a new home, let down my guard, and then find out they were sending me back. I was too old, too quiet, too loud, too stupid, too slow, too ugly..." She sighed. "In the end, the reasons didn't matter. I was like a stray dog they'd taken in, only to realize I was more trouble than they'd bargained for."

Pipe hated the despair he heard in her voice. "That's on them," he said a little too harshly, but unable to tone it down. "You did nothing wrong."

She didn't reply, just seemed to try to get even closer.

Pipe realized with sudden clarity that she probably hadn't had a lot of physical affection in her life. Being in the foster system most likely meant few hugs growing up. He tightened his arms around her. Well, that was done, starting now. He would make sure this woman knew she was worthy of love. Of being loved. Of being touched in an affectionate way. He'd never been a demonstrative guy, but for Cora? He could change.

They lay like that, Cora plastered against his chest, for a long time. Pipe thought she'd fallen asleep, and he loosened his hold on her, intending to go back to his room. But as soon as he tried to slip away, she whimpered and grabbed for him.

"Stay?" she whispered, as soon as his arms were around her once more.

"Are you sure?"

In response, Cora nodded against him. "I'll probably be embarrassed as hell tomorrow, but I...Will you stay? It's not an invitation for...you know. I just...you feel so good. Safe."

Pipe forced his anger down. He hated that she had to spell out that she didn't want him to stay for sex. Of course she didn't. She'd had a bad dream and was feeling off-kilter. He wasn't the kind of man who would ever take advantage of that. "No need to be embarrassed," he told her. "I've never been as comfortable as I am right now, love."

Neither of them said anything else. Pipe didn't feel the need for words. He was content to hold the woman in his arms and be her shelter from the storm of memories that were doing their best to overwhelm her.

She fell asleep a few minutes after he'd promised to stay, and Pipe lay awake holding her, his mind going a million miles an hour.

He'd heard the saying, "Be kind. Everyone you meet is going through a battle you know nothing about," many times, but tonight was the first time he truly understood it. From the outside, Cora looked like she had things together. She had a job, a best friend, and gave off vibes that said she was tough and content, if not happy. But deep down, she was struggling. Just like he was some days.

For the most part, Pipe was satisfied with his life. But he still held resentment for what had happened on that last mission. For feeling as if he had no choice but to move to a different country and join forces with men he didn't know in order to survive.

Those men had become his best friends. The Refuge was as much a part of him as being an SAS soldier had been. And yet, there were days he didn't want to do a damn thing but sit on his rooftop and be bitter about his past.

Cora had been through much worse, and at such a tender age. When she should've been worrying about boys, or makeup, or test scores, she'd had to think about where she'd be sleeping night after night. Wondering if an adult entrusted with her care might try to abuse her in the worst way. And the emotional toll of all that trauma was clear. Here she was, almost forty, and she still had nightmares about her childhood.

Pipe rested his chin on the top of her head and closed his eyes. He wished he could go back in time and make things right for her, but of course that was impossible. What he *could* do was make sure that the one person in the world she knew without a doubt loved her exactly how she was, Lara, was all right.

After that? He'd work hard to prove that she *was* loved by others. That she had friends and support. That just because others had turned their backs on her, didn't mean *he* would.

He should've been way more panicked at the direction his mind was going, but instead, Pipe felt only peace.

He'd already decided that if she was receptive to the idea, he'd happily move to Washington, DC, to see where things between them might go.

But lying there with Cora in his arms...he changed his mind.

Instead of immediately offering to move across the country, he'd first try his best to convince her to stay *here*. In New Mexico. At The Refuge. Brick, Spike, and Tonka's women had done the same thing, and they were deliriously happy.

Cora loved The Refuge, that wasn't hard to see, even after the short time she'd been there. She fit here. It was a place of peace and healing, which she needed. And going back to DC, where people like Eleanor and others couldn't see the amazing person Cora was, felt completely wrong.

There were preschools in Los Alamos where she could work...and hadn't they all talked about opening up The Refuge to people with children? Maybe she could be in charge of a childcare center right there on the property.

The more he thought about it, the more Pipe loved the idea. Of course, just because he liked it didn't mean Cora would. Too many people in her life had said the right words, but when push came to shove, they'd turned their backs on her. He'd have to show her *without* words that he was serious about what was developing between them.

And he'd start doing that by finding Lara and reuniting the best friends. Afterward? He'd have to take things one day at a time. But he knew something for certain...even though he'd drawn the short straw and hadn't wanted to go, attending that auction was the best thing that he'd ever done in his life. It had led him straight to Cora.

# CHAPTER FOURTEEN

Cora woke in the morning to Pipe kissing her forehead. He was standing at the side of the bed, leaning over, his arms caging her in.

"Good morning."

"Morning," she mumbled.

"We need to get up and get ready to go."

"Okay."

He smiled. "You awake?"

"Yeah."

"You sure?"

"Uh-huh."

His grin grew. "Right. I'll start the coffee. If I don't hear the water running in three minutes, I won't let you have any of the special black cherry brew that I'm gonna make."

"Mean," Cora grumbled.

In response, Pipe leaned down and kissed her on the lips this time. "Get up," he repeated, then stood and headed for the door. Cora couldn't help but admire his ass as he went.

DESERVING CORA

It was then that she realized he wasn't wearing anything but a pair of boxers. She should've felt embarrassed or shy or something, but instead she felt...mellow.

At the door, Pipe turned. "Cora?"

"Yeah?"

"Slept better last night than I can remember sleeping in a very long time." He grinned at her. "Three minutes."

Then he was gone.

Cora sighed and closed her eyes as she stretched. She'd also slept like a rock. Well, after her nightmare, that was. She hated the dreams she still had occasionally. She'd tried really hard to put her past behind her, but there were times her brain still liked to dredge up her crappy childhood, as if to remind her that things can always go bad—or get worse.

The second Pipe's arms had wrapped around her last night, she'd felt safe. Safe from the horrors of her childhood, from the taunts of other kids about her lack of a family, from the fear of being homeless, from all of it.

"Two and a half minutes!" Pipe called from down the hall in his room.

Cora couldn't stop the laugh that escaped her lips. It was hard to believe she was finding anything humorous right now, considering what lay ahead of her and the others later in the day, but she did.

"I'm going!" she called back as she swung her legs over the side of the bed and headed for the bathroom. Instead of dwelling on her nightmare, or the fact that Pipe had spent the night in her bed, holding her tightly, she let the tiniest bit of excitement flow through her veins. She'd been doing everything in her power to get to this moment, to find out what was really happening with Lara. And today it was happening. The police might not believe her, or Lara's parents, but she was more certain than ever, especially after everything that Tex guy had found out, that Lara was being held against her will.

All she needed to do was get to her, get Lara to admit that she wanted to go home, and they were out of there. Ridge wouldn't be able to stop them, not with Pipe, Owl, and Stone at her back.

Cora grit her teeth in determination. She wasn't leaving Arizona without Lara. Whatever it took, she'd make sure her friend was safe.

* * *

Hours later, Cora's determination had waned a bit and nervousness had taken its place. The flight had gone without any issues and the four of them had rented a Jeep Wrangler. They were now parked on the street, a ways from Ridge Michaels's mansion.

"So I really *am* just going to go up and knock on the door?" Cora asked nervously.

"I'm thinking that's better than skulking around the grounds and risking a trespassing charge," Stone said with a shrug.

"I'm okay with it, but you aren't going by yourself," Pipe said.

Cora looked over at him and realized he was extremely tense. They were sitting in the back seat, while Stone and Owl sat up front. The latter had his attention on the house, taking pictures from the passenger seat as they waited for...something to happen.

"I might have a better chance of talking with Lara if I'm by myself," Cora argued. "You guys aren't exactly nonthreatening."

"And Michaels could decide to grab you too," Pipe countered. "If Stone or Owl is with you, that won't happen."

Cora tilted her head as she studied Pipe. "Why them? Why not you?"

Pipe snorted. "Yeah, right."

"No, seriously, why not?"

"Look at me, love. A rich bloke like Ridge Michaels isn't going to let someone like me into his home. He'll take one look at me and know something's up."

Cora frowned, not happy at the way he disparaged himself. "Or maybe he'll take one look at you and realize he messed up. He'll poop his pants and let us have Lara without any fuss."

Pipe's lips twitched.

"This isn't funny!" Cora argued.

"Poop his pants?" Pipe asked.

Cora tried not to smile, but she was so worked up, so full of nervous energy, that she couldn't stop herself. "Yeah, well, cussing hasn't exactly made me any friends, so I'm trying to tone it down."

"We don't give a shit if you cuss," Owl said from the front seat.

"Nope," Stone agreed. "We aren't exactly non-cussers ourselves."

"And, for the record, I agree with Cora," Owl added. "Michaels will see you with her and know she's got reinforcements. There's no guarantee he'll hand over his girlfriend, but—"

"She's *not* his girlfriend," Cora growled.

"Right, sorry."

"Still don't think this is a good idea, but all right. I'm not letting you go up there by yourself. But you should all be forewarned, if this Michaels guy tries anything, if he touches Cora, I can't promise I'll hold my temper."

"Noted," Stone said.

"Cool," Owl added.

"So, what's the plan?" Cora asked. "Do we have a cover story?"

"Cover story? Cora, he knows who you are, that you live in DC, and the fact that you're suddenly on his doorstep, wanting to see Lara, shouldn't come as a huge surprise. Not with how close the two of you are. We don't need a cover story."

"Right. Sorry, I'm just nervous."

Pipe reached out and took her hand in his. "I'll be right there."

Taking a deep breath, Cora nodded. "I know. And I appreciate it."

"Owl, is there anything you can see that we didn't get from the satellite pics Tex sent us?"

"Yeah, you know that large, flat space we saw that we thought were tennis courts?" Owl said as he stared through a pair of binoculars toward the house. There weren't a lot of trees in the fancy neighborhood to block their view of the house. The perimeter was surrounded by a low brick wall, easy enough to see over and scale, if need be. There were cacti sprinkled around the entire neighborhood, and the house they were surveilling had a gate across the driveway.

"Yeah? What about it?" Pipe asked.

"It's *not* a tennis court." He lowered the binoculars and turned to grin at Stone. "It's a helipad."

"No shit?" Stone asked, sitting up straighter and staring at the house.

"Yup. I can just see the blades of a chopper sticking out from around the house."

"Ridge has a helicopter?" Cora asked. The base of her spine was tingling. She remembered Ryan's words about stealing the chopper, just like Ridge had stolen Lara, and wondered anew if the other woman had somehow known about the helicopter or was just guessing.

"Apparently," Owl said, lifting the binoculars again. "Looks like an R66 Turbine."

Stone whistled low. "That's not cheap. I mean, it's not the most expensive civilian chopper out there, but it's not exactly inexpensive."

"How the hell can he afford that if he's using Lara's credit cards?" Cora asked.

"That's what I'd like to know. Although, it could be Daddy's. And why does he even *need* it?" Pipe added.

"Well, I guess right now it doesn't matter. I'm getting more and more nervous sitting here. Can we just go and do this?" Cora asked. "I want to see Lara for myself."

Stone turned around. "Be careful," he said.

Cora wanted to roll her eyes, but instead she simply nodded.

"Intel only at first," Owl added. "We need to know what's going on inside that house. If the hired help is assisting him with whatever he's doing with Lara or if they're clueless. Best-case scenario, Lara leaves with you, but if he doesn't let you see her, don't lose your cool, Cora. We'll simply come back with another plan."

"You guys and your plans," she mumbled.

Stone chuckled.

"Okay, let's do this," Pipe said.

He squeezed her fingers before letting go and reaching for the door handle.

Cora got out on her side and was having a hard time believing she was actually here. And that she had three badass ex-military guys at her back. It was so much more support than she'd dreamed she'd have. "Please let this work," she mumbled under her breath, then Pipe was there. He reached for her hand, and the feel of his warm fingers around hers went a long way toward easing her nervousness.

Pipe started walking toward the house, talking under his breath as he went. "Stay calm, no matter what he says. Don't let on that you know about the credit cards. Just say that you're here because you're worried about Lara, and you took vacation time to come out and make sure she's okay."

"I know," Cora told him. They'd been over this before, but she was still afraid she was going to screw everything up by saying the wrong thing.

They headed for the long gate to the driveway. There was a walk-in entrance next to the gate, and to Cora's surprise, it wasn't locked. They walked right inside and down the driveway.

The house was large, but not as huge as some mansions she'd seen. It had huge white columns on the front, which looked a little tacky here in the southwest, where something that blended in with the xeriscaping would be more appropriate. There wasn't a lot of grass in the yard, it was mostly crushed rock. Cora saw one person to the side of the house, doing some work on the yard, but otherwise felt as if she and Pipe were the only people on the grounds.

"Deep breath, you've got this," Pipe told her, squeezing her fingers.

Cora didn't think she'd be able to do this at all if it wasn't for the man at her side. She'd do anything for her friend, but this was actually kind of scary, especially after learning more about Ridge. If she hadn't known anything, she probably would've marched up to his door with her usual bravado, but now that she knew he was lying his ass off for some unknown reason, and not knowing if Lara was even still alive, she was kind of freaking out.

Before she was ready, they reached the front door. She turned to look at Pipe and saw his head was on a swivel. He was on the lookout for...what? Danger? Bad guys jumping out from behind a cactus with a knife? She had no idea, but again, she was glad he was there.

Without hesitation, he reached for the door knocker and slammed it down a couple of times. The loud bang it made each time it hit the metal plate made Cora flinch. Her hands felt sweaty, but she held onto Pipe for dear life.

It took a couple of minutes, and Pipe even knocked again, before they finally heard someone on the other side of the door. Cora couldn't help but wonder if it had taken so long because Ridge was trying to hide Lara. Or threaten her. Or something else equally scary.

When the door opened, it wasn't Ridge on the other side. It was a man probably around Cora's age. He was a little taller than Pipe and extremely muscular. He immediately intimidated her.

"Whatever you're selling, we don't want," he said, crossing his arms over his chest.

His attitude irritated Cora, making her find her backbone. She straightened her shoulders and met his glare with one of her own. "Good for you, but we aren't selling anything. My name is Cora Rooney, and I'm here to see Lara Osler."

"She isn't seeing visitors," the man replied without hesitation.

"She'll see me," Cora told him, lifting her chin stubbornly.

"No, I mean she's not well enough to see anyone."

Cora's stomach flip-flopped. "What's wrong with her?"

"I'm not going to disclose the lady of the house's issues with a stranger who shows up on our doorstep," the man sneered.

"Look, I'm her best friend. I know everything there is to know about Lara. I know she gets cramps really bad when she has her period and nothing but a heating pad and Advil will help her. She hates seafood, and she has to pick those little mushroom pieces that you can't even taste out of any dish made with cream of mushroom soup. Trust me, I'm no *stranger*. I've known her since we were fifteen years old, and I've come all the way from Washington, DC to see her and make sure she's all right."

"She's fine," the man said, not persuaded in the least by Cora's statement.

"I'd like to see that for myself," she argued.

The man didn't budge. "Sorry, no," he told her, not sounding sorry in the least.

"It would be a shame to have to involve the authorities in this matter," Pipe said. "All she wants is to see her best friend, make sure she's all right. She hasn't heard from her in a while, and Lara left DC very suddenly. You let us in, let Cora see Lara, and we're out of your hair."

Creepy Guy's gaze swung to Pipe, and it made Cora's skin crawl when he studied him from head to foot before narrowing his eyes. "Ms. Lara isn't feeling well. I'm sure she'll be happy to know you came by to see her. I'll tell her to text you later."

"No!" Cora practically shouted. Her heart was beating a million miles an hour. Something was very wrong, she felt it in her gut. She thought something was wrong before, but now she was convinced.

The man's arms uncrossed and his legs shifted so he was more secure on his feet. Ready for some sort of...what? Cora didn't know. Confrontation? Did he think she was going to jump him?

But the man's eyes weren't on her—they were on Pipe.

She glanced over and realized why the man's stance had changed. Pipe's outward appearance could be intimidating to some people, Cora was aware of that, though she'd never been scared of him. Not once.

But right this moment? If she was the recipient of the look he was giving Creepy Guy, *she'd* be the one pooping her pants. His jaw was ticking, his eyes narrowed, and the hand that wasn't holding hers was in a fist at his side. His muscles were tense, as if he was one second away from losing his shit on this guy. Which probably wasn't a wrong assessment.

"Tell Michaels we'll be back," Pipe said in a tone that seemed like it was an octave lower than his usual voice.

"Right, sure," Creepy Guy said.

"Please tell Lara that I was here," Cora rushed to say. She had no illusions that anyone would tell her best friend that help was on the way, but she could hope. "Tell her that Jenny Thompson sends her best wishes too, and that I'll see her soon."

As far as clues went, it was lame, especially because she felt there was less than a two percent chance this jerk would pass along any messages to Lara...if she was still alive to get them.

Jenny Thompson was a girl who used to pick on Cora in high school. She was nothing but a bully who'd loved to torment her by making fun of the fact she was a foster kid and no one wanted her. One day, Lara got sick of the taunts by the other girl and got right up in her face—saying it was better to be a foster kid with no family than have a murderer for a father.

It was harsh and cruel, but it had the desired effect. Apparently, it wasn't common knowledge that Jenny's dad had been found guilty of first-degree homicide and was doing life in prison. Jenny had left Cora alone after that, then had switched schools not too much later.

Cora wanted to remind Lara that she had her back. That no matter what, she wasn't going to give up on her.

Creepy Guy didn't respond to her request, just continued to stare at them both.

"And let Michaels know that maybe I'll see him at the Blue Moon later. I've heard it's the best around," Pipe added, before taking a step back.

Cora followed, not that she had a choice, since his fingers were like a vise around hers.

Creepy Guy narrowed his eyes, his own jaw ticking now, before turning and shutting the door in their faces.

"Bloody hell," Pipe muttered, before hustling her off the front porch and back down the driveway.

"I'm guessing that gate we went through is gonna be locked from here on out," Cora said in a daze.

"Probably," he agreed.

They arrived back at the Jeep and climbed into the back seat.

"Well?" Stone asked impatiently. "I take it you didn't see her?"

"No, we didn't. And if the gorilla that met us at the door is any indication, things aren't good," Pipe said.

"Any sign of Lara at all?" Owl asked.

"No," Cora said, her shoulders slumping.

"Next up...Blue Moon," Pipe said.

"You think he'll be there after you made it clear you know Ridge frequents the place?" Cora asked.

"No. But I do want to talk to people. See if he's got a specific stripper he's been spending money on."

"I still want to know about that chopper," Owl said under his breath.

"Gotta be his father's. Though it would make sense for Ridge to use it if he doesn't want anyone to know he's got money issues. Flying around in that thing would portray a certain image," Stone said with a shrug.

The men continued to speak, but Cora tuned them out. She felt incredibly disappointed. She'd truly thought that maybe, just maybe, she'd get to see Lara today. That they'd knock on the door and Ridge would take one look at Pipe and let her talk to her friend. But to be blocked as firmly as they'd been, to not even know if Lara was, God forbid, alive or not...it was a blow she was struggling to absorb.

"Hotel," Pipe said abruptly, jerking Cora out of the fog she'd been in.

"Right," Stone said, turning the key in the ignition and pulling away from the curb.

Cora's eyes stayed glued on Ridge's house as they drove past. It sucked to be so close, and yet just as far as she'd ever been to finding out what was going on with her friend.

Pipe squeezed her hand again. He'd only let go long enough for them both to get into the car, and she was grateful for his silent support.

She also appreciated that he didn't give her platitudes about how he was sure Lara was fine. They both knew that likely wasn't the case...not with the way that man so firmly refused to let them in the house.

Cora turned to look out at the passing landscape. Tears filled her eyes, and the scenery blurred as she struggled to keep her composure. She couldn't lose Lara. She just *couldn't*.

Feeling as alone as she'd ever felt growing up, Cora desperately tried not to start bawling.

Then she felt Pipe lean toward her. She didn't turn to look at him because she didn't want him to see her tears. "I give you my word, love, that we're going to help her."

Cora closed her eyes. He was close enough to her that his breath warmed her neck as he spoke directly into her ear. She nodded but didn't turn. She couldn't imagine a world without Lara. She was her rock. Her anchor. She was quiet, kind, dependable, and a perfect balance to Cora's brashness and tendency to act before thinking. Without her, Cora would be lost.

She had to be all right. She simply had to be.

# CHAPTER FIFTEEN

Pipe didn't like how quiet Cora had gotten. More often than not, she exuded a sense of relentlessness. Of stubbornness. But after meeting with the arsehole who'd refused to let them see Lara, she seemed subdued. Almost despondent. And he hated it. He much preferred the woman who wasn't afraid to disagree with law enforcement and Lara's parents. Who stood up to him and his friends. Who did what she thought was necessary without hesitation.

He'd left her in their hotel room, which he was relieved she had no problem in sharing, to talk to Owl and Stone. He'd originally wanted to go to the Blue Moon and investigate himself, but he'd easily let his friends talk him out of it. He felt a bone-deep need to stay with Cora. To make sure she was all right. It wasn't as if he thought she'd do something rash, it was more that he couldn't bear to watch her suffer and not be there to try to ease her pain.

When he returned, Cora was sitting in the exact same position as when he'd left half an hour ago, seemingly lost in thought. Pipe didn't hesitate to walk over to the chair and crouch down in front of her.

"Cora?"

She brought her gaze to him. "Are you leaving soon?" she asked in a flat tone.

"No. Owl and Stone are going."

She frowned slightly at that. "I thought *you* were."

"I changed my mind. They'll go, see what they can find out, then brief us in the morning."

"Then what?"

"We'll see what they discovered and go from there."

Her gaze went distant again. "Right."

"Look at me," Pipe ordered.

Cora sighed, but complied.

"We're going to get in there and find Lara." He waited for a reaction, but didn't get one. "I swear."

"This sucks, Pipe. We're so close, but just as far away as we've ever been in finding answers. I hate this. *Hate* it," she said vehemently.

"We're going to figure this out," he told her, putting his hands on Cora's shoulders.

She shrugged off his touch and stood, pacing the small area next to the bed. "We need to do something *now*! Not sit around waiting for that asshole to hurt her even more. To possibly *kill* her, if he hasn't already!"

Pipe was surprised at the sudden change from despondency to anger...but he was also glad to see it. He much preferred this Cora to the shell of the person he'd walked in on.

Standing, he approached her carefully.

"Don't touch me," she warned, holding up a hand.

Pipe ignored her words and the hand and pulled her roughly into his embrace. Cora struggled for just seconds before giving up and melting into him. Her arms went around him and she clung to him so tightly, Pipe wasn't sure she would ever let him go. Which was perfectly all right with him. He walked backward toward the bed and managed to climb on with her still wrapped around him.

He rolled until she was under him and took her face in his palms. "She's alive," he said firmly.

"You don't know that."

"I do. If she wasn't, why does Michaels have a bloody bodyguard answering the door for him? He needs her alive for some reason, probably to access her money. Tell me this—would her trust continue to pay out if she didn't make contact with her family occasionally, or whoever is in charge of it?"

Cora frowned in surprise, as if she hadn't considered that question before. "Actually, no. I don't think so. She's complained on more than one occasion that it's a pain in the ass to call the man who releases the money into her account every month. Apparently, he's a talker. She has a tough time getting off the phone."

"Right," Pipe said. "And if she wasn't alive, I have a feeling Ridge would have no problem meeting with you himself. He'd simply tell you she left. He'd make up some story about how they got into a fight and she stormed off and he hasn't seen her since. That's what murderers do to try to get away with what they've done. She's alive, Cora, I believe that with all my heart, and I'll do whatever it takes to get her away from him."

Cora stared at him for what seemed like minutes, but in reality, was probably only a few seconds.

Then she lunged upward, locking her lips to his.

She kissed him almost desperately. Grunting, Pipe

rolled until she was on top. Cora lifted her head and stared down at him, breathing in harsh pants.

"I want you," she stated baldly.

Every muscle in Pipe's body tightened. He wanted her too. So bloody much it scared him. But there was no way he was going to take advantage of the current situation.

As if she could read his mind, she frowned. "Don't," she ordered.

"Don't what?"

"Don't think that I don't know what I'm saying. That I'm not in my right mind, or I'm influenced by grief or whatever. Every time I do something that should turn you off, should make you think, 'wow, this woman is crazy, I need to get away from her,' you actually do everything in your power to pull me closer. I've never known anyone like you, Pipe. And I've never felt this way before."

"What way?" he couldn't help but ask.

"Like if I don't get you inside me, I'm going to explode into a million pieces. Like being around you grounds me, makes me feel as if I'm actually worthy of affection. Of...of being loved."

"There's no doubt about that," he said firmly.

Cora shook her head. "You don't get it," she whispered. "My entire life, I've felt as if I'm on the outside looking in. Watching people find love, connect, feeling as if I'm missing the gene that allows me to do the same. But with you...from the second I saw you on that stage, something inside me just clicked. It was as if I was waiting for you."

Pipe licked his lips. He'd felt exactly the same way. It was uncanny. He wasn't a big believer in fate or love at first sight. But with this woman, everything he thought he knew was turned on its head. As if fate was laughing at him and saying, "See?"

"Are you sure?" He couldn't deny this woman anything. And Lord knew he wanted her just as badly as she apparently wanted him.

In response, Cora reached for the hem of her shirt. She whipped it off over her head before he could blink. She sat astride him in her bra, and Pipe's mouth went dry. She was so bloody beautiful, it almost hurt to look at her.

His Cora was a curvy woman. He supposed some people would call her fat, but all he saw were feminine curves that his palms literally itched to touch.

He didn't know how long he lay frozen under her, but it was long enough for her brows to furrow and a look of uncertainty to cloud her expression.

He hated that he'd caused her one second of doubt.

He sat up suddenly, and Cora let out a small screech of surprise before he was kissing her. His tongue plunged into her mouth, and he held her tightly against him with one hand at her neck and the other palming her back. Without thought, he trailed the latter up until he fingered the clasp of her bra. He deftly undid it, then tore his lips from hers and leaned back.

She smiled almost shyly at him, and dropped her arms, letting the straps of the bra fall down her biceps, the cups covering her tits following suit.

"Bloody hell!" he exclaimed as he saw her bare for the first time. She was perfect. Literally perfect. As he stared, her nipples began hardening, and he couldn't stop himself from dipping his head.

She helped by arching her back and giving him room as he closed his lips around one of her nipples. He sucked. Hard. And was rewarded by the shimmy of her hips and a long groan from her mouth. The nipple hardened further, as if reaching for more of his touch.

And he gave her what she asked for without words. He devoured her. Sucking, biting, licking. And with every caress, she squirmed harder. His Cora wasn't a passive lover. Her fingernails dug into his skin as she rocked into him, demanding more.

Abruptly, Pipe let go of her, causing her to fall onto her back on the bed. His hands went to the button on her jeans and he roughly jerked the denim down her legs. To his relief, he heard Cora giggle as she lifted her hips to help. He'd forgotten she was still wearing shoes, and it took a moment for him to get those off, as well as her socks, before removing the jeans altogether.

She smiled up at him as she put her thumbs under the elastic of her underwear and shoved them down. Pipe helped by pulling them off her legs and throwing them aside. Then he lunged with a groan and shoved her legs apart.

"Yes, Pipe...please, yes."

He needed to taste her more than he needed to breathe. He hadn't expected this when he'd decided to stay at the hotel with her while Owl and Stone went out to investigate the Blue Moon. But now that she was under him, he couldn't slow himself down.

Cora's hands went to his head and gripped his too-long hair almost roughly as he licked up the seam of her pussy. She tasted like heaven. He'd never enjoyed this, had only gone down on women a small handful of times. But with Cora, he didn't think he'd ever get enough of her taste.

She kept herself neatly trimmed and it was easy to find her clit. Using a finger to pull back the hood, exposing the small bud, Pipe lowered his head and sucked as hard as he had with her nipple.

In response, Cora shrieked and almost pulled the hair out of his head. "Pipe!"

He didn't respond. He was too busy. He closed his eyes and lost himself in the feel and taste of Cora. Her thighs closed around his head and it became hard to breathe, but Pipe didn't care.

Her pussy was soaking wet now, and he eased a finger inside her as he sucked and teased her clit. She jerked once more, then suddenly opened her legs as wide as she could. "More, Pipe. Harder!"

Smiling against her, Pipe lifted his head and watched as his finger disappeared inside her body. When he pulled the digit out, it was glistening with her juices. Looking up and meeting her gaze—he was thrilled she was watching him pleasure her—he sucked his finger into his mouth. Her eyes went wide before she dropped her head back down onto the mattress.

"That should be kind of gross, but it's honestly the hottest thing I've ever witnessed," she said to the ceiling.

Pipe lowered his head once more to lick at Cora's clit. Over and over in a steady rhythm. As he concentrated on her clit, he used one finger, then two, to gently thrust.

She began to move her hips, fucking his fingers and making it difficult to keep his mouth on her sensitive bud. Pipe's cock was so hard in his jeans, it physically hurt. But he wasn't about to stop to undo the zipper to give himself relief. No way was he taking his hands or mouth from between Cora's legs until she'd come.

Her entire body began to shake as she neared orgasm. Pipe licked faster, then locked his lips around her clit and sucked. For a moment, Cora froze, and he wondered if he was hurting her. But then she shoved her hips up, pushing his fingers even farther inside her body, and began to convulse. His fingers moved even easier as she slickened with her orgasm.

The way she shook in his arms made him feel as masculine as he'd ever felt in his life. *He'd* given her this pleasure. When he felt her begin to flinch away from his tongue, Pipe lifted his head, but only enough to watch the steady stream of come leaking from between her legs. He couldn't keep the smile of satisfaction off his face.

"Pipe...I need more."

His Cora needed more? He'd give it to her.

He scooted back, noting that she seemed boneless, not moving when he got to his knees to whip off the shirt he was wearing. Pipe wasn't ashamed of his tattoos, but there had been times when he'd taken off his clothes in front of a woman when he'd seen a look of distaste as they viewed his ink. His chest and arms were a mishmash of tattoos. There wasn't a coherent theme, he simply got inked because of the peace the needle gave him.

To his relief, the look in Cora's eyes wasn't one of abhorrence. Instead, she licked her lips and sat up, reaching for the zipper of his jeans.

Pipe could've brushed her hands aside. Could've taken off his jeans himself. But he was enjoying her hands on him too much to stop her. The woman in front of him was a literal goddess. Her tits bounced as she moved, her thighs were still spread, and he could see more of her come leaking between. *He'd* done that. And would do much more by the time they both passed out from exhaustion.

\* \* \*

Being with a man had never felt so right. She wasn't the kind of woman who slept with a guy so soon after meeting him, but Cora didn't feel one iota of regret for what was happening. Pipe had made her come harder than she ever had in her life. He seemed to know exactly how to touch her and didn't care that she couldn't lie passively under him while he was doing it, making his job harder. Which was a good thing, because considering how he'd made her feel, she couldn't have remained still.

Seeing him now, on his knees above her, his tattooed body on full display, Cora felt a fresh spurt of wetness leak out of her body. She wanted him. But she also wanted to make sure he felt as good as she did.

For once in her life, she wasn't self-conscious about her body as she sat in front of him. She didn't feel the need to suck in her stomach, to try to make some of the folds around her middle disappear. She didn't care that her boobs were uneven and a little too saggy for her liking. How could she when Pipe looked at her and licked his lips as if he couldn't wait to make her his own personal lollipop again?

The pleasure he'd taken while going down on her hadn't been faked. And when he'd sucked his finger covered with her juices into his mouth, she'd almost spontaneously orgasmed right then and there. But as much as she enjoyed him eating her out, she wanted him inside her. Wanted him to fuck her. Hard and fast.

She smiled at him and unzipped his pants, making sure to caress his cock as she did. His hips pushed toward her, and her smile grew. She shoved his pants and boxers down and without giving him a chance to stand to remove them, leaned forward. She tilted his rock-hard dick toward her and took the head into her mouth and sucked hard, just as he'd done to her nipple.

To her delight, he swore—she loved when he said

"bloody hell" in that sexy British accent—then grabbed hold of her head as she did her best to pleasure him in the awkward position. He swayed on his knees as she sucked his cock.

Cora loved sex. That didn't mean she had it indiscriminately. In fact, she was very picky about who she chose as a sexual partner, and she loved the power she held when she had a man's dick in her mouth.

Pipe was no different...and yet he was. This wasn't something she was doing simply for his pleasure. No, it went deeper than that. She wasn't sure why, or how, but she knew that sex with Pipe was life-changing.

Instead of letting it scare her, she welcomed the feeling.

Cora slurped and sucked and used her hands to caress Pipe's balls as she pleasured him. At one point, he held her head still and began to fuck her mouth—and Cora loved every second of it. She dug her nails into his thighs and held on as he got lost in the pleasure she was giving him. Just when she thought he was going to spurt down her throat, Pipe seemed to get himself under control.

He pulled his cock out of her mouth and stared at her for a long few seconds. His cock dripped with her saliva and his precome. A drop hit her leg, and she shivered.

Pipe moved, growling deep in his throat and practically throwing himself off the bed. He promptly fell on his ass as he struggled to get his jeans off over his shoes, with no luck.

Cora giggled. Had she ever had fun while having sex? No. The answer was definitely no. She moved up the bed and pushed the covers down so she was lying on the sheet. Feeling sexier than she ever had in her life, she put her arms over her head, spread her legs, and waited for Pipe to untangle himself from his clothes and rejoin her.

The look of lust on his face when he popped up from the floor and saw her made Cora suck in a breath.

Before she could blink, Pipe was over her. Covering her from head to toe, and she loved it. Her hands grabbed hold of his biceps as she felt his still-dripping cock smear come on her belly.

She looked down and sighed in pleasure at the sight of his dick so close to where she wanted it. Needed it.

"Please, take me," Cora pleaded.

He hesitated.

"What? What's wrong?" she asked, suddenly afraid he was having second thoughts.

"I want to be in there more than I want to breathe, but I don't have anything to protect you with. I didn't expect this, not in a million years, so I don't have any condoms."

Cora fell in love right then and there. Any other man would've taken what she was so clearly offering without a second thought. She hadn't brought up birth control, and some men wouldn't even have thought of it. Pipe wasn't one of those men. And she loved him all the more for it.

"It's not the right time," she told him.

"You aren't on anything?" he asked.

Cora's belly clenched. Was this a deal-breaker? She shook her head, not willing to lie to him.

"You could get pregnant," he said, an odd glint in his eye.

"It's possible, but again, I don't think it's the right time."

"I should do the right thing. Wait until I can protect you. But I can't, Cora. If you get pregnant, I'm going to want to be part of the baby's life. I won't be an absentee father."

Her eyes widened.

"Yes or no, love. And be sure about your answer. Because if it's yes, I'm going to have you all night. One time won't be enough. I need you like I need air to breathe. I don't understand it, don't even care to. I know down to my bones that you're it for me. But if you aren't sure about being a mother, if you aren't sure about *me* being your kid's father, you need to say no. Right now."

Everything about Pipe's words made Cora's entire body tingle. It was hard to believe this man was real. There was a chance that once the heat of the moment calmed down, once their lust was sated, he'd regret what he'd said. But Cora didn't think so.

"I can't imagine a better father for my child," she whispered.

In response, Pipe reached down, took his cock in his tattoo-covered fingers—which was hot as hell—and ran the head up and down her slit. Cora opened her legs wider.

The next thing she knew, he was balls deep inside her. He stretched her as no man ever had, and the small bite of pain made her arousal ramp up even more.

"Okay?" he asked between clenched teeth.

"More!" she begged.

Pipe grinned and shifted, until he was impossibly deeper inside her. His hair fell over his forehead as he braced himself and stared at where they were joined.

"Like that?" he asked.

"Yes," Cora breathed.

She expected him to start thrusting, but instead he held himself still over and inside her.

"Pipe?" She grinned.

"Yeah?"

"What are you doing? *Move*."

"Can't."

"What? Why not?" she asked, suddenly concerned. She had a crazy vision of them having to call for help, and the paramedics coming into the room and finding him locked inside of her for some reason.

"Because this is the most amazingly perfect thing I've ever felt in my life, and I don't want it to end. You're so bloody hot. And wet. And you're squeezing me so hard, I feel as if I move a muscle, I'm gonna blow."

Cora relaxed. Thank goodness nothing was wrong. "You feel good too," she said, the words completely inadequate for what she was feeling, but she didn't have the brain space to come up with better praise at the moment.

Pipe stared at her as he pulled his hips back slowly, then sank back inside her.

They both moaned.

He did that a couple of times, and while it felt good, Cora needed more.

"Harder, Pipe."

He ignored her, choosing instead to torture her with his slow, measured thrusts.

In retaliation, Cora dug her fingernails into his butt. He simply grinned down at her in response.

"Love your claws, love. Go ahead, make your mark on me."

Narrowing her eyes, trying to think of what she could do to hurry him up, Cora's gaze landed on his pec. As he held himself over her with his arms, his chest muscles undulated with his steady thrusts. An impulse grabbed her, and she acted.

Lifting herself to her elbows, she latched onto his chest

with her mouth, right above his nipple, and sucked as hard as she could.

That seemed to work. Pipe grunted. Then Cora felt his hand at the back of her head, supporting her as she did her best to give him the biggest hickey he'd ever had in his life.

To her delight, his controlled thrusts became more erratic. By the time she thought she'd sufficiently marked him, at his request, and dropped her head back to the pillow, his thrusts had sped up exponentially.

He looked down and smiled at seeing the red bruise on his chest.

"Better than any tattoo. Maybe I'll go and get it immortalized in ink."

Cora grinned at him. "Fine. Whatever. *After* you fuck me," she ordered.

The smile faded from his face as Pipe finally, *finally*, began to take her harder.

She drove her hips up to meet each of his thrusts, and the sound of their skin slapping together was loud in the otherwise quiet room. Before she knew it, Pipe was pounding her hard and fast, and it felt amazing. Each time he bottomed out, there was a small pinch of pain, but it all added to the experience.

"Gonna come," he warned, still holding himself up over her. "Gonna fill you with my come and watch it leak out between those puffy pussy lips, then do it all over again."

"Do it," Cora breathed, egging him on. She wasn't close to a second orgasm, but she couldn't wait to see him lose it. She'd never seen anything sexier than Pipe hovering over her, her legs spread around his thighs as he took her.

He grunted, then shoved himself so far inside her body, Cora squeaked. He snarled loudly as he came.

But instead of collapsing on her, as she expected, Pipe

sat up. He shoved her legs farther apart, stayed buried inside her pussy, and began to thumb her clit.

"Pipe!" she exclaimed as the orgasm that seemed so out of reach crested quickly.

He was staring at where they were joined, concentrating on giving her pleasure, and it was almost overwhelming. She'd never had a guy so intent on making sure she came. She would've been happy with the orgasm he'd given her earlier.

"That's it. Come on my cock. I can feel your muscles fluttering around me and it's indescribable. Let go, love, let me feel it."

Between one breath and the next, Cora broke. She felt as if she was flying and the only thing holding her to Earth was her grip on Pipe's arms. Her thighs shook as she tried to pump her hips on Pipe's cock, but he was holding her so tightly, she couldn't move. All she could do was feel. She had no idea how long her orgasm lasted, but when she finally came back to herself and looked at Pipe, his gaze was still locked between her legs. She could feel wetness leaking down the crack of her ass.

"Look at us," he whispered when he realized she was back with him.

Lifting her head, Cora looked down and inhaled sharply.

Pipe's half-hard cock was still buried deep inside her body, her pussy lips stretched around him. Their pubic hair was meshed together, and his tattooed thighs pushed her legs apart. It was carnal and erotic, and made her squirm in his hold.

He looked up at her face and smiled. He rolled suddenly, his cock slipping out of her as they moved. Cora sat perched on top of him, his cock between their bodies, wet with their combined juices, peeking out from between her swollen and slightly sore pussy.

"I can feel our come on my cock," he said.

Cora never would've guessed this man was a dirty talker. But she liked it. A lot.

"That's what happens when you don't use a condom," she said with a shrug.

He frowned. "You've done that before?"

"Well, no. But I read."

The smile returned. He craned his head down to look at his chest, where she'd given him the hickey.

"Sorry?" Cora said with a small smirk.

"No, you aren't. But turnabout's fair play," he said—a second before he lifted himself up and latched onto the skin next to her nipple.

Cora squealed and tried to shift away from him, but his grip on her was absolute. She wasn't going anywhere. She giggled and laughed as he sucked on her skin. When he pulled back, a satisfied look spread across his face as he stared at what he'd done.

"Good Lord, Pipe. That's gonna leave a huge mark," she complained.

"Yup," he agreed.

"I guess I forgot to tell you that my skin is sensitive," she said with a laugh. "I sunburn easily. When I get bitten by bugs, I get the worst welts. I think that hickey is gonna be there until I'm old and gray."

"Good. If it wears away, I'll leave another," Pipe told her.

"You're impossible."

"No, I like my mark on you. Just as I like your mark on me."

The moment got intense in a heartbeat.

"What are we doing?" Cora whispered.

"No clue. But it feels more right than anything I've ever done," Pipe said solemnly.

Cora couldn't argue that point because she felt the same.

She felt his cock twitch against her and looked down, surprised to see he was getting hard again.

"Already?" she asked incredulously as she shifted over him, caressing him with her still soaking-wet pussy.

"Apparently," Pipe said dryly. "Put me in and ride me."

Cora mock frowned at him. "Bossy. Maybe I don't want to."

"You do," Pipe said with a cheeky grin.

She did. She totally did. Without another word, Cora went up on her knees and reached for Pipe's dick. She notched it between her legs and sank down.

They both gasped.

"Seriously, if I could live here I would," Pipe told her.

Cora giggled.

Pipe let out a sexy little moan. "Bloody hell, woman. I felt that on my dick."

Which made Cora laugh harder.

But laughter quickly gave way to more moans when Pipe's thumb began to rub her clit, and his other hand came up to palm one of her breasts.

"Ride me, love. Hard and fast. Let me fill you up again."

And just like that, Cora's belly clenched. How could dirty words be so damn sexy? But she didn't complain, she simply did as he asked, and as she wanted. Rode him until she orgasmed, and until he lost it again, shooting his load deep inside her just as he promised.

# CHAPTER SIXTEEN

Pipe woke up and knew exactly where he was, who was lying in his arms, and what they'd done. All night.

They'd slept for a bit, then woke up and made love again. He'd never been so ravenous for anyone. Honestly, he was surprised he'd been able to get it up as many times as he had. Without a doubt, he wouldn't be able to do that every night, but for their first time, he was pleased that he'd been able to pleasure Cora as much as he had.

Looking down, he saw the mark she'd made on his chest. It was red and blotchy, and easy to see even with the tattoos under and around it. She was pressed against his side, one arm over his chest, one leg over his thigh, and she was drooling a little against his bare skin.

Closing his eyes, Pipe wished they could stay there forever. Wanted this every morning for the rest of his life.

Even as he had the thought, Cora stirred against him. Pipe waited for her to realize where she was and what they'd done. He wasn't sure if she'd be embarrassed, or if she'd maybe pretend that it was no big deal. But that wasn't true. Something big *had* happened.

Pipe had fallen head over heels in love.

"Morning," she mumbled as she snuggled closer.

For a moment, Pipe was surprised. Pleasantly so. He tightened his hold around her back and pressed her harder against him. "Morning," he returned.

She sighed then. "I needed that. You," she said.

Pipe nodded and turned to kiss the top of her head. "Me too."

"But we need to get up and get Operation Get-Lara-Away-From-Those-Wankers started."

Her words startled a snort out of Pipe. "Yeah," he agreed.

But neither moved.

"Pipe?"

"Yeah, love?"

"Last night…that was…I'm not usually like that."

"Like what?"

"So lusty."

He chuckled. "Me either."

Cora lifted her head so she could see him. "I don't believe that. You ooze sexuality."

"Nope. You bring it out in me."

"We bring it out in each other," she countered.

"Apparently," he said with a shrug.

"I…I don't regret it. I just wanted you to know."

Pipe's respect for this woman grew. "Good. Because if you did, I wouldn't be happy. Last night was…" He searched for the right word. "Perfect," he finally said.

"Yeah."

"And since we're being honest…I'm gonna want to see where this goes after we find your friend."

She smiled at him. "I like that. Both the idea of continuing this, and how certain you sound that we'll find Lara."

"Good. Go ahead and take the bathroom first. I'll text the guys and see what's up."

"Okay. Pipe?"

"Yeah?"

She stared at him for a while, then gave him a small smile. "Nothing."

"You can tell me anything. You know that, right?" he asked.

"I do. It's just...if I *am* pregnant...not that I think I am, but if it happens...I won't hold you to anything."

Pipe frowned. "What did I tell you last night?"

"I know, but I thought maybe that was just the heat of the moment."

"It wasn't," he said firmly. "I *will* be a part of my son or daughter's life...just as I want to be a part of their mother's life. I'd never turn my back on my own flesh and blood. Ever."

"Okay."

"Okay," he agreed.

He expected Cora to be shy when she got out of bed. She didn't have a robe and wasn't wearing a stitch of clothing. Of course, he'd examined every inch of her body the night before, and loved everything he'd seen, but now it was morning and she wasn't in the throes of passion anymore. But he was surprised again when she flipped back the sheet and climbed out of the bed, heading for the bathroom without even trying to hide from him.

Pipe felt his cock twitch, and he shook his head in amazement.

She turned at the last minute, giving him a frontal view of her naked perfection. He could see the mark he'd left on her chest clearly. It was dark red and huge and she was clearly right, her skin was extra sensitive. He'd have to keep that in mind the next time he gave her a hickey. And he was determined that there *would* be a next time.

He could also see small bruises on her thighs and waist from where he'd held her a little too tightly. She wasn't walking as if she was in pain, and he assumed she'd tell him if he was too rough, so he let himself feel a smidgen of male pride that *he'd* been the one to mark her. Not only that, as she stood there staring at him, Pipe saw a bead of their combined come slowly make its way down her inner thigh.

She wrinkled her nose, then said, "No matter what happens. No matter if we find Lara or not, I'll never forget or regret last night. You made me feel wanted, Pipe. Loved. Thank you." With that, she turned and disappeared into the bathroom.

Pipe wanted to get up and go to her. Tell her that she *was* loved. That she *was* wanted. But they had stuff to do. And if he admitted his love for her, they'd probably end up back in bed. While he didn't regret what they'd done either, and was anxious to do it again, he also felt the pressing need to find Lara. He couldn't shake the feeling that the clock was ticking.

They'd made the first move, and Michaels had to know Cora wouldn't turn around and leave town just because his goon wouldn't let her see her friend. No, he'd be panicking, trying to fix the situation to his benefit. And Pipe had a feeling that wasn't good news for Lara.

He needed to talk to Owl and Stone and see what, if anything, they'd found out last night at the strip club. Then they needed to make their move. Before Michaels could make his.

\* \* \*

After meeting Owl and Stone for breakfast, they all headed upstairs to Owl's room to discuss what the two men had learned the night before.

Cora sat in the only chair in the room, while Pipe found himself hovering near her. Owl was propped up against the headboard of the bed, and Stone paced back and forth.

"It was weird, man," Stone said. "I went in there fully expecting to find out that Michaels had a favorite girl, and that's why he was spending so much money. You know how it goes, a guy showers money and gifts on one of the girls because he has the delusion that they'll marry and live happily ever after...and have really great sex for the rest of their lives. But that's not what Michaels is doing. Yes, he's throwing around money, gift cards, and crap he's bought from those high-end stores as if he's the money-fairy. But he gets lap dances from *all* the girls. He hasn't shown a preference for any of them."

"That's not exactly true. He likes all the ones with big tits," Owl said mildly.

"Does he have a schedule? When he goes to the club?" Pipe asked.

"Yeah. Every night. He's only missed a few nights here and there in the last month," Stone said.

Pipe frowned. "Was he there last night?"

"Nope," Owl said.

"Bloody hell," he swore, running a hand through his hair. "We freaked him out."

"That's what I'm thinking," Stone agreed.

"Where does that leave us?" Owl asked.

"We could try going back and asking to see Lara again," Pipe said. "Or we could see if we can break into the house and find her ourselves. Or call the cops and bring our concerns to them, see if they'd do a welfare check."

"I'm thinking Brick wouldn't be thrilled with the second option," Cora suggested.

Pipe nodded. "Maybe not, but he also wouldn't be surprised. Besides, who said we'd get *caught* breaking in?"

"Uh...alarms, cameras, bodyguards," Cora said with a shrug.

"I'm sure we could work around them, if we really needed to," Owl said dismissively. "Should we go over the list of employees Tex sent?" Owl asked. "When I got back last night, I looked it over and there are some people who we could maybe use to our advantage."

"Wait, what time did you get home last night?" Cora asked, the concern clear in her tone.

It was one more thing Pipe loved about her. How she was always worrying about others.

"Around two. Couldn't sleep. It's not a big deal. Anyway, after asking around at the club, it seems the same bodyguard always accompanies Michaels to the Blue Moon. Arlo Harvey."

"Arlo. What kind of name is that?" Cora mumbled.

"What's his background?" Pipe asked, trying not to laugh at Cora's question.

"He's twenty-seven. Was in the Marines for a few years right out of high school. Was injured, fell while walking across the base where he was stationed and broke his wrist pretty badly. Got a medical discharge and got a few jobs doing security at warehouses and businesses, before being hired by John Michaels after the lawsuits began to roll in for that drug he'd manufactured. He's been with Ridge for a couple of years now," Owl told the others.

"And?" Pipe asked.

"And what?"

"That's it? What's his background? Does he have any convictions on his record?"

"Normal background. Good childhood. Was a decent Marine. No convictions. He seems to be loyal, makes sure no one hassles Ridge, follows him where he wants to go and keeps his mouth shut."

"Well, that seems like a dead end," Cora sighed. "He has to know if Lara's in the house, right? I mean, if he's that close to Ridge, shouldn't he know?"

"Maybe, maybe not," Owl said. "He doesn't live at the estate. He shows up when requested and for his scheduled shifts, and that's it."

"Is he married? Have a girlfriend?" Stone asked.

"No and no."

"Hmmmm. What about that guy who answered the door yesterday?" Pipe asked.

"Carter Grant," Owl said, looking back down at his phone. "He's also Michaels's bodyguard. But he was hired by Ridge himself, not his father. From what Tex could find out, they met online. Carter was interested in bitcoin from Michaels's company and they started talking. One thing led to another, and Michaels hired him to be a bodyguard when Arlo wasn't on shift. Not married, no girlfriend, and his background is actually pretty boring. Thirty-five years old, a handful of not very interesting jobs, no college degree. And no, before you ask, no convictions of any kind."

"Wait—Carter Grant?" Cora asked with a small grin.

"Yeah, why? You know him?" Owl asked, sitting up straighter on the bed.

"No, I don't know him at all, but it's just a little funny. I was calling him Creepy Guy in my head, because, well, he was creepy. It's just a little ironic that his initials, CG, are the same as the initials for Creepy Guy."

Pipe's lips twitched. This wasn't funny, not at all, but somehow Cora's observation eased some of his tension. His friends also smiled and shook their heads.

"Anyway, sorry, go on. Arlo and CG are bodyguards. CG obviously knows about Lara because he didn't seem confused when we asked to see her, and he had that excuse about her being sick ready to go. Does CG live on the estate?" Cora asked.

It was a good question. Pipe wanted to hear the answer too.

"I'm guessing so, yes, as there's no address listed for Grant. And you're right, after what you said about the encounter with him yesterday, he's obviously in the know about Lara, or what might have happened to her."

Pipe frowned. He'd avoided even thinking that Lara Osler might be deceased. He didn't want Cora to dwell on that at all. He'd rather keep thinking that this was a rescue mission and not a body recovery.

"Yeah," Cora said quietly, and Pipe tensed. It hadn't escaped her notice what Owl meant.

"Anyway, there are others who live and work in the house. Sarah Latimer is the chef. She lives onsite, which makes sense, since she's responsible for all the meals. Alice Green is the head housekeeper. She's responsible for the other hourly employees who come in to clean and do laundry and anything else involved with keeping the place spotless. Steve Browning does maintenance. Neither he nor Alice live onsite, but they're close by and their rents are paid by the estate. Nora Walker is in charge of the grounds, Joel Ackerson is both a driver and the pilot for the chopper. He flies Michaels, and his father when he's in residence, to conferences in California and Vegas, or when they decide they want to go to dinner in Flagstaff or on other frivolous outings. And Benjamin Fox is the estate manager. He oversees all the employees and generally makes sure things run smoothly. He's also responsible for mundane things like paying the utility bills and ensuring the trash people are picking up the garbage."

"So once again, the question is...do any of these people know anything about Lara?" Stone asked.

"If you're asking me, I don't know. It looks like, other than Grant, they were all hired by Daddy. But if anyone knows, it would most likely be one of the live-in employees. Even when Ridge isn't there, they retain their schedules and keep the place ready for members of the Michaels family to show up at a moment's notice," Owl said.

He looked up from the phone and said, "But you might be more interested in knowing that Michaels's Bitcoin company..." He paused dramatically for effect.

"Spit it out," Stone growled.

"It's toast. Apparently, he's a shit CEO and spent more money than he made. It's hemorrhaging cash left and right. He's managed to maintain his outward appearance of being loaded, but it's pretty much bullshit."

"Which explains why he needs Lara's money," Cora said.

"I think so," Owl agreed with a nod.

"That, and the fact that his daddy cut the money he's getting every month to almost nothing," Pipe added.

"Since I'm on Lara's account, do you think I'd be able to go in and cancel her cards? Make it harder for him to use her money? He might let her go if he can't access her money."

"Or he could decide that since she's no use to him anymore, he needs to get rid of her," Stone said bluntly.

Cora's face turned white. It was obvious to Pipe that Stone's suggestion was a surprise. He was kind of mad at his friend for not using more tact.

"Oh, shit, I hadn't thought of that," Cora whispered. "So what do we do? I hate the idea of Ridge draining her accounts, but I don't want him to freak out and hurt her if he can't access her money anymore."

"I'm thinking we go back to the house," Owl said. "Maybe this time I go with you. Make sure Michaels and his goons know that this is about more than Cora wanting to talk to her friend."

"So we threaten him," Stone said sternly.

"Yeah," Owl agreed.

"But they could still refuse to let us see her," Cora said. "I mean, I'm happy to have you there, Owl, but how is that going to make CG or Ridge give in and let us see Lara?"

"It might not," Owl said. "But we make it clear we aren't leaving until we see her, and if they don't bring her to us in a timely manner, we'll call the cops. It's not like they'll call the police themselves and say we're trespassing. I'm guessing they don't want the cops anywhere near the estate."

"And we'll be armed," Pipe told her. "In case they try anything."

Cora's face leeched of even more color. "Oh, God, this is getting out of hand," she muttered.

Stone walked over to where Cora was sitting and crouched down in front of her. He didn't touch her, but he definitely had her attention. "You think we can't handle ourselves? That we can't protect you and Lara?"

SUSAN STOKER

"It's not that," she protested.

"Then what is it?"

She took a deep breath. "When I decided to try to win a date with a representative from The Refuge at that auction, I didn't think this is where we'd end up. And I don't want any of you to get in trouble or—God forbid—shot because of what I've asked you to do," Cora said.

"We aren't going to get shot," Stone reassured her.

"No way," Owl added. "Stone and I may not be quite as good as the others when it comes to certain aspect of special forces training, but we aren't slouches either."

"It's not that, I just..." Cora sighed. "You guys believed me almost from the start. You might've had some doubts, but you never treated me as if I was crazy or blowing things out of proportion. I've never...I can't...I'm not used to this," she blurted.

"Used to what?" Pipe asked, nudging Stone, who got the message and stood up and took a step back, letting Pipe take his place in front of Cora. He immediately reached out and put his hands on her knees. He needed to touch her, needed her to know he was there for her.

"Feeling supported. Or believed. Or important. And letting you walk into potential danger is no way to repay you."

"We support you, Cora. We believe you. And you're *very* important. Your worth isn't determined by who your parents were, how much money you have, or what kind of job you do. It's what kind of person you are. And you, Cora Rooney, are a shining light in what can be a dog-eat-dog world. Your loyalty is..." Pipe shook his head as he tried to come up with the best word.

Owl beat him to it. His friend had shifted so his legs

hung off the side of the bed and his eyes were glued to Cora. "Everything."

Pipe nodded. "Yes. Your loyalty is everything. It's worth a little danger. We're going to find Lara. Get proof of why Michaels kidnapped her. He's going to pay for what he's done. If you believe nothing else I tell you, believe that."

"We aren't scared of this Michaels guy. Or his so-called bodyguards. Owl and I have been through hell and back, and we aren't going to let these rich assholes get one over on us," Stone said firmly.

"I want to say something, but Pipe gets weird when I do," Cora said.

"Pipe is weird no matter what," Stone said with a laugh. "Say it."

"Thank you," she said, the sincerity coming through loud and clear. "I don't know what I would've done if you guys weren't here."

"You would've figured it out," Owl said. "From what I know of you, you're stubborn and resourceful."

"True," Cora said with a small laugh. "So...Plan B is to go back to the house and knock on the door again?" she asked.

"Tryin' to keep it simple," Stone told her. "I think adding Owl to the mix is good though. A show of force isn't a bad thing."

"Not to mention a little threat thrown in for good measure. I'm guessing Michaels isn't going to want a bunch of cops tromping through the house. There's no telling what he's hiding in there...besides Lara."

"Is it weird that I feel a little bad for his dad? I mean, he probably doesn't even know what his son is doing," Cora asked.

Pipe hadn't moved from his crouch in front of her. "Don't," he said a little too harshly. When Cora frowned, he took a deep breath and did his best to moderate his tone. "I don't know how many houses that family has, but they made money off the people in this country and beyond who took the drugs John Michaels pushed. Yeah, they're legal, but he had to know how addictive they were long before it was announced to the world. There's no telling how many people moved on to more hard-core drugs when they couldn't get prescriptions for the shit he developed. And through it all, he's still flaunting his wealth. I mean, he has a bloody *helicopter*. For what? It's excessive and unnecessary."

"I don't know, I wouldn't mind having a chopper," Stone said as he laughed.

"Right? Think about how fast we could get to Albuquerque if we had one. Maybe we can convince Brick to add a landing pad and hangar," Owl agreed.

"Tax write off!" Stone exclaimed. Then he got serious and said, "You know, I hadn't thought I would ever want to fly again. But after that mission to save Reese from those asshole drug dealers, I realized how much I'd missed it."

"Same," Owl said with a nod. A look passed between the two men. They'd been through hell together, and it was obvious they were on the same page now.

Pipe turned back to Cora. "If you aren't comfortable with this, Owl and I can talk to Michaels and his goon by ourselves."

"Nope. No way. If there's even a one-percent chance this will work and they'll let us see Lara, I'm not missing it."

"That's what I thought, but I had to offer."

Cora stared at him and bit her lip.

"What?" Pipe asked.

She shook her head and asked quietly, "Is this what it feels like to have family? I mean, to have people willing to help you when shit goes south? To have your back no matter what?"

"Yeah, love. This is what it's like," Pipe told her, his heart breaking that she'd never had this kind of support before.

"Yep, we're your brothers now," Owl told her with a grin.

"Annoying older bros who'll meet your date at the door with a shotgun and make sure he knows that if he doesn't return you before your curfew, he'll have *us* to answer to," Stone added.

Cora's eyes were twinkling when she looked at Pipe.

"*I'm* not your brother," he told her with a small growl.

Her grin widened. "I would hope not." She giggled.

Owl and Stone laughed at them both.

"All right, no more sitting around," Pipe said, as he stood and held his hand out for Cora. "We have work to do."

"Hey, some of us were working late into the night," Owl retorted.

"Oh, we were working too," she replied, her smile huge on her face. "Working *hard*."

Pipe couldn't help but love how unembarrassed Cora was about the two of them. It boded well for their future relationship.

"Happy for you guys," Stone said. "And it's about time."

At that, Cora's smile slipped. "We haven't known each other that long," she hastened to add.

Stone waved off her trepidation. "When you know, you know. And if you're thinking we're going to judge you, stop," he told her. "With guys like us, with the shit we've been through, when we find the right person, we aren't gonna hesitate to act. Life's too damn short to not go after what you want."

"Damn straight," Owl agreed.

"Right," Pipe added with a nod.

For a moment, Cora looked a little surprised, but relief crossed her face. "Right," she finally said.

"On that note, let's get going. I'm not feeling comfortable with the fact that Michaels didn't follow his usual routine last night by going to the Blue Moon. If he's panicking, he could be packing right now to head out of town, and that's the last thing we want," Stone said.

Pipe was in full agreement. The sooner they made it clear that they weren't going away, and that the jig was up and Michaels might as well produce Lara, the better.

He squeezed her waist before reaching for her hand, loving that she didn't shy away from holding onto him. "Let's do this," he said firmly. "Owl and Stone, we'll meet you at the car. I need to stop and get my pistol before we head out."

His friends nodded and Pipe headed for the door. He wanted to find Lara almost as much as Cora did at this point. For her own safety, but also so he could give Cora peace of mind...and bring her back to The Refuge, spend more time getting to know her. He had no idea what would happen between them, if they could figure out how to be a couple long-term, but he was going to do his best to make that happen.

Stone was right. Life was too short to not go after what you wanted. And Pipe wanted Cora. He just prayed she wanted him right back.

# CHAPTER SEVENTEEN

"Okay, I'll be here waiting for you guys," Stone said solemnly. "If anything looks hinky, I'll text, and I expect you to do the same. Watch your six," he warned.

Pipe and Owl nodded.

"Six?" Cora whispered to Pipe as they headed for the driveway and the gate they'd used to enter the grounds the previous afternoon.

"Back," Owl answered before Pipe could.

"Oh, right."

She was nervous and on edge. She stayed close to Pipe as they neared the gate. This time, as she suspected, it was locked, and the gate across the driveway was also closed.

"As if that'll keep us out," Owl grumbled as he headed for the brick wall that surrounded the property. He jumped over it as if it was only a foot high, rather than the four feet that it actually was.

Pipe also cleared it without any issue, then he turned around and held out his hand. "You got this," he encouraged.

It wasn't as if Cora couldn't get over the wall, she just

wasn't as graceful as the two guys were while doing so. She hopped up and got her belly on the wall, then one leg up and over the edge. Pipe took it from there, lifting her without making it seem like it was a big deal, putting her on her feet on the grass on the other side.

"You good?" he asked.

Cora nodded. She wasn't sure she was, but she'd insisted on being here, so she wasn't going to back down now. Everything about today felt more ominous than the day before. The area was quiet, the air still, as if the very environment was anticipating...something. Which made no sense, but that was how it felt.

They didn't see anyone on their walk toward the front door, and before she knew it, Pipe was reaching for the knocker. Like yesterday, he slammed it down on the metal plate.

Cora was standing a little behind Pipe and Owl, which, to be honest, she was all right with. It wasn't as if she expected Creepy Guy or Ridge to open the door and start shooting, but knowing both Pipe and Owl were armed and more than ready and willing to use their weapons to protect themselves and her, if necessary, had ratcheted up the danger she felt.

It took several minutes, and several more knocks, before they heard the locks clicking on the door. Cora held her breath as it slowly opened.

Creepy Guy stood there staring at them. She supposed she should start calling him by his name, but now that she'd been calling him Creepy Guy in her head, it was hard to stop.

"What do you want?" CG growled.

"To see Lara," Pipe told him in an equally menacing voice.

"I told you yesterday, she's sick."

"Don't care. We're seeing her today whether you like it or not," he countered.

CG laughed. And not in a humorous way. "Yeah?" he asked.

"Yeah," Pipe confirmed. "We've done a little inquiring about Mr. Michaels and his *staff*." He emphasized that last word, making sure CG was aware that the inquiries included him. "And we were surprised not to see him at the Blue Moon last night. The girls were also disappointed...you know, considering how much he's spoiled them in the last month."

Cora held her breath as she waited to see what CG would say to that. He looked just as intimidating as he had yesterday. Had on a pair of black cargo pants, a short-sleeve gray polo shirt that showed off his bulging biceps, and black boots. He towered over her. His blond hair was cut short, in a military buzz, and his hazel eyes were cold as he looked down at them. The muscle in his square jaw ticked as he stood there with his arms crossed over his chest.

She felt the urge to apologize for interrupting him and flee, but Cora locked her knees. She wasn't the kind of woman who was easily intimidated, but this guy? Yeah, he scared the crap out of her for some reason.

"And it's fine if you don't want to let us in," Owl added. "We'll just call up our contact in the Phoenix Police Department and have him come out with a dozen of his brethren to do a welfare check on Ms. Osler. There's no telling what else they might find in the house...is there?"

At that, Cora was certain she saw alarm flare briefly in CG's eyes, and her heart rate sped up. This was going to work. They were going to get in.

"There's no need to get the cops involved. Nothing untoward is happening here. I'm sure Lara will be glad to see her friends." With that, CG stepped away from the door, inviting them in.

As happy as Cora was that they were finally going to see Lara, something about stepping across the threshold made her hesitate. An old poem by Mary Howitt that she'd read in high school suddenly flashed into her mind. About the spider inviting the fly into his parlor. And everyone knew what happened to the poor fly. Right about then, she felt as if she was the fly and CG was the big bad spider.

She desperately wanted to grab hold of Pipe, but he'd warned her that he needed his hands free at all times...just in case. Cora didn't want to think about what "just in case" entailed, but she could guess.

So she stayed glued to Pipe's back as he stepped over the threshold behind CG. Owl was at her back, and she shivered as the door shut behind them with a loud clang. CG took the time to relock it, which was another thing that didn't give Cora the warm fuzzies, before gesturing for them to follow him.

Looking around as they walked, Cora noted that the estate was pristine. There were no dust bunnies on the floor or in the air, there weren't any knickknacks out of place. She was constantly putting crap on her counter, dropping bags on the floor when she got home, and she didn't want to think about how many pairs of shoes were lying around her place. Her apartment was lived in. Well, before she'd sold everything.

This place was...hollow.

The thought of Lara being here made Cora want to weep. Her friend was full of sunshine. Despite being shy, she was a happy person, always thinking the best of people. Her apartment was even more chaotic than Cora's, but it was full of love, and she'd always felt right at home there.

Their steps echoed on the tile floor as CG led them down a long hall. Cora noticed that Pipe's head was on a swivel, just as it was anytime they were in any kind of situation he wasn't familiar with. He was obviously taking note of their surroundings and the route they were taking.

Just when Cora thought CG was leading them to some back entrance and was going to shove them all out, he stopped. He opened a door and swung it open.

"If you wouldn't mind waiting in here, I'll go get Ms. Osler. It might take a few moments because she'll need to change out of her sleeping clothes. There's a small wet bar on the side of the room and the seats are comfortable. It's the most restful room in the house. Figured you'd want privacy to speak to your friend."

Pipe hesitated before he stepped into the room, and that small pause spoke volumes to Cora. But she followed close behind him, not wanting to be more than a few steps away, just in case. If shit *did* hit the fan, she wanted to be where Pipe was.

The space they entered was some sort of media room. There were three rows of large leather recliners on gradually elevating platforms, like at a movie theater. The seats were facing a big screen, and there was a projector on the back wall. As CG said, there was a wet bar to the right of the door with well-stocked shelves of what looked like an impressive array of liquor.

"Ten minutes," Owl told CG as he turned to face him.

"Pardon?" CG asked. He might be a bodyguard, but he

had the mannerisms and tone of a privileged and snotty staff member down pat.

"You've got ten minutes to bring Lara here, before we call the cops."

An angry look flashed across CG's face, but he simply nodded. "Ten minutes," he agreed, then began to shut the door behind him as he left.

It went against everything inside Cora to let the asshole shut that door, but she didn't want to do anything to jeopardize their chance of getting to see Lara. Apparently, Pipe was on the same page.

"I don't like this," he said the second they were alone.

"Me either," Owl agreed.

"Me three," Cora joked uneasily.

"That seemed too easy," Owl said. "Although he definitely didn't want us to call the cops. Did you see his face when I mentioned having the police doing a welfare check on Lara?"

"Oh, yeah, there are some secrets in this house for sure," Pipe agreed. "I'm beginning to wonder if *Michaels* is all right. I mean, we haven't seen him yet."

"No, but the women at the Blue Moon said he was there the night before last," Owl argued.

"That was before we showed up," Pipe said with a shrug.

"You think maybe Michaels isn't the bad guy here?" Owl asked.

Cora's head swung from one man to the other, like she was watching a tennis match.

"No. He's in this up to his eyeballs. He's not innocent in the least, but I do think it's odd that we haven't seen hide nor hair of him yet."

"So what do we do now?" Cora ventured to ask when no one had spoken for several seconds.

"We wait," Pipe said firmly. "And no, we aren't drinking any bloody thing from that wet bar. We have no idea if they've drugged the alcohol. Or the ice."

"Wait—you can drug ice?" Cora asked.

"Absolutely," Owl said with a nod. "I know of a case where terrorists were able to take over a plane by drugging all the passengers through the ice in their drinks. Thankfully, there was an astute chemist onboard who realized what was happening, and she informed the Navy SEAL sitting next to her."

"Holy crap! Were they okay?"

"Yup. The SEAL didn't drink anything, and he and his two buddies—who were also on the plane—overtook the hijackers."

"Wow, I had no idea ice could be drugged," Cora said with a shake of her head.

"It's why I'll never ask for ice on a plane," Owl told her with a small smile.

Pipe remained quiet, and when Cora looked up at him, she saw he was checking out the room, his gaze running over everything. The chairs, the projector, the signed movie posters on the walls.

"What are you looking for?" she whispered.

"I don't know. I'm just looking," he replied.

Cora nodded. She felt out of her league. All she'd wanted was to make sure her friend was all right, and instead, she'd found herself in a situation where she had no idea what to do. She was very thankful that both Owl and Pipe were with her. She was safe with them, she had no doubt about that.

She tried to think positively. Soon, she'd get to talk to

Lara, and hopefully leave with her. At this point, she didn't care *what* Lara said. If she told her that she was fine and wanted to stay. After everything the guys had said, and after what Tex had found out about her so-called boyfriend, there was no way she was leaving her friend here. Even if Lara got mad at her and ended their friendship, it would be worth it to know she was safe.

Cora frowned at the thought of not having Lara in her life, but she'd rather have her best friend alive and hating her, than stuck in a bad situation.

"I hate waiting," she admitted softly.

"You and me both, sister," Owl said with a nod.

Pipe crossed the room and pulled her into his side. Cora gladly leaned against him, doing what she could to soak up his confidence and warmth. She couldn't shake the feeling that something was very wrong, but she had no idea why or what to do about it. All she could do was wait for Creepy Guy, or maybe even Ridge, to come back with Lara in tow. Once she saw her friend, they'd figure out what to do next.

* * *

Stone sat impatiently in the car. The others hadn't been gone all that long, but he couldn't shake the feeling that they'd walked into a shit show. He'd sometimes gotten these feelings when he was on a mission, and when he did, every single time, the shit had hit the fan.

He stared at the brick wall about thirty feet from where he was parked. The Jeep was at the corner of the estate's property line. Out of sight of the front door, but close enough that if needed, he could get to his friends to evacuate them.

Looking down at his watch, Stone swore as he realized only two minutes had passed since he'd last checked the time. He hated not knowing what was happening. But the fact that the three hadn't immediately returned had to mean they'd had some success. Hopefully they were inside, meeting with Lara and finding out what the hell was going on.

The sudden vibration of his phone in his hand startled Stone so badly, he jerked. Laughing at himself, and shaking his head, he looked down at the screen.

A text had arrived—and Stone frowned as he read the preview.

*Unknown: You need to back off.*

He quickly unlocked the phone and clicked on the text to read the entire thing.

*Unknown: You need to back off. Michaels is not the threat. It's Carter Grant. The bodyguard. That's not his real name. He's got several aliases, Alex Hansen, Daniel West, Connor Smith, among others. He's wanted by the FBI for over a hundred counts of sexual assault, rape, and murder. He gets off on drugging women and holding them hostage while he does unspeakable things. To date he's been connected to thirty-five deaths. He's a serial killer, and if Lara Osler was in that house, it's likely she's no longer alive. If Cora goes in there, I have no doubt she'll be his next victim. I've called the police and the FBI but there's an active shooter situation at a school on the other side of town. Literally everyone is tied up with that. They've called in agents from the*

*Sedona office to check out the situation. But you need to back off. Abort!*

Stone's heart rate shot up to levels he hadn't experienced since he'd gone down in the chopper on his last mission. His fingers raced over the screen as he texted the person back.

*Stone: Who are you? How do you know this? We got intel from Tex and he's the best of the best. He didn't tell us any of this.*

Three dots immediately blinked on the screen, letting Stone know whoever had sent the text was typing a reply. He didn't have to wait long for it to come through.

*Unknown: Who I am doesn't matter. And how did I know where Jasna was? How did I know to track Reese's tile? I hacked into Tex's computer and dug deeper than he ever could on the names of Ridge's employees. Get the hell out of there!*

Holy shit. The mysterious person who'd already helped them—*twice*—was back. And if their intel was right, his friends were in extreme danger.

Stone believed the unknown person. Tex hadn't been able to track who he was, and he was a computer genius. But now...

It seemed obvious to Stone that it *had* to be someone connected to The Refuge.

There were a lot of people who'd known about Jasna's disappearance—but that wasn't the case with Reese. There were supposedly no witnesses when she was taken from that parking lot in Los Alamos. And the fact that this person now knew where Cora was—and what they were doing—pointed at someone who had to know they were headed to Arizona in the first place. And very few people had that information.

But at this point, with this new intel? It didn't matter who the unknown person was. All that mattered was getting his friends out of that house in one piece.

He immediately clicked on Pipe's name and sent him a text.

*Stone: Get out. Now.*

He sent the same message to Owl, just to be on the safe side.

To his horror, he didn't get the little check mark next to the messages saying they were delivered. He immediately clicked on Pipe's name again, but this time to call him.

It went straight to voicemail.

Stone swore viciously and clicked on Owl's name...with the same result. Out of desperation, he tried Cora. Again, no luck.

The situation felt worse and worse with each minute that passed. He desperately wished that the other guys were there. Brick, Tonka, Spike, and Tiny were better at this kind of thing. He was a helicopter pilot. Yeah, a hell of a good one, but he didn't have the time in the field that his friends had. He'd been sufficiently trained in every type of combat situation, but the vast majority of his time had been spent in the air, not with boots on the ground. He had no doubt his friends would have probably formed three different plans by now and be halfway to executing them.

He frantically tried to think about what he should do next. Call the cops? Go up to the door and get his friends? Sneak up to the house and look through windows to see what intel he could gather?

All he knew was that if he didn't do something, he might never see Pipe and Owl again. Both of them—as well as Cora and Lara—could end up dead.

He hadn't lived through a helicopter crash and two weeks of torture to lose Owl now. They'd vowed to stay together through thick and thin, and no way was he gonna sit back and let anything happen to his best friend...or anyone else.

He had to come up with a plan. Pronto.

# CHAPTER EIGHTEEN

Pipe resisted the urge to pace. He held Cora against him as they waited.

After what seemed like hours, but was probably only minutes, Owl swore. "Something's definitely wrong," he said.

Pipe didn't argue. How could he when everything within him was screaming that the situation was FUBAR? He pulled out his phone and typed out a text to Stone. He hit send, but to his surprise, after a few seconds, a notice came up that the message hadn't been delivered. Pipe clicked on the message and tried to send it again, with the same result.

"Bloody hell," he swore, clicking on Stone's name. But the phone wouldn't connect. "Owl, can you get a hold of Stone?"

His friend pulled out his phone and clicked a few buttons, then looked at him. "It won't go through."

Pipe's lips pressed together. He didn't need the hair standing up on the back of his neck to know they were screwed.

"Jammer?" Owl asked.

"That would be my guess," Pipe agreed.

"What? What's jammed?" Cora asked.

"The phone signal," Pipe told her in a voice that sounded much more calm than he felt.

"I thought that kind of thing was just something made up from the movies," she said.

"Unfortunately, it's not," Owl told her.

"Obviously," she said, sounding very disgruntled. "They aren't going to let us see Lara, are they?" Cora asked.

Pipe sighed and shook his head. Although seeing Lara was the least of their worries at the moment.

"Shit!" she said. "Right, so...fuck them. What now? Go out there and kick Creepy Guy's ass? Search the house? What's the plan?"

"Get the hell out of here and come back with the cops, like we probably should've done in the first place," Pipe said grimly. He was an idiot for letting Cora accompany him and Owl to the house. He'd let her desperation to see her friend outweigh his common sense. And now she was in the middle of an unknown fucked-up situation.

He headed for the door, grabbed the doorknob and twisted—but froze when it didn't move. Pulling on the door didn't help either.

Fuck. They'd been locked in.

He *knew* he shouldn't have let Carter close the door. It went against everything he'd ever learned in his training. But he'd been trying not to rock the boat. To piss the man off before he produced Lara.

It was a mistake that could cost the woman her life, and possibly cost them their own.

"Bloody hell!" he swore, turning to Owl and Cora. "Locked," he said unnecessarily.

Pipe hated seeing the fear on Cora's face. He was so stupid for blindly following Grant. He should've known he and Michaels wouldn't simply change their minds about letting them see Lara. He was obviously rusty if he'd been fooled so easily. And Cora and Owl might pay the price.

They'd showed their hand, and Grant and Michaels were probably right this moment hightailing it out of there. Possibly with Lara, if she was even still alive. At this point, that was looking less and less likely. His heart hurt for Cora.

Looking around, Pipe tried to get his bearings. Ran through their options in his head. Unfortunately, there weren't a lot. As a typical media room, there were no windows to let in light or, in their case, escape through. Pipe wasn't even sure if there was an exterior wall. For all he knew, this room was in the middle of the building, so busting through a wall wouldn't do them any good. But if there was even a remote possibility they could get out of there, he'd take it.

But first...he pulled his firearm from the holster at the small of his back. He gestured to Cora with his head, indicating the other side of the room. "Step back, love."

Her eyes got wide. "What are you going to do?"

"Shoot out the lock," Pipe said flatly. Discharging his weapon would not only alert Grant, Michaels, and anyone else in the vicinity that he was armed, but it would let them know that whatever their plans were, they were fucked.

Owl stepped forward and took Cora's elbow, pulling her backward and moving so he was standing in front of her. Pipe nodded at his friend then turned back to the door. It had been a while since he'd been at the firing range, but he was a good shot, always had been. He raised the weapon and aimed it at the lock. He shot off one round...

And immediately swore when the bullet ricocheted.

He dropped into a crouch and saw Owl pulling Cora down with him. Of course, it was way too bloody late to try to dodge a bullet. But thankfully, none of them were hit by the ricocheting projectile.

"Fuck!" Owl swore.

Pipe was too pissed to respond.

"What happened?" Cora asked in bewilderment as she slowly stood.

"The door's steel," Pipe answered.

"Oh, shit. This was planned, wasn't it? I wonder how many other people they've trapped in here."

Pipe kind of wondered that too, but at the moment, he was more concerned with breaking the hell out. He hoped maybe one of the other employees in the house had heard the shot and would come investigate, but he doubted they'd be so lucky. Grant and Michaels had clearly thought this far ahead, so he guessed the room might also be soundproofed. It was the perfect place to put anyone you didn't want wandering around...or that you wanted to incapacitate.

Urgency hit him hard. He went over to the first row of chairs and yanked on the leather recliner. It didn't budge. Leaning down, Pipe realized he wasn't going to be able to move the chair. There were huge bolts keeping it in place.

He heard Cora cough behind him, but he didn't glance her way, too focused on looking for some sort of tool to try to break through the drywall.

Walking to the top of the tiered platforms, Pipe peered at the projector on the wall. To his disappointment, he didn't see anything there that would be useful.

"Uh, Pipe?" Owl asked.

"Yeah," he asked without turning around.

"Something's wrong," his friend said.

At that, Pipe spun to see Owl leading Cora to one of the seats. Frowning, he moved toward them. "What's wrong?"

"I don't feel good," Cora said, coughing again, harder.

Then Owl coughed.

Only then did Pipe realize he was breathing faster than normal himself, and his head was pounding. He'd been in plenty of stressful situations in his lifetime and hadn't ever had this kind of reaction. Of course, he'd never been responsible for the safety of a woman he didn't want to live without, so he could probably be forgiven for having a more extreme reaction now.

He shook his head—and immediately regretted it as he stumbled to the side. He was dizzy.

Cora moaned, and Pipe went to his knees in front of her chair, reaching for her shirt. "Pull your shirt up over your nose and mouth," he ordered, tugging on the material, trying to help her.

She raised her head, and he saw she had little to no color in her cheeks. But she did as he asked, her eyes huge in her face. "What's happening?" she asked.

Pipe's limbs felt uncoordinated as he pulled his own shirt to cover his nose and mouth. When he turned, he saw Owl had done the same thing.

Looking around, Pipe tried to find the source of the sudden weakness in his limbs. He saw nothing.

"Gas," Owl said, coughing harder.

"Gas?" Cora asked, standing up in alarm.

Pipe grabbed her and pulled her back into the chair. "Stay calm," he ordered.

"Stay calm?" she echoed almost hysterically. "How can you even say that? We're being gassed!"

Pipe coughed to try to clear the fuzzy feeling from his head, but it was no use.

"Are we gonna die?" Cora asked.

"No," Pipe reassured her, although honestly, he had no idea what the assholes who'd locked them into this room had planned.

"I don't smell anything," Owl said. "No smell, no taste, and we can't see any vapor."

Something niggled in the back of Pipe's mind. One of the guys on his SAS squad had a unique hobby. When they weren't on missions, he had a workshop in the garden of his small house. He was an artist, and he made the most amazing metal figures. Some were small—Pipe had one back in his cabin at The Refuge. But his specialty was life-size sculptures. Mostly of animals. He and Pipe had talked once about the process of creating them, and his mate had gone on for almost an hour about the ins and outs of welding and how it worked.

And the one thing that came back to Pipe now, was how the guy had used argon gas to protect the metal being worked on.

He didn't remember exactly how it worked, or why, but he clearly remembered the conversation they'd had about the dangerous properties of the gas itself. His mate had joked that it was probably one of the best agents to use if someone wanted to render someone unconscious. It was legal to buy and easy to procure.

And argon gas was odorless, tasteless, and completely transparent.

He had no idea if it was being used to incapacitate

them right now, but it was as good a guess as anything else he could think of.

And speaking of thinking, Pipe was having a hard time doing anything other than trying not to puke his guts out.

"Pipe?" Cora asked in a thready tone.

He tried to reach for her and almost fell over. "Bloody hell!" he exclaimed. "Come here, love," he said, opening his arms.

Cora practically threw herself at him, and Pipe fell back on his arse, but he clasped Cora against him firmly. She buried her cloth-covered face into his neck, and he could feel her trembling against him.

"Fuck, man," Owl said as he slumped in the chair next to the one Cora had been sitting in.

For the first time in his life, Pipe was truly terrified. He'd been through some scary shit in his previous career, but nothing was more frightening than the possibility of Cora being hurt. He felt himself swaying and knew it was only a matter of time before they were all overcome by the gas. Once they were unconscious, he had no doubt the bodyguard would return...and who knew what would happen to them then. What would happen to *Cora*.

Ridge Michaels had already kidnapped one woman, and done who knows what to her. There was no telling what he'd do to his Cora.

And she was. His. Right then, with all the bullshit stripped away, Pipe knew what was truly important. Cora. His friends.

He'd always looked death in the eye, ready to give his life for the greater good, the safety of others. And he'd had no doubt the men fighting at his side had felt the same way. But things were different now. He didn't want to die.

Didn't want Owl to die. And he certainly didn't want anything to happen to Cora.

As a last-ditch effort to do something, Pipe shifted until he could get his phone out of his back pocket. His fingers shook as he clicked on Stone's name. He needed to tell his friend what was happening. Get help.

But as he stared down at the text string, he frowned.

Oh, yeah, he'd already tried to contact Stone and the message wouldn't go through. Bloody hell, he was so confused. He needed to get up. To do something. But he couldn't seem to move. His limbs were heavy, his head hurt, and he felt as if he was going to hurl.

Looking up, he saw Owl sitting in the chair with his head back, his eyes closed. That seemed like a fine idea. He was so tired. A nap would be good.

Pipe leaned back, keeping Cora in his arms as he did so. She snuggled against him, and he smiled. Yeah, he liked when she curled into him. He remembered that so vividly from this morning. Except now, oddly, their bed was much harder than before.

It didn't matter. He was so tired, he could sleep anywhere.

He'd just close his eyes for a moment, then he'd get up and do whatever it was he was supposed to do. And he definitely needed to do *something*...but for the life of him, he couldn't remember what. He was simply too tired. And dizzy.

The room was deathly silent as Pipe slipped into unconsciousness, a boneless Cora in his arms.

\* \* \*

Stone tried not to panic. He kept hoping that any second now, Owl, Pipe, and Cora would reappear. But the more time that passed, the more he knew that wasn't going to happen. Something had gone wrong inside that house, and he had no doubt that his friends were in trouble. He should call 9-1-1...but what would he tell them?

He could do what they'd planned to threaten Michaels with, ask for a welfare check.

But something told Stone he didn't have time for that. Michaels had every right to deny the cops entrance, and it would take way too long for them to get a search warrant. No, he had to do something *now*.

Stone's hands started shaking and he couldn't help but think of a different situation where he'd felt just as help-less. When he and Owl had been prisoners.

Once upon a time, he'd been a cocky son-of-a-bitch who didn't think anyone could ever get the drop on him. Then he'd found himself being held hostage. Tortured. That experience had changed him. Made him doubt his abilities.

It took a moment for his head to clear, to shake the memories of the pain and absolute terror he'd felt as a POW.

Stone straightened in his seat. He had to do more than simply sit on his ass. Pipe, Owl, Cora, and even Lara, if she was still alive, needed him to figure this out. To do *something*.

He realized he was holding his phone so tightly, his fingers were tingling. An idea came to him. Stone had no idea who the unknown person was who kept saving the day, but maybe, just maybe, they would have some sort of idea on how to reach his friends. His fingers flew over the keyboard.

. . .

*Stone: I can't get a hold of Pipe or Owl. They're inside the house already and my texts and calls aren't going through.*

*Unknown: Shit. Okay, give me a second.*

Stone didn't know what the person needed time for, but he felt better already for having shared what was happening.

After what seemed like forever, but in reality was only a minute or two, his phone vibrated again.

*Unknown: Bastard has a signal jammer, but I've disabled it. Try to get a hold of them again. Now.*

Stone had no clue how the hell the person knew about the signal jammer from wherever they might be, but he wasn't going to question it. He was also a little annoyed by the bossiness of the unknown stranger, but since he was helping, Stone couldn't complain.

*Stone: Owl, get the fuck out! Now!*

He waited a moment, but Owl didn't respond. Neither did Pipe when he texted him. He replied to Unknown.

*Stone: They aren't answering. What's the FBI's ETA?*

*Unknown: Keep trying. You have to get them out of there. I don't know when the FBI will arrive and Carter Grant is not someone you want near any female, under any circumstances.*

Stone gritted his teeth, unsure how he could get them out. He had zero intel. Didn't know if the arrival of Owl and Pipe had put the entire household on high alert. For all he knew, there were a dozen people just waiting to take him out the second he tried to break in. If anything happened to him, it could mean the end of any hope for his friends.

He continued to try to get a hold of either Pipe or Owl. He called, he texted. He tried Cora. All with no luck.

But his calls weren't going straight to voicemail anymore, and the texts seemed to be going through. That was both encouraging and terrifying. The latter because despite going through—his friends still weren't answering.

He chose to focus on the little glimmer of hope, which gave him the motivation he needed to keep trying.

Pipe and Owl were smart, they'd figure out a way to outmaneuver Michaels. And when they did, Stone would be waiting to get them the fuck out of there.

# CHAPTER NINETEEN

Cora felt like complete shit.

She hadn't felt like this since one night in her early twenties when she'd gone to a bar, feeling sorry for herself, and drank way too much. She had no recollection of how she'd gotten home, but when she'd woken the next morning, she'd had a hangover from hell. It had taken her almost two days to recover from her night of binge drinking, and she'd sworn she'd never do that again.

And yet, here she was. Feeling just as nauseous and out of sorts as she had back then.

But she didn't remember going out. Or drinking anything.

Then in a flash, her memory returned.

Lara. Coming to Arizona. Making love to Pipe.

The house. Creepy Guy. The locked door. Feeling dizzy and confused and then...nothing.

Cora opened her eyes and stared up at a dated popcorn ceiling. She curled her lip. Here she was in a freaking mansion, and they had old, nasty popcorn ceilings? It was ridiculous.

She slowly sat up and looked around.

To her immense relief, she saw Pipe lying to her right. Then she panicked when she couldn't see his chest moving, only for relief to swamp her again when she finally realized he was breathing. The quick seesaw of emotions made her even dizzier.

Looking to her other side, she saw Owl lying in much the same condition. They were on a concrete floor, and she shivered as she realized how cold it was.

As her gaze went around the room, Cora decided they were likely in a basement. There were windows, but they were tiny and at the very top of the walls. The room wasn't huge, but it wasn't a cell either. There was a door on the wall opposite her, and a bathroom—without a door—on the far right.

Moving slowly because every muscle seemed to hurt, Cora crawled over to where Pipe was lying. She put her hand on his chest to double check that he really was breathing. When his chest rose and fell, she sighed in relief. He looked different like this, unconscious and vulnerable. Cora didn't like it. He'd done all he could to protect her when they were locked in that room, but even her badass special forces soldier couldn't protect her from an unseen enemy like poisonous gas.

Honestly, she was completely shocked they were alive right now. *Anything* could've happened while they were unconscious, or the gas itself could've killed them. In fact...why were they moved at all? If Creepy Guy was going to kill them, did it really matter where he did the deed?

Looking around the room again, she spotted something she hadn't before, several feet away from Pipe.

A drain in the floor.

Her entire body shuddered when she considered its

purpose. And it answered the question of why CG had bothered to move them.

*No.* They weren't dying today.

She vowed to do whatever was necessary to protect Pipe while he was unable to help himself, even as she suspected it was probably a stupid thought. What could she do? She was a fairly short, chunky, not-very-educated chick. But then again, hadn't people told her all her life she should probably be a drug addict or homeless by now?

She was neither of those things. She was hardworking, resourceful, stubborn.

Her resolve strengthened. She wasn't helpless, and no way was she going to let an asshole like Ridge Michaels harm her or Pipe.

A quiet noise startled Cora so badly, she jerked, then spun so fast the room swirled for a moment. She blinked when she focused on the object behind her. A bed. Since she was on the floor, she couldn't see who or what was on top, if anything. She wasn't sure she wanted to find out. If Ridge thought he was going to use that bed to do anything sexual to her, he'd find out she wouldn't go down without a fight.

Moving slowly and as quietly as she could, Cora stood. Trepidation filled her as she stared at a lump under the covers. She must've made a sound, because the lump suddenly moved. Whoever was there turned their head, dislodging the covers, which had been pulled up over their face.

Cora blinked, not believing what she was seeing.

Then she made a strangled noise in the back of her throat and leapt toward the bed.

"Lara!" she practically yelled.

Her friend languished on the mattress. Her blonde hair

was limp on the thin pillow. She had a vacant look in her eyes, but it was Lara. Alive.

Tears sprang to Cora's eyes. They'd found her. She never would've admitted it out loud, but Cora was beginning to doubt that she'd ever see her best friend again. She'd never get to talk with her, laugh, enjoy dinner together. But here she was. *Alive*.

"Lara!" she said again, as she sat on the edge of the mattress and pulled the blanket back.

Her friend didn't say anything. Didn't move. Simply continued to stare blankly as if she didn't even see Cora sitting there.

Cora heard Pipe and Owl beginning to stir on the floor, but she couldn't take her eyes from her best friend. Tears welled up and ran unchecked down her cheeks. What was wrong with her? Why wasn't she responding?

She put her hand on Lara's shoulder and shook her gently, but Lara's eyes still didn't focus.

"Oh my God, what'd he do to you?" Cora whispered when she noticed Lara's body for the first time. She was wearing a spaghetti-strap nightgown that Cora had never seen before. It looked odd on her friend, because Lara hated anything with lace. Found it too scratchy. She always slept in an oversized T-shirt. This nightgown had lace around the entire neckline, which was so low her boobs were on clear display.

But it was the bruises that had most of Cora's attention.

They were everywhere. Around her neck. On her upper arms. What she could see of her chest was covered in bruises. Whatever had happened, it had been *bad*.

But the worst part was that the bruises were all different colors, obviously in various stages of healing. She hadn't been abused once, but many times. Over and over again.

Cora's heart shattered. She wanted to scream. Wanted to kill Ridge for doing this to her friend.

And just like that, the tears stopped. Sorrow disappeared, and anger took its place. Cora had never been so angry in her life. Not when she was a kid and had faced rejection after rejection. Not when she was bullied. Not when she was fired unfairly because she'd rebuffed her boss's advances.

Lara didn't deserve what had happened to her. No one did, but especially not Lara. She was the kind of woman who always gave people the benefit of the doubt. She gave her trust willingly. She had the kindest soul Cora had ever met. She was untainted.

Cora knew without a doubt that whatever had happened here would change her friend forever. And it filled her with absolute rage.

"Cora?"

She wiped her cheeks with her shoulder before turning to see Pipe standing next to her. Owl was sitting up, obviously trying to get his bearings.

"Are you all right?" Pipe asked.

Cora shook her head, but said, "Yeah." She couldn't deal with the concern and sorrow she saw in his eyes. "Something's wrong with her," she said, looking back at her friend.

It was Owl who said, "Scoot back, let me look at her."

Without a thought to ask him if he had any medical training, Cora stood and stepped away from the bed, not taking her gaze from Lara. She felt Pipe's arm go around her waist, but she suddenly felt oddly detached, as if she was floating, watching what was happening from above.

Owl leaned down and held his fingers at Lara's throat, taking her pulse. Her eyes had closed, and he lifted each eyelid one at a time to check her pupils. He gently palpated her hands, arms, then eased the blanket down so he could get to her stomach.

Her nightgown had been rucked up, and they all saw she was completely naked beneath the flimsy garment. Owl moved quickly, pulling the nightgown down, preserving her modesty as best he could—but not before they'd all seen the bruises on her belly and inner thighs.

Not to mention the dry, crusted...stuff...on her body.

Cora's fists clenched. Anger swept over her again so fast and hard, it was all she could do to keep breathing.

"Easy, love," Pipe murmured.

Needing to strike out, to try to dispel the fury coursing through her veins, Cora turned on him. "Easy?" she practically shrieked. "Did you see that?" she asked, flinging an arm back to where Lara lay on the bed.

"Yes," Pipe said, sounding too calm.

"She was *violated*! Someone jacked off on her! They *hurt* her! Those are finger marks on her thighs. On her throat! Someone beat my friend. She doesn't deserve this!" She was yelling now, shoving Pipe in the chest to punctuate her words.

He wrapped his hands around her wrists and pulled her against him roughly.

Cora let out an *umph* as she landed on his chest. Pipe wrapped his arms around her so tightly, she could hardly breathe. But it worked. As suddenly as her anger had welled up, it disappeared. She was left feeling hollow. She buried her face in his chest as the tears flowed again. "He hurt her. *Lara*. She's the kindest, gentlest person I know... and he hurt her!"

"I know. And he's gonna pay for that. I give you my word."

Cora pushed the tears back. She didn't have time to cry. Not now. Later, maybe...probably...but for now, she needed to keep herself together.

"She doesn't have any broken bones," Owl said. Cora turned in Pipe's embrace to face the other man. "From the way her pupils are dilated, and given she's so out of it, I'd say she's been drugged."

"Will she be okay?" It was a stupid question. Owl wasn't a doctor, even if he did seem to have some medical training.

But he answered without hesitation. "Yes."

The word was firm and determined, and hearing it made Cora feel a hundred pounds lighter. "Okay, can I... can I clean her?" she asked.

In response, Pipe let go of her and headed for the bathroom. He returned seconds later with a wet washcloth and handed it to her without a word. Cora went to the other side of the bed and began wiping her friend gently. Owl and Pipe turned their heads when she lifted the nightgown, once again giving the almost comatose woman the respect she deserved.

Cora did the best she could and felt marginally better when there were no more traces of what someone had left behind on Lara's skin. She couldn't help but lean down and whisper, "Wake up, Lara. Please. It's Cora. I'm here. I'm with some friends and we're going to get you out of here. But you have to wake up and talk to us. Okay?"

To her surprise, Lara's head slowly turned her way...and Cora swore she saw recognition in her eyes.

"It's me," she told her friend. "We always said we'd be

there for each other through thick and thin, right? Well, I'm thinking this is some pretty serious thick, huh?"

Lara blinked.

"Can you talk to us?" Owl asked.

Lara's head rolled slowly on the pillow, turning toward Owl. She stared at him without saying a word.

"That's Owl. He's with me. His real name is Callen, but people call him Owl because he's got such perfect eyesight," Cora told her.

"Stalker," Pipe said with a small grin from behind Owl.

Cora wasn't ashamed of the research she'd done on the men of The Refuge. Besides, it wasn't as if the information wasn't out there for anyone to find if they looked hard enough.

But at the sound of Pipe's voice, Lara whimpered.

"Easy, it's okay. That's Pipe," Cora told her. "He's mine."

Pipe made a small sound, and Cora looked up at him. He seemed surprised at her words.

She wrinkled her nose. "Too soon?" she asked sheepishly.

"No, not at all," Pipe told her. The bed was between them, but for some reason it felt as if they were the only two people in the world.

"You're scaring her," Owl told Pipe. "Step back."

Pipe immediately took a step away from the bed.

"You're okay," Owl told Lara. "No one's gonna hurt you again. Do you hear me? I won't allow it."

To Cora's surprise, Lara's tongue came out and she licked her lips before croaking, "Hurt."

"I know, and as soon as we can, we'll do something about that. Pipe's gonna figure out how to get us the hell out of here and we'll get you all fixed up. Okay?"

Cora held her breath. She felt no jealousy at all that Lara had responded to Owl and not her. She was thrilled she was talking at all.

In response to Owl's words, Lara's arm inched across the narrow bed. She grabbed hold of his wrist. "Don't leave. Rather die…"

Her voice was thready and weak, but they could all hear the desperation in her words.

"I'm not leaving you. Not a chance in hell. And no one is dying. Hear me? But I need you to fight, Lara."

"Tired," she said, closing her eyes.

But Cora noticed that she hadn't let go of Owl's wrist.

"I know you are," he said gently. "Rest for now."

Lara nodded and let out a long sigh.

Cora pressed her lips together as she lifted the blanket back up and over Lara's body.

Lara's head moved her way, and her eyes popped open again. She still looked out of it, and the thought of someone drugging her friend made the murderous anger return. But Cora did her best to remain calm.

"Knew you'd find me. But…you should've stayed away."

Cora leaned down so she was almost nose to nose with her friend. "No way in hell. You saved me when we were fifteen. I would've moved heaven and earth to save you back. I love you, Lara."

In response, Lara closed her eyes and turned her head away.

Cora wasn't upset. She had to be confused right now. And traumatized. Nothing she said or did would surprise Cora, under the circumstances.

"You guys okay?" Pipe asked.

"Head hurts, and I feel a little off, but okay," Owl said,

not getting up from the bed because doing so would mean Lara would have to let go of him.

Cora fell a little in love with him then. Not a love like she had for Pipe, but a huge, grateful love that he understood Lara needed an anchor right now. And because he was perfectly willing to be that anchor.

"Cora?" Pipe asked.

"Same," she told him. "What's the plan?" she asked before she could think twice about it. It wasn't fair to put that kind of pressure on Pipe, but she honestly had no idea what to do now. They were in a basement, with windows too small to climb out of, and with a half-dressed woman who was mostly out of it. She had a feeling their options were limited.

Pipe opened his mouth to say something, but was interrupted by the sound of his phone vibrating.

"Wait—they didn't take our phones?" Cora asked as she reached for her own in her back pocket. Sure enough, it was still there. "Do you have your gun?" she asked Pipe urgently.

He'd pulled out his phone and was scrolling down the screen, but he shook his head and said, "Nope. Gun's gone."

"Of course it is," Cora said with a sigh.

Then a voice Cora recognized came from the speaker of Pipe's phone.

Stone.

"Talk to me," Pipe ordered.

"Fuckin' shit! Thank God you finally answered. What's going on in there?"

"We were locked in a room, gassed, and now we're in the basement with a drugged Lara," Pipe summed up quickly.

"Fuck. Right, look, they jammed the cell signals, which is why I couldn't get in touch with you earlier," Stone said.

"I know. We realized that when we were locked in that first room. Did they fuck up and unjam it for some reason?"

"No. You know that unknown person who helped us find Jasna and Reese?"

"Yeah?" Pipe asked suspiciously.

"He messaged me after you three had gone to the house and told me some shit. Warned me that you were all in danger and to tell you to get out."

"Yeah, got the forty-seven messages with you saying that. And we would've if we could've. So what's up with the jammer?" Pipe asked.

"Unknown unjammed it. Which is how we're talking now."

"Holy shit," Cora whispered. She moved from around the bed toward Pipe. She put an arm around his waist as he held his phone in front of them, and they listened to Stone.

"Anyway, listen, that Grant guy? He's wanted by the FBI. For multiple murders, among other things. He's got aliases a mile long. He's dangerous, Pipe," Stone said unnecessarily. "He hurts women. Gets off on it. Then eventually kills them. You guys have to get out of there right now."

Cora blinked in surprise. Creepy Guy really *was* creepy. She was kind of glad her internal radar hadn't failed her, but the knowledge was a little too late.

"Gonna need your help, Stone," Pipe said. "Need you to do some reconnaissance. We're in a basement of some sort. There are windows, but they're small. Too small for us to get out of. There's a door to the room we're in, but

272

I'm guessing it's locked and reinforced like the one upstairs. We can't get out without some help."

"Right. Okay, I'm gonna go over the wall and check out the property and see what I can find. Oh, shit!" There was rustling, then silence.

Cora held her breath. This was so nerve-wracking. It was easy to hear the worry in Stone's tone.

"What? What's wrong?" Pipe asked.

"Someone's coming down the street," Stone whispered. "I had to jump over the perimeter wall. I don't think they saw me."

"Lay low. Can you get eyes on them? Who is it?"

The seconds dragged by as they waited for Stone to speak. He was still whispering when he responded.

"It's not Michaels. This guy is stocky. Blondish hair. Tall. He's headed straight for the Jeep. Shit, he's slashing the tires."

Cora closed her eyes as she leaned against Pipe. He was her rock right then. With every minute that passed, things seemed to get worse and worse. With the car out of commission, they wouldn't be able to get away from the house quickly.

"That's Carter," Pipe said.

"Yeah, that's what I figured," Stone said.

"What's he doing now?"

"Preparing a distraction," Stone told them. "He opened the gas tank and stuffed a rag in there."

"He's gonna blow it up," Pipe said.

"Probably. Wait...huh. That's interesting."

"What?" Pipe asked, impatience in his tone.

"He's making a call. Do you think...maybe he doesn't know the jammer was disabled. If hc's out here using his phone, maybe he thought it wouldn't work in the house."

"It's possible," Pipe agreed.

Then they all heard a sound in the background that made Owl's head jerk up from where he'd been staring down at Lara.

"What's that?" Pipe barked.

"Chopper," Owl and Stone said at the same time.

"That's our way out of here," Pipe said firmly. "You need to get to that chopper, Stone. Lara can't walk, so extraction's gonna be tricky."

For the first time since the call had started, Stone sounded confident. "Ten minutes," he said. "I'll be waiting. Owl?"

"I'm here," he said.

"Remember what we did when we realized help had finally arrived for us?"

Cora watched Owl sit up straighter on the bed. "Yeah."

"That's your way out. I wish I could be there to help, but I'll be in the cockpit waiting for you to be my wing-man. Okay?"

"Deal," Owl said.

"Ten minutes," Stone repeated. "Do what you have to do, Pipe, to get out of there. If you don't…" His voice trailed off.

Cora looked up at Pipe. His lips were pressed together tightly and he nodded. "Right. Ten minutes." Then he clicked off the phone and looked at Owl. "What's the plan?"

As soon as Owl explained how their rescue had gone down several years ago, Cora wasn't sure it would work. But they literally had no other choice.

"You okay with taking her?" Pipe asked as he nodded at Lara.

"Absolutely," Owl said.

Cora watched as Owl carefully slid his hand from Lara's and took his shirt off. Before she could ask what he was doing, Owl pulled back the blanket and carefully started to put the shirt over her friend's head.

"Listen to me, love," Pipe said, grabbing Cora's shoulders and physically turning her toward him. "No matter what happens, know that the happiest I've been in a very long time was last night with you. Understand?"

Cora nodded.

"And if this goes right, I'm gonna give you that family you've always wanted. You have a problem with that?"

Did she have a problem with Pipe being her family? Hell no. She shook her head.

"Good. Let's do this."

Taking a deep breath, Cora walked over the door— then started pounding on it and screaming at the top of her lungs.

# CHAPTER TWENTY

This had to work. It *had* to. If not, they were all screwed.

This was nothing like Cora ever thought would happen to her. When she'd decided to try to win a date with one of the owners of The Refuge, she never expected to end up here. From traveling to New Mexico, clicking with the women there, being here in Arizona with Pipe, having the best sex of her life, falling in love, being gassed, finding Lara alive—but in much worse shape than she'd imagined —and now playing the role of a lifetime.

Cora screamed as loud as she could, pounding on the door so hard, she knew she'd have bruises on her hands. They needed someone to come investigate what the hell was happening before Creepy Guy blew up their Jeep. They had to assume he'd then kill Pipe and Owl, and steal away with Lara and Cora in the confusion of all the firetrucks and police cars that were sure to arrive en masse.

And she had no doubt Creepy Guy *would* take her and Lara. He was a rapist and a murderer, and she did *not* want to imagine what he'd do if he was able to kidnap them both. They didn't know the details of everything he'd done to women he'd killed in the past, but Cora had a very good imagination, especially after seeing Lara's condition.

It finally occurred to her, as she pounded on the door and yelled for all she was worth, that it probably wasn't Ridge who'd hurt Lara. Yes, it was possible he'd come home from the strip club every night and messed with her, but she guessed it was more likely Creepy Guy the whole time. Maybe he was the one who'd convinced Ridge to bring Lara to Arizona in the first place. It made her sick to think that this kind of abuse had been premeditated.

They had to get out of this damn room.

Cora looked over at Pipe as she continued screaming. He was standing behind where the door would open, every muscle ready to act. To defend all of them. They'd talked about who might show up before she started her playacting. They hoped the second bodyguard, Arlo Harvey, would be the one to arrive. Or literally anyone else who worked in the house. If they didn't know what was happening in the basement right under their noses, they wouldn't be prepared for Pipe to attack when the door opened.

But if Creepy Guy made it back to the house and heard the commotion, *he'd* be ready.

Even though her throat hurt, Cora didn't stop screaming. She'd yell herself hoarse if that was what it took. She gave the performance of her life, which it literally was.

Finally, after what seemed like ages, she heard the dead bolt scrape along steel as someone began to unlock the door.

Her heart beat a million miles an hour as she glanced at Pipe. To her amazement, he gave her a reassuring nod. Here he was, about to fight whoever was on the other side of the door with nothing but his bare hands, and *he* was reassuring *her*.

"Please! Let me out! My friend needs help! I think she's dying!" Cora yelled, moving back, letting Pipe get in front of her. His muscles were tense as he stared intently at the opening of the door.

To her surprise, instead of waiting for whoever was on the other side to actually enter the room, as soon as the opening was wide enough, he lunged forward, reaching out and pulling the person into the room.

Cora's heart fell to the floor when she saw Pipe wrestling with Creepy Guy. The one person they didn't want to come investigate.

Pipe and CG fell to the floor with a grunt and the fight was on. Cora knew Pipe had hoped to subdue whoever entered the room quickly, but it was immediately clear that CG wasn't going down easy. In fact, as they exchanged blows, it seemed he had way more hand-to-hand combat experience than the average person.

For every blow that Pipe landed, Creepy Guy was getting in one of his own. The impression Cora had gotten while back at The Refuge was that there weren't many men who could match Pipe when it came to fighting. But it was taking all his concentration not to be overpowered or disabled by a blow to a kidney.

Owl leaped into the fray, doing his best to assist Pipe, but Creepy Guy was a monster with muscles. Fighting off both men as if it was nothing. The thought flashed through Cora's head that no woman would have a chance against this guy. She was certain he had either a military background or some sort of martial arts training. The thought of him touching Lara made Cora grit her teeth and want to throw up.

The men were all grunting, none of them speaking as they literally fought for their lives. It was eerie. And brutal. Pipe and Owl weren't pulling their punches, but neither was Creepy Guy. They were all fighting dirty, doing everything they could do to take the other down.

Cora gasped when Creepy Guy landed a hard blow to the side of Pipe's head that had him stumbling back and momentarily stunned. He then kicked Owl in the stomach, which sent him careening across the floor, landing hard on his ass.

In seconds, he'd turned his attention toward her—making Cora's heart stop. The look in his eyes was chilling.

If he got his hands on her, he'd use Cora as leverage to make Pipe and Owl back off. She knew that as well as she knew her name.

Creepy Guy rushed at her before Pipe or Owl could get back up and attack. Cora's life flashed in front of her eyes and she did the only thing she could think of...

She ducked.

Surprisingly, Creepy Guy's lunge had him stumbling past her.

She moved without thought, leaping onto his back as if she were some sort of WWF champion.

Remembering what Pipe had told her back at The Refuge...two days ago? Three? She wasn't sure, but his advice echoed in her head as clear as day.

*I guarantee someone will let go of you immediately if you stick your finger in their eye. That gives you time to get the hell away from him or her and get help. That should be your goal—not standing and fighting, but getting away.*

She screamed, a feral sound that came from deep within her soul as she grabbed his hair with one hand and wrapped her legs around his waist. Then she swung her other hand around, her thumb aimed for his right eye.

The sound his eye made as she pierced his eyeball with her nail made her want to puke. Not to mention the way it squished against her thumb. But instead of letting go at his roar of pain, Cora pushed harder and twisted her hand for good measure.

To make sure this asshole was as incapacitated as possible, she let go of his hair and used her other hand to jam her index finger up his nose.

That was gross...but not as disgusting as the liquid from his eyeball coating her thumb and running down her wrist.

Creepy Guy howled and thrashed in pain.

Satisfaction swam in Cora's veins, but it was brief moment of triumph because CG reached behind him and grabbed a fistful of her hair. He literally pulled her over his shoulder by her hair and threw her across the room.

It all happened so fast. Cora's head throbbed from where he'd pulled out a hunk of her hair, but she barely registered the sensation before she hit the wall. Hard.

So hard her vision went black for a moment and there was a loud ringing in her ears, blocking out all other sound.

She lay slumped against the wall, trying to get her bearings. Shit. She hurt. All over. Her head, her ass where she'd landed, her arm.

She moved slightly, and gasped in pain as she realized she couldn't move her right arm without feeling as if she was going to pass out. Looking down, she saw a huge lump in the middle of her right forearm. It was so deformed, she knew it was broken. Cora had never had a broken bone before, but she'd seen a guy fall down a flight of stairs, and his arm had looked a lot like hers.

Then she saw the blood and gore on her hand from Creepy Guy's eye. She gagged at the sight.

A noise finally registered, and she realized it was Owl, yelling at her.

"Cora! Are you all right? Shit! Talk to me!"

Blinking, Cora turned her head toward the fight that had resumed after CG had thrown her. Owl and Pipe were both punching and kicking their target over and over, with what seemed to be a lot more fury than before she'd been hurt.

"I'm okay," she told him, her voice a little weak.

Looking toward the bed to check on Lara, she saw that her friend still seemed to be unconscious. She hadn't moved, even with the noise of the fight going on feet from where she lay. Cora frowned in worry, but her thoughts turned back toward the fight when she heard a strange noise.

She inhaled sharply at the sight in front of her.

Seconds ago the fight had been full-on, with fists and feet being thrown and Creepy Guy trying to fend off both Pipe and Owl. Now, Pipe had finally gotten the upper hand. He knelt behind CG, his arm around the man's neck, while Owl held his arms tightly so he couldn't break free.

The sound she'd heard was CG gurgling, his breath rasping as he tried desperately to get air into his lungs.

Cora had the brief thought that she should be more disturbed about the scene in front of her than she was, but when she considered Lara's condition, she silently hoped her man killed the bastard.

Blood ran down CG's face from where she'd tried to take out his eye, and from where she was sitting, it looked as if she might've succeeded. Good. Served the sicko right.

One second Creepy Guy was kneeling, and the next, Pipe was dropping his unconscious body to the floor.

As Owl turned to the bed to check on Lara, Pipe said, "We need to go."

If Cora could've, she would've jumped Pipe right then and there. His hair was sticking up all over his head, his T-shirt was torn, he was breathing hard, had blood on his arms—Cora really hoped it was Creepy Guy's blood and not his own—and his lip was also bloody and swollen from where he'd been hit in the face several times. But he was literally the sexiest man she'd ever seen in her life.

"Cora?" he asked as he took two steps toward her. He knelt down and his eyes raked down her body, as if he could see through her clothes to see if she was hurt. He inhaled sharply when he saw her arm.

"I think it's broken," she said, not recognizing the sound of her own voice.

Pipe reached out a hand and palmed the back of her head before resting his forehead against hers so gently, it was as if they were in the middle of some romantic night out rather than in the basement of a kidnapper's house, after being drugged and injured.

"Bloody hell," he whispered.

"I did what you told me to," she whispered. "I went for the soft tissue."

"You did good, love," he said.

Those four words meant more than Cora could express. She half expected him to get mad that she'd put herself in danger, getting hurt in the process. But instead, he understood that they'd all been in deep shit, and she'd done what she needed to do in order to give him and Owl a chance to overcome the threat.

"Is he dead?" she whispered.

"No."

Cora blinked at that. "Why not?"

To her surprise, Pipe drew back and looked at her with a serious expression. "Because unlike that arsehole, I'm not a murderer."

"But we can't let him get away!" she protested.

"We'll call the police as soon as possible. My main concern right now is getting you and Lara away from here and to a doctor."

Cora couldn't argue with that. At least the part about making sure Lara was safe. As for herself, she didn't like doctors. Never had, never would.

"Speaking of which, it's been twelve minutes. We need to go," Owl said.

Pipe nodded but didn't look at his friend. He stood, then reached down for Cora. She stood with his help and promptly swayed.

"What hurts?" Pipe asked urgently.

"Um...everything?" Cora said without thought.

To her surprise, Pipe picked her up as if she weighed nothing at all. She let out a screech and wrapped her good arm around his neck.

"I've got you," he soothed. "Owl, you okay with her?"

Looking over at the bed, Cora saw Owl was holding Lara in his arms. They were about the same height, so she looked a little awkward in his arms, but with the amount of weight Lara had clearly lost, Owl seemed to be able to carry her without issue.

"Yes," he told Pipe curtly.

Without another word, Pipe headed for the door. They were indeed in a basement. The room they were in was at the back of a larger space. The rest of the basement was filled with boxes upon boxes. No wonder no one knew

Lara was there, it didn't look as if anyone had been down there in ages. They went up a flight of stairs and exited into a hallway.

It was eerie how they didn't encounter anyone. The house was completely silent and seemingly empty.

Until a woman holding an honest-to-God feather duster, and wearing an apron, stepped out of a room in front of them and stopped dead in her tracks. She stared at them in astonishment, her mouth open in shock. It was confirmation in Cora's eyes that most of the employees had probably been kept in the dark about what was happening in the basement. That they didn't know Ridge Michaels and his bodyguard were up to no good right under their noses.

"Where's the helipad?" Pipe barked in a low, mean tone.

The woman jerked in surprise at the menace in his voice and pointed down the hall.

Pipe brushed past her. Cora's legs almost hit her in the face, but she stepped back into the room she'd just exited.

Looking over Pipe's shoulder, Cora saw a shirtless Owl right on their heels. Lara's bare legs bounced as he walked, and while his shirt was big on her friend, it wasn't nearly long enough.

Hatred welled up within Cora again. Lara had been through hell, and she didn't know if she hated Creepy Guy or Ridge Michaels more as a result.

"Bloody hell," Pipe swore.

Turning to look forward, Cora saw what had Pipe so upset. Sometime between when they'd arrived at the house and now, a storm had moved in. The wind was blowing so much sand around, they could've been in the middle of the Sahara Desert instead of Phoenix.

"Can Stone fly in this?" Cora asked worriedly.

It wasn't Pipe who answered, but Owl from behind her. "Piece of cake. Come on, move."

Pipe leaned down and managed to open the door without dropping Cora, then stepped outside into the maelstrom.

Cora immediately shut her eyes, the sand hitting her face like little pieces of glass. She huddled into Pipe as well as she could.

Over the sound of the wind screaming around them, she heard the familiar *chuff* of helicopter rotors. She squinted her eyes open and was surprised to see the large aircraft so close. The rotors blades were kicking up even more sand all around them.

Before she knew it, Pipe had placed her inside the chopper on a back seat, then leaped up without seemingly any effort next to her. He helped her scoot over before turning back to the door. He took Lara from Owl's arms so his friend could jump into the chopper. Pipe sat beside her and, as gently as possible, propped up Lara on the remaining seat to his right, buckling her in, then wrapping an arm around her to keep her steady.

"You're late!" Stone yelled from the pilot's seat.

"Sorry, had some trouble!" Pipe yelled back.

Owl turned in his seat next to Stone to stare at Lara for a moment, then met Cora's gaze.

"She's gonna be okay," he told her firmly.

It felt as if there was more he wanted to say, but Stone yelled at him to get his "ass in gear" so they could get the fuck out of there.

Without another word, Owl turned and faced forward. And before her eyes, the man who scemed so uncertain at times morphed into someone Cora had never seen.

Even shirtless, he oozed confidence as he donned a set of headphones and began to flick switches and buttons.

"Hang on!" Stone called back to Pipe and Cora. "This isn't going to be a smooth takeoff!"

Movement in her peripheral vision made Cora turn. She saw several men waving their arms and yelling something, but she couldn't hear them. They were running out of the house, toward the chopper.

It was the man at the back of the group who she couldn't take her eyes off, though.

It was Creepy Guy. He wasn't yelling. Wasn't running toward them. He was simply standing at the door, staring at the helicopter as if his gaze alone could make it crash and burn.

Blood still ran down his face but his expression was blank. He was literally the coldest, creepiest man Cora had ever seen in her life. The thought of him anywhere near her, or Lara, made her blood run cold. No wonder the FBI had him on their most wanted list. He was a menace to society, and any woman unlucky enough to come into contact with him was in extreme danger. She knew that down to her bones.

"Here we go!" Stone yelled.

The chopper lurched upward, and Cora yelped as she reached for something to hold on to. She found Pipe.

"Holy crap, this thing sucks," Owl said, almost conversationally as he struggled to help Stone fly the chopper.

"When we talk to Brick about getting a helicopter for The Refuge, we're getting a Bell. Maybe a 505. This R66 is fine in calm weather, but shit for conditions like this," Stone replied.

Pipe had motioned to her before they'd taken off to put on a pair of headphones so they could all talk to each other, but at the moment, Cora wasn't sure she wanted to hear what else the ex-Night Stalkers had to say.

The two men continued to bitch about the small private chopper they'd "borrowed" as they fought against the wind and sand.

Pipe wrapped his free arm around her, and Cora was relieved. Having him next to her somehow made everything a little less scary. Cora only had one arm she could use, and she grabbed hold of Pipe's hand on her shoulder when the helicopter shuddered. She'd never been in a helicopter before, and this flight was terrifying. She had confidence in Stone and Owl, she'd read about the famous Night Stalker pilots when she'd researched The Refuge, but how the hell they were still in the air with the wind and sand whipping so hard, was beyond her.

When she looked back at the house they'd just escaped, as they rose higher and higher, Creepy Guy wasn't there anymore. He'd disappeared from view—and a shiver ran through her.

She suddenly wished Pipe had killed him. Had made sure he wouldn't be around to haunt them ever again.

Pipe leaned toward her slightly, and Cora turned and buried her nose in his neck, breathing in his familiar scent. So much had happened so quickly, but this man had yet to let her down. When it meant the most, he'd done everything in his power to make sure she was safe. That was more than anyone in her entire life had done for her. She figured some psychologist somewhere would caution her, tell her that what she felt for Pipe was some savior complex, because of her lack of affection growing up. That there was no way she was truly in love with him...but they'd be wrong.

Feeling sick now from the way the chopper was

swaying and jerking in the storm, she squeezed her eyes shut. Her arm was screaming in pain, her butt hurt from where she'd landed on it, and her head throbbed from hitting the wall.

But she was alive, and they had found Lara. She'd go through it all again if it meant being where she was right now. Scared out of her mind, but safe.

As if he could read her thoughts, Pipe spoke softly. She barely heard him over Owl and Stone's conversation about getting them out of there without crashing.

"You're good. I've got you."

Yeah, he did. She was hurt, Lara was obviously traumatized, and they might still die in a horrific helicopter crash, not to mention they might be prosecuted for stealing the chopper...but Cora didn't care. They'd deal with the fallout from the last few hours later. For now, she was content to be alive and with the man she loved.

# CHAPTER TWENTY-ONE

Cora sat on the rooftop deck of Pipe's cabin at The Refuge. To her surprise, he had replaced the two separate Adirondack chairs with a cushioned love seat shortly after they'd returned. He said it was so he could sit closer to her. It was adorable, and considerate, and was even a little hard to believe. Cora had never had a man who wanted to be by her side. And Pipe being so sweet was hard to get used to.

Her arm was in a cast and she'd been given painkillers for her cracked coccyx. She'd literally broken her butt. It was ridiculous. But Pipe had gotten her a wedge cushion to sit on and the drugs cut down the pain significantly.

The helicopter ride had been terrifying and painful, but what had been even scarier was staring down the barrels of a dozen weapons after they'd landed. Owl and Stone had managed to land on a helipad at a local hospital, but since the landing was unauthorized and no one knew who they were or what was happening, the police had been called.

It had taken nearly an hour to straighten everything out—with the help of Tex, Brick, Lara's parents, and even

Owl and Stone's former commander—but eventually they were allowed to enter the hospital.

Cora was discharged that same night after x-rays and getting the cast on her arm, but Lara had stayed for two nights. Owl didn't leave her side. Every time he so much as tried to get up, Lara freaked out. For some reason she'd latched onto him, and when he wasn't in her line of sight, she became hysterical.

Her parents had come to the hospital, and even their presence hadn't calmed her down much. They were obviously glad to see her and know that she was alive, but distraught by everything that had happened. They were filled with guilt over ignoring Cora's warnings...guilt made even worse when Lara didn't seem to want them to stay. Cora suspected it would take a while for their relationship to mend, if it ever would.

Owl wasn't fazed by Lara's need to have him by her side. He had an unending well of patience, holding her hand for two days straight, only reluctantly letting go for the occasional bathroom break.

"You all right?" Pipe asked.

It had been less than a week since their ordeal in the basement, and Cora swore Pipe asked her that question at least twenty times a day, but she truly didn't mind. Him asking meant he cared, which was the best medicine she could've had.

"Yeah. Just thinking," she told him.

"About?"

"Him. Creepy Guy."

Pipe scooted closer and put his arm around her shoulders. He couldn't pull her into his lap with her broken tailbone, but he didn't hesitate to touch her whenever he could. "He's going to be found."

Cora appreciated his confidence, but she wasn't so sure. After all, the FBI hadn't been able to find him before. What made this time any different?

"They will," Pipe insisted, as if he could read her mind. "Someone like that? Someone evil down to his core...he'll make a mistake."

"I just...he's going to hurt some other woman. Or women."

Pipe sighed. "Yeah."

That was all he said, but as much as Cora hated him confirming her worst fears, she appreciated that he wasn't brushing off her concerns.

"Tex hasn't found out any more info?" she asked.

"No. And he's still super pissed that Unknown hacked into his computers."

Cora huffed out an amused breath.

"You don't know him. He prides himself on being the best of the best when it comes to tech shit. And this anonymous person has not only done what he wasn't able to do—three times now—he did it by hacking into Tex's system to get information."

"But he's been helping us. I mean, he unjammed those phone signals so you could talk to Stone. And he figured out who Creepy Guy really was."

"I know. But Tex still isn't happy."

"Who do you think it is?" Cora asked.

"I have no clue."

"Not even a guess?"

Pipe sighed. "Not a good one. I've talked about it with the guys, and previously we'd thought it could be someone from our pasts. One of our teammates, a commander, someone else we worked with. But Stone brought up an excellent point, one we can't dismiss...

that it's more likely someone connected to The Refuge."

Cora gasped. "Really? Like who?"

"It could be anyone. Robert, Jess, Savannah, Ryan, Jason, Luna...even one of the men or women who deliver food and supplies up here. Anyone who might've overheard what was going on with Reese, then Lara."

"Seriously? You think Robert's a closet hacker?" Cora asked with a small laugh.

"Everyone has stuff they don't share about themselves. But I think Stone's right. It has to be someone who knows what's going on here at The Refuge."

"Are you mad?" Cora asked.

Pipe shrugged. "Yes and no."

"I kind of like the thought of having an anonymous benefactor looking over us," Cora declared as she leaned into Pipe's side, feeling content.

They hadn't had a conversation about how long she might stay here with him, but the time was coming when they'd need to talk about the future. She didn't really want to, didn't want to face reality. But she was healing, and she needed to make some decisions about her job and life back in DC.

Complicating matters was Lara. She was a completely different person than who she'd been before Arizona. Cora didn't blame her, not in the least. She'd been through something traumatic, and would be dealing with that for a long time. Cora would do whatever it took to help her heal.

But so far, she wasn't healing at all. Wasn't leaving Owl's cabin.

When she was discharged from the hospital, there wasn't even a doubt that she'd be coming back to The

Refuge with them. They'd actually decided to drive, since Lara didn't do well around groups of people. She didn't speak once during the drive and continued to panic when Owl was out of her sight.

Cora wasn't jealous. Did she want Lara to lean on her because they were best friends? Of course. But knowing she considered Owl her safe space was completely fine, because he was a good man. And there was something in his eyes when he looked at her friend that told Cora he'd do whatever it took to help her.

She wanted that for Lara. So Cora wasn't upset that Owl was the one at her side. She was angry that she was so broken, she couldn't be left alone. Sad that she'd gone through what she had. But not envious of Owl.

"Will you tell me about the investigation?" she asked Pipe.

"I'm not sure I want to," he finally said in response.

"I know," Cora said, and she did. Pipe was her protector. He'd proven it more than once. Wanted to keep her from seeing or hearing anything upsetting. But she'd had time to come to terms with what happened and needed to know everything the police and FBI had learned.

He sighed. "You know that Ridge Michaels was found deceased in the house."

"Yeah. Single gunshot to his temple."

"It wasn't suicide," Pipe added.

Cora gasped and looked up at him. "It wasn't?"

"No. The angle was wrong. And the shot was in his left temple, and Michaels was right-handed. There were a few news stories about it, but just as the publicity was ramping up, that famous actress out in Hollywood was kidnapped, and there was that four-hour car chase to stop her stalker from taking her out of state. That's been dominating the news."

"Yeah," Cora said with a nod, resting against Pipe once more.

"The assumption is that it was Grant who killed him, after we arrived. To keep him from talking."

"That makes sense," Cora mused.

"Also, as we thought, the other employees in the house were in the dark about what was happening right under their noses. If they knew, I'm guessing they'd all be dead right now too. I suppose some of their ignorance can be chalked up to them being used to the quirks of the rich people they worked for. They were used to Ridge's reputation, knew he went to strip clubs when he visited. And they had no reason to think there was anyone being hidden in the basement."

"And the media room? Did they know it was used to knock people unconscious so they could be moved to the basement room, where Creepy Guy could do whatever he wanted?" Cora asked a little huffily.

"They claim to have had no idea."

"But what about that gas? I mean, didn't anyone notice anything weird with *that*?"

"Well, as I thought at the time, it was argon gas. Which is legal to purchase. It's used in welding all the time. So it's not as if having bottles of it in that closet next to the media room was anything to be concerned about."

"Bryson Clark, if I came home and found that you had *ten* bottles of argon gas in one of our closets, you bet your ass I'd wonder what the hell it was doing there, especially since you don't weld," Cora said a little heatedly.

He chuckled, and the sound made her smile, even though the subject they were discussing was heavy.

"Noted. But then again, I'm not a gazillionaire and don't have weird quirks that the hired help is paid to overlook. And...I don't have any hired help either."

"Whatever," Cora muttered.

But she smiled when Pipe kissed the side of her head. She loved this. Loved sitting here on the deck, in the dark, in the cold, cuddled up next to Pipe. Looking at him, no one would ever think he was the cuddling type, but she couldn't help but love that with her, he definitely was.

"So what was the final word about Ridge spending her money? He had to know he'd be caught. I mean, seriously, no woman ever would spend that much at a gentlemen's club."

"Everything is speculation, because he's dead, but the general consensus is that he was just arrogant enough and spoiled enough that he didn't think anyone would question the charges on her cards. After all, she's kind of rich too. If he didn't know much about her spending habits, he might've assumed she liked to shop as much as the next rich girl. And apparently, his dad was sick of his lazy son not working and embarrassing the family name. He reduced his trust enough that Ridge didn't have the money to pay for nightly lap dances and strippers shaking their tits in his face. We don't know if Grant suggested he bring Lara to Arizona, or he did that on his own."

"And he...what? Just thought Lara was crocheting all day or something? Did he really not know she was being drugged with valium and antidepressants and being held hostage in his own basement?"

"We'll never know, but I'm guessing he was aware of everything going on. Grant had been working with him a while, and I heard that he actually did save Michaels's life once. He'd gone to a shit part of town to buy some drugs, and when the dealer jumped him, Grant shot the guy."

"Holy crap, really? And the cops didn't find out who he was *then*? That's awful."

Pipe shrugged. "Grant's good at what he does. And there was video surveillance proving that Michaels was attacked and Grant acted in self-defense."

"So many lost opportunities to get that asshole off the streets," Cora said with a sigh.

"Yeah. The FBI and local authorities are poring over the grounds and the house with a fine-toothed comb. They've found one body buried in the garden already, and expect to find more."

"God. That's awful. I feel horrible for any woman who was unfortunate enough to get mixed up with Creepy Guy. And he's still out there," she whispered. "What if he decides he wants revenge? I saw him when we were leaving in that chopper, Pipe. He wasn't happy. He had this look on his face...it was so cold. So determined."

"He's not going to touch a hair on your head, or Lara's," Pipe growled.

"You don't know that."

"I do," he insisted. "Everyone here at The Refuge is aware of what he's done and what he's capable of. Brick met with the police in Los Alamos, so they're aware of him. We've got cameras everywhere, and after what happened with Alaska, we're more prepared than we used to be for someone trying to sneak through our forest to get to the resort. And...if he does show his face here? Thinking he can outsmart us somehow? He'll find out exactly what kind of training we all have. You and Lara will be safe. I give you my word."

Cora sighed. "I'm just so mad, Pipe. So damn furious at

him. Both of them. What gave Creepy Guy the right to hurt and kill so many people? What happened in his childhood that made him that way? By all rights, *I* should be like him. Bitter, angry, willing to hurt others because I wasn't loved as a kid. But I decided to not let my past determine my future. Though, I admit that I pretty much gave up hope of ever finding someone who could love me. I decided there was something fundamentally wrong with me, making me unlovable.

"But I didn't turn to a life of crime. I didn't hunt down and hold people against their will, doing unspeakable things before killing them. And Ridge? He had *everything*. Lara would've done anything for him. And he took advantage of her. Changed her. I don't know that she'll ever be the same person she was before."

"She won't," Pipe said.

Cora frowned up at him.

"I don't mean that in a bad way, but life changes us. The good and the bad. She can't go back and erase what happened, no matter how much she wants to. She has to live with the decisions she made and move on from there. We all do. No matter what we go through, we have no choice but to keep moving forward. Grant made the choice to act out his sick fantasies and Michaels made the choice to throw his morals aside in return for tits and ass from that strip club."

"It sucks," Cora mumbled.

Pipe kissed her temple again. "Yeah. But Lara will be okay. Want to know how I know?"

"How?"

"Because she has you. The only person who insisted that something was wrong. Who did everything in her power to get help for her. Who went into the lion's den, so to speak, to rescue her. She'll realize that eventually. Right now, she's dealing with the effects of drug withdrawal and the memories of what that sicko did to her. It'll take time, but she'll get there, because she has her best friend at her back and all of us here at The Refuge who understand PTSD. Who understand what she's going through."

He took a deep breath, then continued, "We haven't talked about it, and this might not be the best time, but I want you to stay, love. Here. With me. We'll find you something to do that you enjoy. Or you can sit on your ass on my deck all day. I don't care. I just know that with you at my side, I'm a better person."

Tears welled up in Cora's eyes. "Pipe..." she whispered.

"And I've been thinking about my next tattoo. Where the best place might be to get *you* inked on my skin."

She turned to him in surprise. "What?"

"A wolf, with a skeleton key around his neck. Barbed wire surrounding him. You're the key. I'm the wolf. You trusted me to help you when you needed it the most. And I'll guard that trust with my life. The barbed wire because somehow we made it through all the walls we both put up to keep people at bay, and that wire will also protect what we build in the future. We fit, love. And if you don't want to stay here, I'll go back to DC with you. I just know I want things between us to work. More than I've ever wanted anything in my life."

"I want that too. And I don't want to go back to DC. I mean, I would, if Lara decides that's where she wants to be...but there's nothing there that I'm attached to. If I never see that bitch Eleanor again, it'll be too soon."

Pipe smiled, and she loved how it changed his entire countenance. "Can we send her a wedding photo? To rub it in her face that she lost?"

Cora stilled as she stared at Pipe. "A wedding photo?" she whispered.

"Bloody hell. I let that slip. But it's not like we haven't talked about it before," Pipe said with a grin. "Cora Rooney...I want to marry you. Maybe not today. Maybe not tomorrow. But someday, when you know deep in your heart that you can trust me to always have your back and never let you down."

"Yes!" Cora exclaimed, shifting so she was straddling his lap. Her tailbone screamed in protest, but she ignored the pain. This was too important.

Pipe put his hands on her waist and held her still, as if he knew she was hurting and wanted to do whatever he could to prevent it. "Yes?" he asked softly.

Did he doubt her answer? That was unacceptable.

"Yes, Pipe. I trust you already. I think as soon as I saw you on that stage, I sensed you could change my life, but I didn't let myself believe it because, you know...my history. I promise that I won't let you down. I'll be the best girl-friend and wife. You won't regret being with me."

"Of course I won't," Pipe said, his brows furrowing in confusion. "And I know you won't let me down. You can't." He gently cupped one of her cheeks. "You know, for a moment there in that basement, when it seemed like Owl and I combined were no match for that arsehole, I thought...that was it. I'd failed you. And Lara. But the next thing I know, I see your thumb in his eye and blood drip-ping down his face, and I swear to God, woman, my love for you was so absolute, I was literally frozen for a moment. I'll never forgive myself for giving him the opportunity to attack you, but knowing you were willing to fight, that you had our backs...it meant the world to me."

"Thank you for not yelling at me. Telling me I should've stayed away from him. Stayed safe," Cora countered.

Pipe snorted. "Yeah, right. You doing what you had to do to protect yourself was both scary and sexy as hell. But I'm still gonna teach you more hand-to-hand fighting...if you want."

"I want," Cora reassured him. She cupped his cheek and loved how he gave her the weight of his head for a moment. "I want you, Pipe. For myself. I've never had someone of my own."

"You do now. And we're gonna have that family you've always wanted. We already have ready-made aunts and uncles, but we're gonna have a dozen kids to drive them crazy as well."

Cora laughed. "A dozen?"

He smiled. "Okay, maybe not that many. But like you, I want to foster older kids. Adopt them. Give them the home and family you never had."

Tears welled up once more. This man. He was giving her everything she'd ever wanted. And she couldn't love him more. "I love you," she blurted.

"It's a good thing, since I love you too," he told her calmly.

"And I want you to get that tattoo, but only if I can get one too."

"You still want to get inked?" he asked in surprise.

"Yeah. Maybe not as big as the one you're planning on though. I'm not big on pain."

Pipe guffawed. "Right."

"I want a tramp stamp," she informed him.

Pipe rolled his eyes.

"At the small of my back. Where you always touch me

when we're walking. Where you can see it when you take me from behind. And I want it to match yours. The wolf with the key."

She felt his cock harden under her and smiled, thrilled to feel the evidence that he loved the idea.

"Done," he murmured as he moved one hand to cover the exact spot she wanted to put the tattoo.

Lowering herself against him, Cora curled her arms under her, against his chest, and sighed. They sat like that for ten minutes or so, before Cora shivered.

Pipe immediately moved. "You're cold," he said. "Time to go in."

"But I like it out here," Cora complained.

"And I want my fiancée not to be a popsicle."

Fiancée. She loved that. More than she thought she ever would.

She let him set her on her feet, then smiled as he immediately took her hand and led her to the stairs. He hadn't wanted her to come up here for a while after they arrived back, worried that it would hurt her tailbone more than necessary. And while it *was* a little painful to use the stairs, she wanted to be in her favorite spot more than she wanted to avoid discomfort.

They slowly made their way down the stairs, with Pipe in front of her, making sure she didn't fall.

Cora had no idea what was to come in the future. She hoped and prayed that her and Pipe's relationship would work out. She was well aware that things had been a whirlwind, that when everything got back to normal, and they weren't risking their lives, their feelings for each other might change. But she didn't think so.

She'd clicked with Pipe from the first moment they'd met, something she'd only had with one other person in her life. Lara. And look how well their friendship had stood the test of time.

Thinking about her best friend had Cora melancholy once more. She wanted to help her, but she knew the best thing she could do was give her time and space to heal. She'd be there for her when she felt more comfortable with her surroundings.

In the meantime, she'd continue to get to know the men and women from The Refuge, and if she was lucky, find a way to contribute to the place of healing.

# EPILOGUE

Pipe looked around the barn with a smile on his face. It was amazing how having Cora in his life, his cabin, his bed, made him so much more content than he'd ever been. He spied her standing in a corner with Alaska, Henley, Reese, and the other women employed at The Refuge. Everyone had worked hard to decorate the barn for the occasion.

Tonka and Henley had secretly gone to Los Alamos and gotten married in a civil ceremony, and to placate everyone afterward, had agreed to let them host a wedding party.

One thing Pipe had learned over the last year was that celebrating the good times in life was just as important as working. And more important than dwelling on the crap that had happened in their pasts.

Alaska had organized everything, and the barn looked like a completely different place than it usually did. The stalls had been decorated with ribbons and bows, the animals all had colorful bows around their necks, which were already looking a little ragged. The goats had promptly eaten theirs, and when any of the other animals got close enough, they tried to eat their bows too.

Melba was loving all the people and the attention. The horses were ignoring everyone, the cats were mainly hiding from all the hubbub, the dogs were looking for any scrap of food that had been dropped on the floor, and Scarlet Pimpernickel, the calf Jasna had named—which wasn't a calf anymore—was mooing loudly, looking for someone to pay attention to her. It was chaotic, just like things occasionally were at The Refuge. But Pipe wouldn't want to be anywhere else.

The women separated then. Alaska went to a table and got ready to start the music. Reese, who was just beginning to show from her pregnancy, headed for the doors at the end of the barn. Ryan and Carly handed out champagne glasses filled with Sprite, and Robert and Luna stood by a table heaping with appetizers and finger foods, guarding it from the roving animals and ready to help serve when the time was right. Robert had even used some of his precious stash of Christmas Tree Cakes to make a sweet dip. It was the best endorsement he could've given Henley and Tonka.

"If I can have your attention," Brick said loudly, making everyone immediately stop talking and turn toward him. There were a handful of guests in attendance, but mostly the group that had gathered was Refuge family.

"I have the extreme honor of presenting Finn, Henley, and Jasna Matlick!" Brick said, not drawing out the moment. Reese pulled open the barn doors, and Tonka, Henley, and Jasna walked through hand-in-hand.

They were all smiling, although Pipe noticed that Tonka looked a tiny bit uncomfortable being the center of attention. Everyone was aware that this wasn't the kind of situation he preferred, but for his girls, he'd do just about everything.

Trotting behind the new family were their two rescue dogs. Wally, a beautiful, sleek pit bull mix, and Beauty, a tiny terrier mix.

The family walked over to where a small riser had been created. They stepped up and Tonka immediately wrapped his arm around his wife's waist, pulling her into his side. Jasna was too excited to stand still. She had a huge smile on her face and seemed to be reveling in the attention.

Everyone in the barn was dressed casually, something Tonka insisted on. Jeans and T-shirts were the norm. It was March, and while there was snow on the ground outside the barn, inside it was toasty warm.

Pipe wandered over to where Cora was standing. She had her phone up and was streaming the ceremony. He wrapped an arm around her waist and rested his chin on her shoulder as he cuddled behind her. She turned her head and grinned at him, then turned her attention back to her phone.

Looking around, Pipe saw Brick standing by Alaska at the table with the music. She was ready to hit play as soon as the speeches were done. Spike was standing next to Reese, holding her hand. Stone and Tiny were trying to corral the goats for the couple of minutes it would take for the "official" part of this party to be completed.

The only person missing was Owl.

Everyone knew where he was. He was where he'd been for the last couple of months, since Cora and Lara had joined their Refuge family. In his cabin with Lara.

She was struggling, hard, and it was painful for every-one. It had taken a while for her to fight her addiction to the painkillers she'd been forced to take in Arizona. She suffered from depression, anxiety, and still found it difficult to be around anyone other than Owl.

He knew Cora was devastated that she couldn't help her friend, that Lara still felt uneasy even around her, but she'd vowed to do whatever it took to help her heal. Which was why she was FaceTiming with Owl, making sure both he and Lara were there for Tonka and Henley's celebration, even if it was virtually and not in person.

The only person Lara felt truly comfortable around was Owl. He'd moved her into his cabin the day they'd returned to New Mexico, and they'd spent the last few cold months hunkered down together. Lara wasn't ready to talk to Henley, their resident psychologist, so the woman was giving Owl pointers and tips so he could help her as much as possible.

Pipe hated that Lara was struggling so much. And he hated even more the nights when Cora cried in his arms because she felt so helpless to do anything for her best friend. She wasn't a crier, but the thought of Lara suffering was enough to make her break down. Despite that, Cora refused to give up. She had hope that one day, Lara would be able to break through the bubble of fear she currently lived in. Until then, she continued to do everything she could to make Lara feel as if she was just as much a part of The Refuge as everyone else.

Pipe loved her all the more for it. Her stubbornness was one of the things he adored most about her.

"Thank you all for coming," Tonka told the crowd. "It feels right to be doing this here, surrounded by the animals who were my salvation when I needed it the most. Before getting my head out of my butt when it came to Henley, I hid out here in the barn, feeling as if the four-legged creatures in the world understood me more than any human ever could. Henley saw through my gruffness, and with her patience and understanding, made me see that hiding wasn't going to heal my pain. She shared her love, and her daughter, and helped me understand my past wasn't ever going to disappear. It was always going to be there, lurking, ready to try to steal my joy. But it doesn't have to dictate my future. And my future is here. With my wife, my daughter, our friends...and our new little one, who will be here in the fall."

Tonka gently put his hand on Henley's stomach.

Everyone let out a gasp, then clapped enthusiastically.

"Did you know?" Cora asked as she turned to look up at Pipe.

He grinned down at her, but didn't respond.

"Of course you knew," she mumbled with a small smile, turning back to their friends.

"Yup, I'm pregnant," Henley said when the congratulations had died down. "We'd decided to let nature take its course, and surprise! Now, I'm going to keep this short because if I don't, the goats are gonna overpower Robert and Luna and eat all our food."

Everyone laughed as they looked toward the table and saw the chef and his daughter doing their best to protect it with brooms, wielding them as if they were knights of old brandishing their swords.

"Anyway, I've worked here almost since The Refuge opened, and I knew from the second I stepped onto the property that this place would make a difference in so many people's lives. I just wasn't expecting to be *one* of those lives. When the worst thing in my life happened, you were all there for me and Jasna. That's what family is. And I love you all so much."

She sniffed, and Pipe smiled as Tonka leaned down and kissed the top of her head.

"And I'm so happy to be a big sister!" Jasna said excitedly.

Everyone clapped again, and when the noise settled down, Tonka made a point of meeting the gazes of his friends and co-owners of The Refuge. "This is not my thing, speeches, being the center of everyone's attention, but there's no one I'd rather celebrate my marriage with than all of you. Thank you for your patience with me. For your support. For being there no matter what."

Pipe dipped his head in recognition of his friend's words.

"Now...let's eat!" Tonka exclaimed.

He leaned down and kissed his wife. Jasna ignored her parents and jumped off the short riser and headed to Scarlet to give her some attention. Everyone else made their way toward the food, but Pipe's attention was on Cora.

She clicked off the phone, then turned to face him. She smiled...but he could tell she was sad about Lara.

"She'll be okay," he told her. "And maybe Tonka's words will sink in. About his past not dictating his future."

Cora sighed. "I hope so. I just...I have so many emotions when it comes to what happened. I can't believe the FBI *still* has no idea where Creepy Guy is."

Pipe's lips twitched at her insistence on calling him Creepy Guy, but then he sobered. He also wasn't happy that the man was in the wind. "They'll find him," he told her.

"I know. But I think Lara would feel a lot better, safer, if he was behind bars somewhere. She's terrified he's going to come after her."

Pipe nodded. He and the rest of the guys weren't exactly thrilled by that prospect. They'd discussed it at length, and he knew they'd all do everything in their power to keep that from happening. To stay vigilant. And they'd also had a long talk about actually purchasing a helicopter for The Refuge and putting in a helipad and a small hangar. It would mean cutting other things they'd planned to do on the property, at least for a while, but after Stone's amazing flying had gotten them safely away from the estate in Arizona, they all realized how things could've gone downhill if that chopper wasn't at their disposal. With Cora and Lara both hurt, and Grant having regained consciousness so quickly...

It wasn't the worst idea to have a helicopter at their disposal at The Refuge, just in case they needed to evacuate.

"She's going to be all right," Pipe insisted. "She just needs the time she needs."

Cora sighed. Then nodded.

It was another in a long line of things Pipe loved about her. She was resilient and trusted him with every ounce of her being. He vowed to never let her down. That trust was a gift. He knew it and cherished it.

She'd said something a week after they'd gotten back from Arizona that had stuck with him. They'd been talking about Grant, and why he was the way he was, and she'd commented that she should've been just like him. Angry and bitter. And maybe a criminal. He could acknowledge now that it was a miracle she wasn't. She was wary of people, yes, but Pipe couldn't blame her for that. And there were times when she slipped and questioned why he was with her, but overall, she was remarkably well-adjusted for someone with her background.

He loved her. So much it almost scared him sometimes. But he also embraced it. Cora made him a better person. Kept his demons at bay. Just being with her opened his eyes more to the beauty that was all around him. That was life itself.

"You know how I went to town yesterday with Ryan, Alaska, and Reese?" Cora asked him.

Pipe was glad for the change of subject. He didn't like to see Cora sad. This wasn't a night for sorrow. It was for celebrating Henley, Tonka, and Jasna's new life together... and the new baby on the way. Things were changing on The Refuge, and Pipe was happy with the direction the business was going. "Yeah?" he said belatedly, when he realized Cora was waiting for his response.

"Well, we didn't just go to that chocolate shop and get you those British chocolates you like so much."

"No?" he asked with a lift of his brow.

"Nope. I met with your tattoo guy."

Pipe blinked in surprise. "You did?"

"Uh-huh," Cora said with a small grin. "And...since he still had the art he used to ink your new tattoo, I asked him to go ahead and do mine."

Pipe froze. "What?"

"I got the same tattoo you did," she told him. "Right where I told you I wanted it. In the small of my back. It's a lot smaller than yours though, because holy crap, Pipe, that shit *hurts*."

Without a word, Pipe grabbed Cora's hand and began towing her toward the doors to the barn.

Cora giggled. "Pipe, wait, we can't leave!"

"We can and we are. You should've waited to tell me you got inked if you didn't want me to haul you straight to our bed."

She laughed again. Then turned her head and called out, "Alaska! We're headed out!"

"You told him?" she asked loudly, making everyone turn to look at her, then Cora.

"Yup!"

"Have fun!" Alaska called out.

Ryan and Carly both gave her a thumbs up, and Reese simply smiled.

When they were out of the barn, Pipe growled, "I can't believe you got it without me."

"I know you wanted to be there, and I wanted that too, but I thought it would be more fun for it to be a surprise," Cora said.

Pipe grunted.

He'd wanted to be there to support her when she'd gotten her first tattoo, but he was touched beyond belief that she'd gotten the same art that he'd put on his shoulder blade.

"It's still red," she warned him as he pulled her toward their cabin. "It's gonna get all scabby and gross."

"Tattoos aren't gross," Pipe told her.

"You know what I mean," she muttered.

Pipe looked down and saw she was smiling as he walked them way too fast across The Refuge grounds. "How's your arm feel?" he asked.

"Good."

"And your arse?"

Understanding why he was asking, her smile widened. "It's fine."

"No pain?"

"No. Just a twinge here and there. But it doesn't hurt right now," she said quickly.

Pipe grunted. It had been a long time since he'd made

love to his woman. He'd eaten her out plenty in the last month. Had gotten her off with his fingers, and she'd done the same for him. But because of her arm and her healing tailbone, he hadn't wanted to make love and risk hurting her even more. But after hearing about the tattoo, there was no way he could stop himself from taking her.

The second they entered the cabin, he growled, "Bed."

Cora laughed as she headed toward their bedroom.

Pipe took a deep breath, trying to get control over himself. His cock was throbbing, as if knowing it was minutes away from thrusting home into Cora's tight, wet body.

Then he started after the woman he would follow literally to the ends of the earth.

* * *

Ten minutes later, Pipe stared intently at the tattoo in the small of Cora's back as he eased his cock into her soaking-wet pussy. She was on her elbows and knees in their bed, and he'd already eaten her to her first orgasm. She'd been just as horny as he was, dripping wet before he'd even touched her.

The skin around her tattoo was a bit inflamed. He knew the image like the back of his hand, because he'd designed it with the tattoo artist, down to the smallest detail. The wolf, the key around its neck, the barbed wire. It was perfect.

His woman loved him enough to get him inked onto her body.

He loved her back. So much, he couldn't put it into words. So he showed her instead. He took her slow and steady, loving how wet and hot she was. How her body clenched against him every time he pulled out, as if she didn't want him to leave.

Pipe tried to be gentle. Even though she was healed, he didn't want to do anything that might set her back, but Cora wasn't having it. She began to rock, slapping her ass against him with every thrust.

Her ass cheeks jiggled and that tattoo right in front of his face was burned into his psyche. He ran his fingers over the tender spot on her body. A spurt of precome made his cock glide in and out of her body even easier.

"Bloody hell," he murmured.

Cora laughed under him, and he felt it around his dick. This woman, she was perfect. In every way. And she was his. They hadn't talked about getting married since that night on the rooftop deck. They were getting to know each other in ways they hadn't been able to during the first few days of their whirlwind romance. And everything he learned about his Cora made Pipe even more sure that he wanted her for the rest of his life.

She was his match. It had taken him over forty years to find her, and a lot of heartache on both their parts, but now that she was here, he wasn't going to let her go. Ever. Ring on her finger or not, she was his, just as much as he was hers.

"Pipe," she whined from under him.

"What, love?" he asked.

"Faster. Harder," she ordered.

"I don't want to hurt you," he said.

"I'm going to hurt *you* if you don't fuck me properly," she growled.

Pipe grinned. He put a bit more oomph into his next thrust, and was rewarded by Cora's groan of pleasure. He loved the sounds she made. He loved everything about her.

Focusing once more on the tattoo on her back, Pipe finally let go. He made love to her as he'd wanted to for the last three months. It had been too long since he'd felt the warmth of her pussy. His hips moved fast, faster, and Cora met every thrust. She was beautiful.

Pipe had the thought as her inner muscles fluttered around him that he didn't deserve her. Everything he'd done, all the things he'd seen, he was positive that he shouldn't have been rewarded with such an amazing woman. But he'd spend the rest of his life trying to be deserving of her love. Of her loyalty. Of her trust.

"Oh! I'm almost there!" Cora panted.

She didn't need to tell him. Pipe knew. He shifted so he could reach under her and flick her clit.

She jerked in his grasp as she immediately began to come.

Smirking at how sensitive she was, the fact that he knew just how to touch her to make her explode, Pipe took hold of her hips and fucked her through her peak. She was tighter, wetter, and before he was ready, Pipe felt his balls tingling. He pushed through her spasming muscles as far as he could and held himself still as come burst from the tip of his cock.

The amount of pleasure he got from releasing deep inside her caught him by surprise, just as it had their first night together in Phoenix. An orgasm was an orgasm; at least that was what he'd always thought. But he was wrong. There was something so elemental about coming inside the woman he loved. So primal.

One of these days, he'd come on her back, right on that tattoo.

But tonight wasn't that night. He was going to fill her again and again, until they were both so exhausted they couldn't move.

She shifted under him, and Pipe grimaced when he slowly pulled out of her. The last thing he wanted was to leave her body, but he didn't want her on her knees, putting pressure on her arm or tailbone any longer than necessary.

Before he let her fall to her side, he held her still. Watching as his come leaked out of her folds. It was more erotic than anything he'd ever seen, and Pipe felt his cock twitch. Bloody hell, he'd just come and he wanted her again.

Taking one last look at the gift of her tattoo, he gently lowered her to her side, then immediately followed, taking her into his arms.

Cora sighed against his chest. "I guess you liked my surprise."

Pipe huffed out an amused breath. "You think?" he asked.

She chuckled and kissed his chest.

His breath hitched. Yeah, he definitely didn't deserve this woman.

"I love you," she said softly.

"I love you too," he returned.

They lay there for a few minutes, before Cora lifted her head so she could see his face. "Pipe?"

"Yeah, love?"

"Thank you."

"For what?"

"Everything. Loving me, believing me. Not being a douche. All of it."

Pipe smiled. "You're welcome."

She sighed again and lowered her head back onto his chest. Several minutes went by, and just when Pipe moved his hand down her side to touch her, to start round two, Cora let out a small snore.

Smiling wider, Pipe sighed. His plans for a marathon night of sex would have to wait. His Cora was exhausted. She'd been helping Alaska and the others prepare for tonight's celebration and visiting with Lara every chance she could. Pipe had a feeling she'd work herself sick trying to help others. She had nothing to prove, the others already loved her. She was truly a part of The Refuge. She'd learn that with time. Until then, he'd watch over her and make sure she rested when she needed to.

Pipe pulled the blanket up higher around them and closed his eyes as he held the most precious and amazing woman in his arms. Life was full of twists and turns, and while he hadn't understood why he'd had to endure the things he had in the past, he got it now. He needed those experiences to be the man his woman deserved. Without his past, he wouldn't be who he was today.

Turning his head, he kissed Cora's temple, smiling when she mumbled under her breath and burrowed into him. Being the man Cora deserved was his lifelong goal. One he took just as seriously as his military oath.

"I can hear you thinking way too hard," she complained with a mumble. "Stop it. Rest, Pipe."

"Yes, ma'am," he said with another smile.

\* \* \*

Lara huddled in the corner of Owl's couch and stared blankly at the television. She felt hollow. Numb. Earlier, she'd watched Cora's FaceTime call with Owl, also without feeling much of anything...beyond a touch of guilt that she was keeping Owl from celebrating with his friends.

She wanted to shake herself out of the weird headspace she was in, but couldn't figure out how.

She was letting everyone down, yet she couldn't seem to care.

Her parents had come to visit her in the hospital in Phoenix, and even though they'd said all the right things, Lara knew they were relieved when it was decided she would go to The Refuge with Cora. They called Owl to check in, but Lara hadn't spoken to them since arriving in New Mexico.

The detectives had pushed her to tell them what had happened in that house. Lara couldn't. She'd told them the basics. That yes, she'd gone to Arizona of her own free will, and once there, she'd quickly changed her mind. But Ridge had taken her phone. She'd been kept in the basement almost from the beginning, only dragged out occasionally for appearance's sake. But always drugged...and then that man, the one she knew as Carter Grant, had hurt her.

But she didn't elaborate. Couldn't. What she'd been through was embarrassing and horrifying and unbearable. And speaking of it would only make the memories more real.

She was ashamed that all too soon, every time he'd shown up with pills in his hand, she'd taken them willingly. Gladly. She'd needed them. Needed to enter that floaty world where she barely knew what was happening, and it didn't hurt when Carter touched her.

Now that she was free of that house, she should be fine. Relieved. Should be getting on with her life. But how could she, knowing that Carter was still out there?

The last words he'd ever said to Lara echoed in her head, over and over.

*You're my favorite. I'm never giving you up. You're mine.*

She shuddered.

"Are you cold?" Owl asked, not waiting for her response, but standing to grab another blanket from the back of the couch. She was cold all the time. Owl had turned up the heat in his cabin, but she could still never seem to get warm.

Lara didn't understand Callen Kaufman. He was the first person she remembered seeing when she was rescued, and she'd latched onto him like a toddler with separation anxiety. He'd instantly represented safety for her, and while she'd gotten slightly better over the last few months, she still panicked when he wasn't around.

There was something about the man that made her feel protected. Sheltered.

And that was all it could *ever* be. She was done with love. With the fantasy of happily ever after. She wished nothing but good luck to the men and women who'd been so amazing, who'd let her stay here at The Refuge, but her desire to be loved, to have a family one day, had died a spectacular death.

There was no such thing as happily ever after. Disney and Hallmark movies were a scam. Romance novels were nothing but fantasies.

Lara swore that as soon as she was able, she was leaving here and moving to Alaska and living in one of those off-the-grid cabins. She'd grow her own food, hunt for meat, use candles for light. That was preferable to being hurt over and over again by people. By *men*.

Owl draped the fuzzy blanket over her, and Lara forced herself to look at him and nod.

"I've said it before, and I'll say it again. As many times as you need to hear it. You're safe here, Lara," Owl told her gently.

Lara's gaze dropped to her lap. It was obvious Owl believed what he was saying, and while she trusted him as much as she could trust anyone right now, and she was definitely using him as a crutch, she knew down to her soul that she *wasn't* safe.

And anyone close to her wasn't safe either.

She'd overheard Owl talking to one of his friends—she didn't know which—at the door the other day. They'd kept their voices low, trying to keep their conversation from her, but Lara had heard.

Carter was still out there. The police hadn't been able to find him. Ridge was dead, which she felt a smidgen of relief about, but the real danger was Carter. Had always been him. And he was free. He was going to come for her.

She needed to leave. Hide. Because no matter what, Carter wasn't going to rest until he'd taken her back. He'd claimed her, whether she wanted him to or not, and he would make her pay for escaping his warped basement prison of humiliation and pain.

Lara would rather die than be back in his clutches again.

In the meantime, she'd regain her strength. Try to get better, try to endure longer lengths of time without Owl by her side. Once she was capable enough, she'd disappear.

Cora would be fine. She'd found herself a protector as well, which made Lara happy, but also sad. She'd miss her friend. But she'd be safer with Lara gone.

Lara took a deep breath. First things first, though—she needed to shake herself out of the pit of despair she'd fallen into, at least on the outside. Needed to convince everyone she was okay, so she could leave. She didn't know where she'd be safe from a monster like Carter, but she refused to drag others into the horror that had become her life.

She looked up at Owl and smiled tentatively.

He tilted his head as he studied her.

"Can we watch a movie?" she asked.

"Yes! Absolutely," Owl responded quickly.

It was the first time she'd asked for anything, and it was obvious Owl was ready and willing to give her whatever she wanted. She didn't like lying to him, and by pretending to be getting better, she *was* lying. But it was for his own good. He'd protected her when she'd needed it the most, and it was time she returned the favor.

Owl settled on the other end of the couch from Lara and continually switched his attention from the movie to the woman sitting just three feet from him. In reality, was miles away. Yes, she'd asked to watch a movie, the first time she'd requested anything since he'd brought her to his cabin after her discharge from the hospital in Phoenix.

But she wasn't okay. She might've asked to watch a movie, but she wasn't actually paying any attention. She was lost in her head, just as she'd been for most of the last few months.

Owl had tried everything he could think of to help her, but nothing seemed to work. She didn't want to talk to Henley, didn't want to talk to her parents the few times they'd called. Even Cora's regular visits didn't seem to make any difference.

So yeah, her taking the initiative and asking for something as simple as a movie was a huge step...but it wasn't a genuine one. Lara still had that haunted look in her eyes. She was deeply traumatized by whatever had happened to her in that basement, and it hurt his heart.

He didn't know what it was about the woman that had gotten under his skin so much. Maybe it was the look in her eyes when she'd briefly connected with him in that basement. Terror. Hopelessness. Resignation.

He'd felt the same way when he'd been a hostage. Every day brought new horrors, and he couldn't help but feel as if he and Lara were two peas in a pod.

Looking over at her once more, Owl clenched his teeth. She was planning something. He didn't know what. But he could sense it...and all he could do was continue to promise that she was safe.

This woman deserved more than just barely surviving. More than a life of living in fear. More than a broken helicopter pilot like himself as a guardian.

Owl would do whatever he could to release her from the clutches of whatever fears lived deep within her. Then he'd set her free to find the happily ever after that Cora said she'd been looking for all her life.

Owl himself was no prince charming, not even close. But if he could help this woman outrun the demons that lived in her head, maybe, just maybe, he could find a way to rid the ones that lived in his head too.

\* \* \*

Carter Grant, aka Carl Glick, aka Connor Smith, aka Daniel West, aka a hundred other aliases, sat in the rundown motel on Albuquerque's Central Avenue...and plotted.

His eye throbbed, which pissed him off. It was proving difficult to get used to having only half his vision. The patch over his ruined right eye made people stay the fuck away from him, which was a small blessing. But it also *drew* attention, something he hated.

In the months since his cushy arrangement had imploded, he'd picked up a few prostitutes who frequented the area, had drugged them and done whatever he'd wanted. It was mildly enjoyable.

But none of them were Lara.

She was perfect. Blonde, beautiful, delicate. And her skin was so soft. Unlike the girls on the streets. They'd lived hard lives, and it showed in their bodies.

No. Lara was the one. He wanted her back. And he'd get her too. He knew where she was. Up in the mountains near Los Alamos. But he couldn't just walk into the fancy lodge where she was hiding and take her back. Not with the kind of men who ran the place.

They'd been professional soldiers, just like him. He knew what he was up against because he'd had similar training. The men who'd fought him in the basement of the Michaels's estate had been good. Really good. But he would've beaten them both if the bitch hadn't jumped on his back and taken out his eye.

Carter would get his revenge. On her. On the men. And he'd have his Lara again.

His dick twitched in his pants as he thought about what he'd do to her when she was back in his bed, where she belonged. Carter didn't get off on rape. That was too easy. He liked seeing fear in his women's eyes. Liked touching them, hurting them. Marking them with his fists...with his come, so they knew who they belonged to. That was his kink.

And Lara was his perfect woman. His perfect captive. The terror in her eyes was intoxicating. The way her pale skin bruised...beautiful.

He unzipped his jeans and took out his cock, masturbating to the images in his head of the recent past. Of his Lara.

When he was done, Carter impatiently cleaned himself up and zipped his pants.

He had a lot of planning to do. Needed to find a hideaway, somewhere he could live the life he wanted with Lara. He'd stolen plenty of money from Ridge Michaels throughout his employment, before he'd ultimately put a bullet in his brain. He had more than enough to live comfortably. Away from prying eyes. But before he holed up, he needed his Lara. Needed revenge against the men who'd stolen her away.

Yeah, Carter had a lot of planning to do...but in the end, Lara would be his again. He couldn't wait.

*

As you've guessed, we haven't seen the last of Carter! He'll be back...and Owl will need to use every one of the skills he learned while in the military to keep Lara safe. And even that might not be enough... Find out what happens in *Deserving Lara*.

*Want to talk to other Susan Stoker fans? Join my reader group, Susan Stoker's Stalkers, on Facebook!*

**Scan the QR code below for signed books, swag, T-shirts and more!**

## Also by Susan Stoker

### The Refuge Series
*Deserving Alaska*
*Deserving Henley*
*Deserving Reese*
*Deserving Cora*
*Deserving Lara (Feb 2024)*
*Deserving Maisy (TBA)*
*Deserving Ryleigh (TBA)*

### SEAL Team Hawaii Series
*Finding Elodie*
*Finding Lexie*
*Finding Kenna*
*Finding Monica*
*Finding Carly*
*Finding Ashlyn*
*Finding Jodelle*

### Eagle Point Search & Rescue
*Searching for Lilly*
*Searching for Elsie*
*Searching for Bristol*
*Searching for Caryn*
*Searching for Finley*
*Searching for Heather (Jan 2024)*
*Searching for Khloe (May 2024)*

### Game of Chance Series
*The Protector*
*The Royal*

*The Hero (Mar 2024)*
*The Lumberjack (Aug 2024)*

## SEAL of Protection: Legacy Series
*Securing Caite*
*Securing Brenae (novella)*
*Securing Sidney*
*Securing Piper*
*Securing Zoey*
*Securing Avery*
*Securing Kalee*
*Securing Jane*

## Delta Force Heroes Series
*Rescuing Rayne*
*Rescuing Aimee (novella)*
*Rescuing Emily*
*Rescuing Harley*
*Marrying Emily (novella)*
*Rescuing Kassie*
*Rescuing Bryn*
*Rescuing Casey*
*Rescuing Sadie (novella)*
*Rescuing Wendy*
*Rescuing Mary*
*Rescuing Macie (novella)*
*Rescuing Annie*

## SEAL of Protection Series
*Protecting Caroline*
*Protecting Alabama*
*Protecting Fiona*
*Marrying Caroline (novella)*

*Protecting Summer*
*Protecting Cheyenne*
*Protecting Jessyka*
*Protecting Julie (novella)*
*Protecting Melody*
*Protecting the Future*
*Protecting Kiera (novella)*
*Protecting Alabama's Kids (novella)*
*Protecting Dakota*

## Delta Team Two Series
*Shielding Gillian*
*Shielding Kinley*
*Shielding Aspen*
*Shielding Jayme (novella)*
*Shielding Riley*
*Shielding Devyn*
*Shielding Ember*
*Shielding Sierra*

## Badge of Honor: Texas Heroes Series
*Justice for Mackenzie*
*Justice for Mickie*
*Justice for Corrie*
*Justice for Laine (novella)*
*Shelter for Elizabeth*
*Justice for Boone*
*Shelter for Adeline*
*Shelter for Sophie*
*Justice for Erin*
*Justice for Milena*
*Shelter for Blythe*
*Justice for Hope*

*Shelter for Quinn*
*Shelter for Koren*
*Shelter for Penelope*

## Ace Security Series

*Claiming Grace*
*Claiming Alexis*
*Claiming Bailey*
*Claiming Felicity*
*Claiming Sarah*

## Mountain Mercenaries Series

*Defending Allye*
*Defending Chloe*
*Defending Morgan*
*Defending Harlow*
*Defending Everly*
*Defending Zara*
*Defending Raven*

## Silverstone Series

*Trusting Skylar*
*Trusting Taylor*
*Trusting Molly*
*Trusting Cassidy*

## Stand Alone

*Falling for the Delta*
*The Guardian Mist*
*Nature's Rift*
*A Princess for Cale*
*A Moment in Time- A Collection of Short Stories*
*Another Moment in Time- A Collection of Short Stories*

*A Third Moment in Time- A Collection of Short Stories*
*Lambert's Lady*

### ***Special Operations Fan Fiction***
http://www.AcesPress.com

### **Beyond Reality Series**
*Outback Hearts*
*Flaming Hearts*
*Frozen Hearts*

### **Writing as Annie George:**
*Stepbrother Virgin (erotic novella)*

# ABOUT THE AUTHOR

*New York Times*, *USA Today* and *Wall Street Journal* Bestselling Author Susan Stoker has a heart as big as the state of Tennessee where she lives, but this all American girl has also spent the last fourteen years living in Missouri, California, Colorado, Indiana, and Texas. She's married to a retired Army man who now gets to follow *her* around the country.

She debuted her first series in 2014 and quickly followed that up with the SEAL of Protection Series, which solidified her love of writing and creating stories readers can get lost in.

If you enjoyed this book, or any book, please consider leaving a review. It's appreciated by authors more than you'll know.

www.stokeraces.com
www.AcesPress.com
susan@stokeraces.com

facebook.com/authorsusanstoker
twitter.com/Susan_Stoker
instagram.com/authorsusanstoker
goodreads.com/SusanStoker
bookbub.com/authors/susan-stoker
amazon.com/author/susanstoker

.

Printed in Great Britain
by Amazon